The Un...

– A Formula One Novel

About the author

Mike Breslin was born in South Wales in 1964. A lifelong motor racing fan, Mike first attempted to carve a career as a racing driver, competing in Formula Fords at club level in the 1980s after attending the Winfield Racing Driver School in France.

After hanging up his helmet Mike gained a degree in Philosophy at the University of Wales, Lampeter, and he now works as a freelance motorsport journalist and PR consultant following an award-winning spell on a regional newspaper.

Mike has worked in Formula One on a freelance basis as a technical adviser for F1's own digital TV station.

The Unfair Advantage is Mike Breslin's first novel and its sequel, *Mulsanne*, is due out in the autumn.

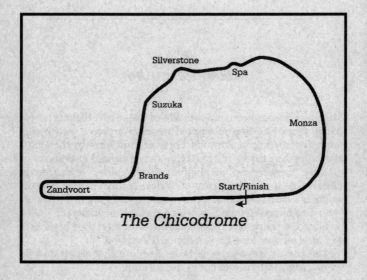

Silverstone

Spa

Suzuka

Monza

Brands

Zandvoort

Start/Finish

The Chicodrome

Mike Breslin

The Unfair Advantage
– A Formula One Novel

Rough Diamond

Rough Diamond is an imprint of Rough Diamond Media Limited
Diamond House, 55 Oxford Street, Reading RG4 8HN

A CIP Record for this book is available from the
British Cataloguing in Publication Data Office

ISBN 0-9537714-0-7

Cover illustration by Simon Taylor.

Printed and bound in Great Britain by Cox & Wyman Ltd, Reading, Berkshire.

Cover design by Conservatree, The Courtyard, 36b Church Street, Caversham,
Reading RG4 8AU

Author's Note.

Actually, this is more confession than 'note'. You see, some of you might think me a thief – because of the title, *The Unfair Advantage*, which is also the title of the late Mark Donohue's autobiography. It's just that by the time I found out, the thing had a life of its own and no other title seemed to fit. Apologies to him then.

And apologies for the anoraks out there too, for there are some things in this that will surely grate. I have tried to make the work as authentic as possible, but for the sake of narrative I've had to change the shape of F1 a little – personally I'd like to see 26 cars back on the grid again anyway.

There are one or two other things too, but I hope that as you find yourself getting into the story you will be able to forgive me.

Finally, in true Hollywood style, all the characters in this book are fictional – but if you want to see the shadows of the real in them... Well that's up to you...

Mike Breslin
London 1999

Chapter One

SOME shunts go beyond spectacle. They have a sickening quality about them, something that touches the caveman – the frightened animal – in us all. Reminds us of death – reminds us of the ultimate rule of the game... Don't get yourself killed Kinsella...

It had been a hot lap, as hot as he could make it. And that Bianchi was just a dot at first, a minor distraction, a fly worrying away at the distant horizon beyond the exit of the esses. Kinsella had clipped the first segment of the turn, almost inch perfect. Then he fed in the power, feeling the rear end of the car squat slightly, feeling the firm push of the DBM's motor through the back of his moulded racing seat, feeling the neck snapping surge of power as he wound on more revs to guide the car through the second part of the turn. Perfect. The rear of the DBM hardly hinted at a wiggle as he exited the corner and let the car drift out to the fringe of the track as it hit the straight: carry the speed Kinsella, carry the speed...

Focus switched. His mind was already on the next corner as the engine wound up to maximum revs, little glottal stops breaking its scream as Kinsella worked the steering wheel mounted paddles of the semi-automatic gears through third and fourth and fifth, now sixth. All on song, he let the luxury of the thought – *yes, a hot lap* – seep into his concentration: could be close to Chico this one, could beat Chico this one. But too early for that Kinsella. Concentrate. Just concentrate on the filament of grey asphalt stretching out before you, nothing else matters – not the smeared palette of greens and blues that form the funnel for your experience, nor the insistent, solid, strangely muted yet high-pitched hum of the engine behind you. He dipped his eyes, glancing at the electronic display, the surge of red wedge that was the rev counter and the number of the chosen gear that glowed bright-electric on the boss of the butterfly shaped steering wheel. And then, on looking up again, just an instant later, the Bianchi was there. All too big, all too soon.

Later, when there was time to think, he might say that it was like those films of sky-divers, where the parachutist pulls the cord and is gone, shooting up into the air it seems, leaving the cameraman behind – all back-to-front. It was the Bianchi that had slowed after all, slowed suddenly. Kinsella was at full chat, flat out. The driver of the Bianchi was a novice. Christ, Kinsella had barely heard of him, done something in Italian Formula Three, little else, wasn't ready for this. He had a problem with the car obviously, eased off: too much, too quickly, still hogging the line. No, this one wasn't ready for F1, not ready for Eoghan 'Egg' Kinsella on a hot lap at any rate.

It was a split second thing, just time for reflex – you store up a lot of that in 12 years of motor racing, four of those in Formula One – get to know where a car will go, or at least should go. But if the man's a sprog, well shit, he could do anything... go anywhere. He went right. But so did Kinsella, braking hard.

Kinsella let go of the wheel just as the car speared into the back of the Bianchi – learnt that early on he had, too easy to snap a wrist by hanging on as the steered wheels took a pounding. The DBM's low, raked nose dug in beneath the sponsor emblazoned rear wing of the other car, ripping away the aerodynamic diffuser and the lower element of the wing as it did so. And then, a fraction of a moment later, the searing Australian sun was lost to Kinsella, obscured by the blue smoke from his own skidding tyres and the underside of the Bianchi sliding up the sloping cowling in front of him. Up the cowling and over the forward lip of his cockpit...

Too much was crammed into that eighth of a second: the smoky texture of the grounding plank on the floor of the Bianchi as it passed close to Kinsella's head, the flaying of carbon fibre body-work as the wheels of the Bianchi hit the roll hoop above and behind him... And the noise – mostly the noise. The noise of his own tyres, still squealing as his foot remained planted on the brake pedal, but more than that the unearthly scream of the Bianchi's engine, just inches above him. For the sprog had panicked, that was clear. Giving it loud, had probably seen Kinsella come up on him in his mirrors at the last moment, tried to accelerate away, and now his foot was hard on the gas, buzzing the engine mercilessly and spinning the wheels close to where Kinsella sat.

The roll hoop just above and behind Kinsella's head had stopped the Italian's car with a jolt, so that the rear end of the Bianchi was directly on top of Kinsella, just inches clear of the crown of his helmet. But now, as the interlocked machines slowed to almost a stop, the Bianchi started to slide off the DBM, rotating anti-clockwise, very slowly, as it did so. The still-spinning left rear wheel inched towards Kinsella just as he caught sight of the sky again, just as he was about to breathe his sigh of relief.

He couldn't move, couldn't even make himself small – strapped tightly in for safety – and in that moment Kinsella had an insight into time, into the tricks of Zeno, and into true fear. The spinning left rear wheel of the Bianchi arched towards him as the car fell away from him very slowly. Kinsella wanted to close his eyes, but somehow couldn't, and instead he focussed on the spinning black mass in front of him, picking out white trails from the studs of stones plucked from the trackside by the hot rubber as the Bianchi had slowed... Christ, he could even smell and feel the heat from its sticky well-worked surface. And then the tyre struck Kinsella's helmet, ripping away the visor, and snapping his head back against the headrest with the force of a mule kick – an 800 horsepower mule kick. At that very point of impact with Kinsella's helmet the spinning wheel began to fall away from him...

The digital TV station was re-running the shunt. Some of the DBM team, Kinsella and Chico among them, gathered around one of the slim, carbon effect, monitors that were suspended from the ceiling of the pit garage to show a list of practice or race times, but also to convey the action from the track. The hesitancy of the Bianchi driver was there for all to see, the camera focussing in just as the green and black car moved on to the racing line – it would be difficult for them to pin this one on him, Kinsella thought. Then there was the tyre smoke pouring from the silver and blue DBM's wheels as it came into picture: the moment of impact, the shredding of carbon fibre, and the flailing of the tethered front wheels before it was lost beneath the Bianchi.

There was a collective intake of breath from those assembled around the screen as in a split second the Bianchi's wild ride across the top of the DBM was arrested by the DBM's air box with its integral roll hoop, just behind Kinsella's head. Then the green and black car lurched forward and swivelled slightly, its rear wheels still spinning impotently against the azure Melbourne sky. It was here that the TV director chose to freeze the action, just as the spinning rubber made contact with Kinsella's helmet, which he now held by its vented chin guard, swinging it slowly, rocking it almost.

3

He knew that they would be looking at him, some of them – Chico perhaps? Looking for a reaction, a wince even: it was that sort of shunt. The picture, frozen there, flickering there, just in front of him, loaded with 'what ifs'. They would want to know what it had done to him, could it slow him? Lose him a tenth on the lap? He pushed at the bridge of his mirrored shades, bringing them tighter to his face, closer to the eyes. Christ, and they were right to look, this time at least, for he had done the sums. These days, he'd figured, 9.5 times out of ten you could bet on coming out of an accident without a scratch. But when the exposed head was involved the odds shifted. He turned and coughed a little to hide the shiver that ran down his body. Someone said something: 'close one', something like that, the end of it lost in the roar of a low passing Australian Air Force jet, keeping the crowd entertained in the run-up to qualifying. Kinsella turned to see Chico looking right at him, looking for something? Looking for that shiver perhaps? For a moment eyes met shades... And past those languid Latin eyes was there something? A shadow of doubt in the other man? Something Kinsella could take from this? Something in Chico he could use? Had Chico played the 'what ifs'? If he had, Kinsella could have him. That was for sure...

And so the game went on. He held up his helmet for all to see. Its green and red bands with cap of green, all on a field of white, were smeared from top to bottom with ugly black marks where the hot rubber of the Bianchi's tyre had done its level best to erase Kinsella. He said nothing for a moment, waiting until he had everyone's attention. Then he just held up the helmet, a jagged piece of tinted visor poking out at an angle, catching the sunlight, throwing a dancing spectrum across the spotless, white interior of the DBM garage. He ran his finger along the thick black smear of the tyre-mark until it too was black, and then he inspected it and said:

"Well, at least we know what tyre compound they are using now..."

The first of the laughing was nervous, one or two mechanics. But then others joined in, a mechanic slapped him on the back, even Chico was smiling a little – before turning to talk with DBM technical director Gordon Fraser, who was ready with a sheaf of papers – data from Chico's last qualifying run for them to go over. Business as usual.

Yes, business as usual. They showed the shunt again, but Kinsella didn't watch – old news now, had to be, no place for memories and imagination in this game. Certainly no place for 'what ifs'. The only thing that mattered was the last lap and then the next, it was the way it had to be. Kinsella searched the DBM garage for his own engineer.

4

A group of mechanics worked on his car, most of the damage seemed superficial, and it would take no time for them to replace the broken front suspension and steering components. At least he wouldn't have to take out the spare for qualifying that afternoon. It was set up for Chico anyway, his advantage: fair enough, quicker in winter testing by a long chalk, half-a-second at most places, more than that at Barcelona. Yes, Chico was top dog at DBM for now, as all – except Kinsella – had expected.

Kinsella picked out his race engineer, Burgess, towards the rear of the pit, communications headset still in place, hunched over a laptop computer which was resting on one of the gleaming silver tool cabinets that lined the rear wall of the pit garage. Burgess was tapping away furiously, looking for some way to find that half-a-second, half-a-second that would translate into half a minute across a race distance. Half-a-second, an aeon in F1. Kinsella had seen the times, he could only hope that the telemetry from that 'hot lap' would show something different, show that the speed was at least there somewhere – wayward sprogs aside.

Other mechanics – Chico's crew – were working methodically on his team mate's car, which sat on low stands to the left of Kinsella's. He watched as they went through the process, stepping over the myriad electronic umbilicals, monitoring the patient at rest, checking its heart, its fluids, all done with that happy familiarity that comes when things have gone right. Although a couple of the mechanics lay on the floor to work on the car their DBM uniforms – of silver grey polo shirts, with blue piping and sponsors' logos, and blue baggy shorts – remained spotless.

In fact, everything in the DBM garage was spotless, functional, surgical even – aside from the shards of splintered carbon fibre from Kinsella's machine. Even the oil collected from the gearbox of Chico's car was as clear as thrice pressed olives. Kessler and Fraser would have it no other way. More importantly, the suits from K-Corp, the team's main sponsor, would have it no other way. A snapshot of memory came before Kinsella's eyes: him, a friend, the corner of a wind-blown paddock in England, them working on the old – even then old – Formula Ford in the rain and the mud, running out of time before the race was due to start. Time moves on Kinsella, time moves on...

Burgess was beside him now, shouting above the noise of a revving Sultan in the pit next door. He had printed off the telemetry from his and Chico's best laps onto transparencies, and had overlain them for comparison. At the top he had written in black marker: *Saturday morning – untimed session. Australian Grand Prix.* There were other details too: date, time, weather conditions, track temperature, wind direction, wind speed, wing settings, tyre pressures, damper settings, suspension settings, gear ratios... many other details. Details to be studied microscopically. For in the details lie the hundredths, the tenths. And string a few of them together, then you might just have a half-a-second. Might just catch Chico.

Kinsella looked at the chart in front of him. Two jagged mountain ranges, one with steep curves, dropping off in precipices, the other a mirror image of the first, shifted to one side as if it peeped from behind it. While in the distance there was a cityscape of thin rectangular plateaux with little shelves of indecision, or triangular peaks spiking from top to bottom where he had jumped on the throttle for an instant. Every movement he had made over his fastest lap was recorded there, everything: the slight lift at Turn One when he had run wide, the wheel-spin out of Three when he had put the power down just a little early, and the tenth he had lost locking up into Ascari. All represented in peaks and troughs across the page. And behind was the handiwork of Chico, all too bold a peak, or a trough, where his team mate had excelled: hit the power earlier, braked later, all too bold... Christ, there was no hiding from it. The guy was good.

Kinsella asked for the trace from the hot lap, the lap spoilt by the green Italian. It was better, but still a bit off what Chico had managed up to that point, would probably have been 0.4 off on the lap. A worry.

"The set-up?"

"There's not a lot in it to be honest, perhaps a tad less wing... But he has you in the twisty bits too..."

The DBM mechanics started Chico's car up and Burgess' words were whipped away. Kinsella watched as one of the engine technicians attached to the team revved the V10 motor via a hand controller – similar to a trigger from a slot-car-set – that was attached to the keyboard of his laptop. The engine man's eyes were glued to the dancing graph on the screen in front of him, while all around pressed their fingers to their ears as the blip of the engine spoke its hooma-hooma-hooma, before momentarily rising to an air tearing rasp of half throttle. Kinsella turned back to the monitor that hung from the ceiling. The replays from the morning session had stopped now, to be replaced with a long list of times, not the times that would decide the grid, no, those would come later in the day. But some of the first shots in the campaign nonetheless, the first shots in a multi-million dollar campaign that would take them to fifteen countries across the world in the next seven months.

At last they knew where they stood – and DBM were standing very tall indeed. The double bluff of winter testing – where some ran lighter cars to clinch lucrative sponsorship deals – was out of the way. Friday's rained off session counted for little too. But this, this list, meant something, a taste of all to come. And so caught up had he been in his efforts to beat Chico he had hardly noticed how quick the DBM, at least in his team mate's hands, was.

Chico was top. Then came the two Sultans of Guido Solé and Thierry Michel. Then came Kinsella. Next up were the McLarens and the Ferraris, with the under-financed Spando of Bobby Drake Jnr splitting them. Then the others filled out the usual slots. Much the same as the year before, all that fighting talk and the hype over for another season. As they always say: 'when the flag drops the bullshit stops'. Now, for them – the slower runners – it was back to business, scraping a few points where they could, bringing in the money where they could. But without the right package, the best of everything: engine, chassis, design team, driver – and some thought in that order – they were nothing. Christ, a team like Bianchi could put Chico behind the wheel and be nowhere.

Which was why beating your team mate was everything. Beat your team mate in a Bianchi often enough, then you might move up – up to a Spando perhaps, a sniff of a win there, podiums often. Then you beat your team mate there and you find yourself knocking at the doors of the big boys, teams like DBM and Sultan, McLaren and Ferrari. Well, at least that's the way that Kinsella had played it. Only now he was up against the best... And in F1 the only guy playing on the same field is your team-mate, your only measure: your value. Kinsella had signed for $2m. Chico for $15m.

He had to find that half-a-second.

He looked at the car again, Chico's car, which was still shivering slightly as the engine technician continued to tickle at the throttle. Even like this, sans much of its sweeping bodywork, it was still a thing of magnificent beauty, a fusion of the functional with the aesthetic that he would never tire of, he thought. Yet this was a thought that he was always careful to keep to himself – it would do little for the Kinsella image to let them all know that he actually liked these bloody things. Couldn't let then know that even now he would allow himself a little smile when he just thought of sliding into the cockpit of an F1 car. Couldn't let them know that he could still grin to himself when he thought of how lucky he was: Eoghan 'Egg' Kinsella – Formula One driver. A man entrusted with the control of a car valued in millions; a car weighing much less than a Mini but with the power of fifteen sports-styled road cars; a car which can easily top 200 mph and can accelerate from nought to 100 mph – and then brake to a standstill again – in just over six seconds. And, most importantly of all, a car which would ultimately allow him to show the world that he was the very best.

The engine of the DBM had burbled, farted and died. Burgess started to talk to him again, pointing to the graph, showing where Chico was up on him, rubbing it in. The mood elsewhere in the garage was lighter, they had a car this year after all, should be bonuses aplenty. A girl, usual paddock sort, with a photographer or two in tow, was prancing about near Chico's car. They shouldn't have been there really, but with the joviality – with the first happy flush of success – no one had bothered to stop them as they slipped beneath the elasticated tape that bounded the DBM pit area. It wasn't unusual here anyway, wasn't unusual anywhere the F1 circus visited, always plenty of fluff. Already that day the DBM pit had been visited by a couple of buxom Aussie soap stars, a pop starlet and a model painted in the colours of K-Corp, wearing – as far as Kinsella could tell – little else but the silver and blue non-drip. All good grist for the PR mill though, and that's what mattered. This new girl's outfit left little to the imagination either – even an imagination never stretched too far beyond 'what ifs' after a good buffing from a spinning disc of hot rubber. Kinsella, like the rest, found himself staring.

It was just an old string vest really, the diamond mesh stretched by the heave of her breasts, so that one nipple forced its way through, hard and dark. The vest was about four sizes too big for the girl, hanging low over her thighs and off her shoulder at the neckline. A leg, long and bronze, was lifted and swung over the cockpit side of the DBM. There was a peep of darkness, and a gasp from one of the mechanics close by, and then she lifted the other leg into the cockpit and she was standing in the DBM, standing on Chico's seat. Kinsella turned to find him, but the South American was nowhere to be found: probably huddled up with Fraser already, poring over the telemetry, missing the show, missing the fun...

She slid herself down into the cockpit and Kinsella saw her face for the first time, the smile of a showgirl in control of the audience, in control of the situation, the watchers – the snappers – reflected in the lenses of her dark glasses. Her hair was cut short, in a spiky cap, black against the deep tan of her skin. He thought he recognised her, one of the usual crowd of camp followers perhaps, the usual crowd of racer chasers, but he could not be sure. As she slid herself into the cockpit of the DBM Kinsella found himself framed precisely in the reflective lenses of her glasses. She smiled at him, the sort of smile that says so

8

much: forget about that half-a-second, stuff like that... He smiled back – a reputation to enhance – but then he was distracted, pushed from behind as others tried to get into the pit garage.

The DBM PR man – Kinsella had little time for him – was trying to clear away a mass of photographers who, smelling the sex, had come running to the pit garage and were now pushing against the elasticated tape fence to get a better view of the action. Kessler wouldn't like this, Kinsella thought, not ordered at all... He allowed himself a little laugh. Back at the car a friendly mechanic was pointing out some of the more interesting features of the controls to the girl, not really knowing where to look as he leaned over the cockpit orifice. Kinsella heard her ask him where the detachable steering wheel was and then he saw the sudden flash that lit the cockpit, and the compact camera that the girl clutched tightly.

No harm, she protested – souvenirs that's all... But Kessler and Fraser had been drawn back into the garage by the commotion and had not seen it that way at all. They chewed off Chico's crew for the lapse, and the PR man struggled to wrest the little camera from the girl's hands while the photographers around the entrance to the DBM pit gave him hell for his efforts. Fraser shouted at her and she started to cry, pulling off her shades and rubbing at her eyes.

Poor Fraser, poor Kessler, neither of them knew where to turn, both embarrassed and angry, while none of the mechanics knew what to do either – where do you hold the thing, it was virtually naked, and those tears..? Finally, the PR man grasped the nettle and pulled her clear of the car, shepherding her out of the front of the pit, a scrum of photographers pressing close to them. Kessler shouted after him: "Get the camera, get the camera..." As she passed Kinsella shrugged in sympathy, before allowing himself another little laugh. Kessler's paranoia was well known. Ever since a nosy snapper had scooped the team's trick braking system at Hockenheim a couple of years back cameras were banned from anywhere near a DBM cockpit. For his part, Kinsella could only wonder where she had hidden the thing.

As the furore died down Kinsella motioned for Burgess to follow him to the back of the garage, where a door opened onto the paddock. He still held the buffed-up helmet by its strap, and glancing down at it he felt the ghost of a shiver dance along his spine. Another knot of pressmen waited in the paddock, among the piles of tyres and equipment. Kinsella told Burgess to wait for him in the motor-home, peaceful there, somewhere to go into the detail of the telemetry. And besides, he could do without someone from the Chico camp clocking the worry on their faces.

The press wanted to know about the shunt, something juicy for the back pages, no doubt there would be pictures, it was a good spot for pictures. He tried to see if Mossup was in the press of scribblers. If Chico's early speed was anything to go by he might need to stock up on favours – and an exclusive now could help him later.

Chapter Two

Yeah, it wasn't professional. But the rain was pissing him off. The job was pissing him off. He had thought he'd seen the last of this type of work, tailing the cheating husband. How had he let himself be talked into it? Bloody Sarah. Bloody money.

The case sat in the barber's chair. Stubbs could see the little hairs on the back of his neck – no, never tailed this close before. The barber was already snipping at the case's fringe, pulling it back with a comb and cutting it down, cutting it level. The case eyed Stubbs in the big mirror, natural enough, where else to look – a little shop, one barber, Stubbs next in line – though he wouldn't take the chair of course. No, he'd be off, after the newly shorn one.

Stubbs looked past the streaks of racing raindrops that clouded the window a pearly grey, and into the even greyer street beyond. A cabbie argued with a punter kerbside, and couples, huddled beneath the water stained cupolas of umbrellas, hurried past the shop front without glancing in. But there was little to hold his interest in a wet Ealing afternoon and he turned to the case again and their eyes met in the mirror once more. Stubbs shifted his gaze to the corner of the mirror. His own eyes now, tired, red-rimmed, set deep in a soft, round face – fat face, Sarah said. The case was still watching him though, he felt sure of it, and Stubbs found himself fingering the shiny scar beneath his nose, as always – always under stress. He picked up a magazine from the top of a pile that sat beside him, big and glossy, he opened it and lifted it to his face.

The magazine was called *F1 Racing*, it would do. It was a sport he watched sometimes, fell asleep to it after a good Sunday roast down *The Lion*. Plenty of pictures of girls too. One in particular had caught his eye: a stunner in a rag of a string vest, tits on the point of bursting free, clambering all over a silver and blue racing car. Then there

11

was a sequence of pictures showing another silver and blue car, perhaps the same one Stubbs thought, but on flicking back he saw that the numbers were different: that one seven, this one eight. The number eight car was pictured burrowing beneath another car, a green car. The last picture in the sequence had been enlarged. It showed the rear wheel of the green car spinning against the helmeted head of the driver of number eight. He'd seen the picture before, a few weeks ago it had made the back page of *The Brit*, an exclusive – but then they were always saying that. An interview with the driver had accompanied it, laughing the whole thing off, laughing a bad race off. Ice cool. But to look at that, what: an inch to the left, a nothing on the pic', a nothing to the left and he would have been chewing on the rubber. He allowed himself a little shiver, other people's danger, what it's all about, he supposed, this racing game: a vicarious thrill on a Sunday afternoon – before dozing off. Over the page was the report from the Australian Grand Prix, the first round of the Formula One World Championship. The South American, Chico, had won. At a canter the stand-first said. The other silver and blue car, the number eight car, was pictured beached in a bed of what looked to be blue-painted gravel.

He turned the page again. Another girl. The sort of girl you never really see, never in the street – just for the pages of magazines this one. Almost boringly beautiful he thought: the sort of face you could take a protractor to, perfectly spaced eyes that belonged in a jewellers, hair that was spun from softened ebony shards, flecked with the essence of flame itself, and arranged into a tumble of elaborately organised mayhem. A neck that was long and slender, fluted it seemed, meeting the shoulders in a way that suggested design – no art – no design... as if, if you were to continue the lines into her head, they would meet at some point, some fulcrum of her beauty.

Oh, and that body, tagged with a minuscule bikini, the orange of which was almost lost in a deep tan of newly minted copper coinage. The clavicles protruded a little, curving outwards like the lip of a bodice, forming their own little hollows. And then, of course, there were the breasts: not too big, bunched and brown, straining against the orange cloth, hinting at that independence that all the best breasts have: even functional, professional breasts. The stomach was flat, save for a ripple – she sat on a rock – while the curve of the hip bone played teasing geometry with the stretch of the bikini bottom, opening a gap, enough for a finger he supposed. Then the legs, crossed and curving to the bottom of the picture – too long for the picture, cropped at amber ankle.

Sitting on the rock with this vision, this thing of fiction, this glossy goddess, was a man. Stubbs instantly recognised him as Chico, a face of the time. Like the vision he wore nothing but a bathing costume, minimalist – the sort of thing that South Americans seem to be able to get away with, the sort of thing that would look bloody ridiculous on an Englishman. You could easily make out the curl of his penis through the wet cloth. His tightly curled hair was wet too, and his athletic, long muscled body shone with the salt water, painfully reminding Stubbs of Sarah's jibe the night before – 'lose some weight Justin'. Chico's arm was around the goddess, both sat on the rock: both visions framed by the bright sun-bleached sands stretching to the white flecked sea in the background... *Bastard*, thought Stubbs, allowing himself a wry little smile to go with the jested jealousy.

Stubbs thought himself an expert at interpreting body language, part of the game he supposed, you need to know when you're rumbled after all, need to know when they've sussed you, following them, following them all bloody day long. And he was certain of one thing here. This superstar on the page in front of him was not comfortable, was not comfortable at all, posing with the model: the professional vision with the professional tits. Which was why he almost gasped aloud when his eyes were drawn to the caption beneath the picture: *Relaxation: time to reflect on the perfect start to the season with wife Teresa on the their private – yes private – beach. All three miles of it...*

His wife? He found himself reading the feature.

What's it like to have everything? That's the question I wanted to ask José Chico Perez – universally known by middle name alone. What's it like to have absolutely everything a man could want? What's it like to have a beautiful wife, a talent recognised by his peers as the best of its generation, and a pay slip black with noughts?

Thing is, I never did ask him. Why? Simple. Within a minute of speaking to the great man I realised that he did not have everything after all. And what it was that he thought was missing was eating him up was filling every waking moment of his life, a want so great that it is a part of him... You see, Chico wants the comfort zone.

The comfort zone? What could be more comfortable than this you ask? A luxuriously appointed ranch by the sea with its own beach, five other homes across the world, a $5m yacht, a stable of auto exotica that would make the likes of you and me dribble, a private jet...

And the list goes on. While he can take extra comfort in the thought that he already has two world crowns under his belt and every early indication suggests that he has every chance of adding a third this year. Just how much comfort can one man take?

He laughed at that, a little, then weighed the question for some long moments, thinking it through, analysing it I supposed.

"Yes, it must seem strange. But it is never enough. Not the money I mean, not here... not all I have... Of course that's plenty for one man. But the car, that is never enough. For sure, we have half a second on the Sultans now. It is nothing. They could catch us, and Melbourne is not typical. It is slippery, we worked the rubber well. But we can never be complacent – it may all be upside down when we get to Interlagos for the Brazilian Grand Prix, so we must continue to work... There is much more work..."

So it seems I'm lucky to catch him at home, spending a day or two between tests with wife Teresa – a former beauty queen he married last year – almost a royal wedding here in the Republic such is the esteem that Chico is held in by his countrymen. He is recharging his batteries before jetting trans-Atlantic back to Barcelona, and yet more testing.

"It is a shame we had to stop for a while. But they wanted to get back to England, work on some new aerodynamic parts in the wind tunnel – and Gordon Fraser's always in touch anyway."

A touch of guilt there? Was he guilty that he was here, in paradise with his wife, rather than laboriously pounding around a race track 4,000 miles away, making the tiny settings that might, just might, shave off a tenth – a hundredth – of a second. Just might help to build the comfort zone.

"Perhaps... I can never feel comfortable when there is work to be done on the car, and there is always this advantage we must find... It's what I always look for. One-and-a-half seconds, maybe two seconds. Then we have won. When my engineer and I can get that from a car, then there is satisfaction... For me at least."

But surely the satisfaction is in the winning from behind, I suggest, like at Silverstone last year, when in the worst conditions in living memory he slithered the DBM from a mid grid position to the top step of the podium?

"There is satisfaction in that. For sure. But it is a small part of it all, it has always been there: through the go-karts here, then in Europe, and Formula Three in England. Just the racing.

"The extra step is what we do with the car. It's about perfection. First we find the perfect car, then we dominate, and then there is the chance of the perfect lap. That's the dream, that's the comfort zone."

Perfection then. It could be the motto of the DBM team, from the meticulous Otto Kessler down to the humblest van driver at the 200-strong Oxfordshire based operation. The sort of perfection that has

DBM technical chief Gordon Fraser – who also doubles as Chico's own race engineer – individually checking almost every single component that is bolted onto the twice world champion's car.

I asked Chico about Fraser, about the successful relationship the two have built up since the latter transferred from McLaren three years ago.

"He is very good. He is very, very good. Some people do not understand the situation, how he can engineer my car and yet still control the design team back at the base. But I see this as his strength, he is always there, at the sharp end – as he calls it – it compresses the line of communication... and it's good to know that he is behind me, someone I can rely on. That's important, yes?"

Yes, of course, someone to rely on – very important. Which brought us nicely to Eoghan 'Egg' Kinsella, the self-styled wild man of F1 and reluctant number two driver at DBM, who joined the team from Jordan with the fully stated intention of knocking Chico off the top spot but has – thus far – failed to shine.

It's a mark of the man that there were no digs, just understanding on Chico's part: "He has had a bad time. The crash in Melbourne, it wasn't his fault, it could have happened to any one of us. And I was impressed that he was fairly quick in qualifying later in the day. It was a shame for the team that he went off in the race. But it is early in the season, and I think he will be quick.

"But," and here Chico's eyes narrowed, just a little, "he has to learn that we must race as a team. I have the speed, I am the number one driver at DBM at the moment and it is up to him to back me up. I think for now he tries too hard to make a reputation, to make a reputation by beating Chico – it would be better for the team if both cars finished, no? But he will improve, and I am confident that as the season moves on he will be in a position to help me take the fight to the Sultans."

Others, it must be said, have yet to be convinced. But back to Chico, what about that perfect lap he spoke of. How often has it happened?

"Never." He said, that's all. But noting my confusion – disbelief even – he smiled that broad polar white smile of his and continued: "No, it's true, believe me. I have come close, and before I would have said that I have done it, on some qualifying laps. But now I see it different, the best lap is so much more, and the car must work with you, otherwise it is compromised, too much sliding. The perfect lap is right on the edge, but no more, right on the line, not a micron off. It can be done, I think – maybe this year. No?"

And how? "Again, it is about getting the package right. Driving a racing car is a little like slicing a loaf of bread. You have to learn to use the whole of the knife, every part of the blade – it is a tool, there to help you. But the cutting edge of that blade is much more than just the car, it is the team, it is the sponsors, it is every one at DBM. Only after you have used the whole package, the whole organisation, to the very best of its potential can you hope to go from centimetres to millimetres, half-seconds to tenths, excellence to perfection..."

His eyes shine as he speaks, there is obsession there it's plain to see, the sort of obsession – or passion – that all the greats have possessed. A single-mindedness of purpose that seems to exclude all else, maybe even the beautiful girl who sits next to him, who knows? Easy to think then that here is a man with a one track mind. But you would be wrong. For Chico has another track very much on his mind, the venue for the final round of this year's world championship – the first time a Grand Prix has been held in the Republic.

That fact alone, his first chance to perform in front of his almost fanatical home fans, adds spice to this year's season-closer for Chico. But this is just the start of it, for the circuit on which the race is to take place has also been designed and financed largely by Chico himself, and by all accounts it should be something to look forward to.

"I have set out to design the best track possible for the greatest Grand Prix possible. Many of the circuits these days are nothing more than glorified go-kart tracks, and many of the drivers miss the challenge of the great circuits. So we have tried to identify the best kind of corners the world has to offer and stitch them into one circuit, with plenty of gradient and some long straights for passing. I am convinced that it will be a challenge for the drivers and – this is important – it will be good for the spectators too, for the people of the Republic."

The press in the Republic have already christened the track the Chicodrome and despite Chico's modest protestations it looks like a name that is set to stick. If, that is, the project is finished. For rumours coming out of the country suggest that all is not well, with financial problems hindering the construction, while questions about the safety of such a circuit have also been raised.

"Yes, of course there have been problems. It is a giant undertaking. But now all the funds are in place and much of the draining of the marshland is completed and we are about to start blasting clear many of the rock faces to make ample run-off areas. I am confident that all will be ready in time for the race."

And what price Chico managing that perfect lap on this, what may well be the perfect track?

"Well, for that we will have to wait and see – there are many races to go before we come to the Republic... But it would be nice, Yes?"

Yes. And perhaps then I will be able to ask that question: what is it like to have everything Chico?

Stubbs peeped over the top of the page. The case was still there, the barber now scraping away the fine hairs on the back of his neck with a cut-throat razor. Back to the page: more pics, Chico and wife in the house, him in shorts and a T-shirt now – the K-Corp logo proud on the breast – her with a light blue cotton dress, pottering with bits and pieces in a cavernous, brick-lined vaulted kitchen. Stubbs studied the picture of her, posed there, slicing a courgette – not bread – slicing like a model would, not like a housewife would, not even like Sarah would. He looked at her eyes again. Jewels, yes – but empty, no light to make them sparkle. The woman was somewhere else, somewhere darker.

The case stood up, complimented the barber, and paid him. He encased himself in a large overcoat and walked out into the rain, lifting an umbrella over his haircut. Stubbs followed him, tossing the magazine aside.

"Don't you want a haircut, mate?"

Through the window of the barbershop, past his reflection in the rain stained glass and already at one with the grim London day, the case turned to face Stubbs, clocked him proper. Cover blown – but then he'd never liked this sort of job.

Chapter Three

Now he was alive. It always took until this time for Chico to feel truly alive, he sometimes thought. Truly himself, away from the confusion, away from the people – they all wanted a piece of him and he could never give them a piece that was truly Chico. Until now. Now, when it was just him and the car and – on occasion – Fraser's soft, controlled voice over the intercom.

He let the DBM roll to a halt at his grid slot, precisely on the white line, precisely on the white line with the little number 1 painted on it. Precisely on pole. He watched in the little wing mirror as the cars behind found their slots, peeling away from the long Formula One crocodile at the last moment, trying to keep their tyres clean by sticking to the racing line for as long as possible – the line best scrubbed by the passage of cars. The grid was staggered so that Chico lined up on the right – well placed for a good, clean arcing line into the first tight left hander. His DBM was a car's length ahead of Guido Solé in the first of the Sultans, with Thierry Michel in the other Sultan directly behind, a couple of car length's back. Chico tried to pick out Kinsella, somewhere down the grid, somewhere in the confusion of colour, somewhere beneath the blanket of heat that hung liquid above the grid. Gone the wrong way on set up, too much wing, Fraser had tried to warn them. Eighth.

Now concentration. For the fiftieth time that day he pictured the run down to the first turn in his mind, the way it should go, the mental exercise, preparing the way with positive thinking, before it became mechanical. He pulled back the hand-operated clutch with gloved fingers, selecting first gear with another paddle, also located on the underside of the steering wheel – a corresponding paddle for down-shifts to its left. The car seemed to shiver and kick slightly as the gear was selected. His right foot eased on the throttle, letting the revs rise, while his left foot rested firmly on the only other pedal, the brake pedal: insurance – it only takes a slight creep forward to gain a jump start penalty. On the gantry above and ahead of him the first of the three sets of double red lights shone brightly, while behind him the scream of 26 three-litre V10 racing motors roared full throated against the nervous tug of clutch fingers, a many mouthed monster ready to be unleashed. The Brazilian Grand Prix at Interlagos was about to begin.

Kinsella's car was slightly askew, his intentions clear: right up the middle. Some of the guys ahead of him should prove easy meat, the DBM had the grunt to pass them on the run to the first turn, provided his start was clean, was quick. But then he would have to work – own fault: eighth. Not good enough, 1.6 seconds off Chico in qualifying. He had the engine singing, wailing about the point of his chosen starting revs. He allowed himself the music of the engine note as he let it breathe there, little flexes of his right foot letting the revs rise a little, dip a little, rise a little and then settle at the optimum. All around him the noise of 26 Formula One cars was something solid in the Sao Paulo afternoon. He quickly glanced over to his right and thought he caught a glimpse of the eyes of the Jordan driver in front, framed thrice in mirror, helmet aperture and fire retardant balaclava. An old hand that one, wouldn't be intimidated by the Kinsella reputation, wouldn't be intimidated by the silver DBM's nose running up alongside him into the first turn.

Then the bank of red lights – floating and swollen in the distant heat it seemed – blinked off and all was noise and smoke... Fingers extended, clutch out. The car slewed against the camber of the road as the wheels spun frantically, scrabbling for purchase like a gun dog on an iced up river, before finding the grip. Instantly the back of his seat seemed to seize him by the shoulders, hurling him forward so that his stomach felt as if it was being sucked back into the base of his spinal column, a moment later the middle finger of his right hand was tugging back the gear paddle into second, and third an instant later.

Some of those in front had worse starts and he managed to nip between a Jordan and a Spando, easing ahead of them by a nose. An explosion of colour and noise continued to smudge his senses as he headed into the first turn and then, from nowhere it seemed – a nowhere hidden in a bank of thick tyre smoke – a red rear wing sprang up in front of him. A slow starting Ferrari, he was boxed. He lifted, spending momentum, and the Jordan and the Spando rushed alongside, both sides, smearing his peripheral vision with two contrasting explosions of colour. Kinsella was the meat in the sandwich, going into turn one: three abreast there? No chance.

Line of sight. His left front, the Spando's right front, an inch or two between them. His front right, a Jordan front left, two inches apart. In front is the Ferrari, throwing up more smoke as it's late on the anchors for the first turn. Kinsella brakes hard, a gossamer shroud of smoke wrapping itself around the front-left wheel. The turn's here, somewhere in the melee, he has to feel for it almost, no sign of his turn-in point: the advertising hoarding to the right, no sign of his clipping point: the tyre scuff on the low green and yellow banded wall to the left. But they are into the turning in area. The Spando to Kinsella's left is still braking hard, he can see the tyre smoke in his mirrors, the DBM has the room, but it's close. He feels the nudge as his rear left makes contact with the front right of the Spando, but he's into the first part of the turn, plunging downhill to the left. The DBM runs out to the right, drifting out to where the Jordan is crossed up, sliding on the loose stuff that collects at the outside of the turn, rubber thrown off wilting tyres, dirt from the spinners in the supporting races... Kinsella's committed to the line, feeding in the power a little, drifting to the edge of the track where the Jordan driver is having his adventure, holding the slide, holding it... They touch. The Jordan is tipped into a spin, slowly at first, an almost graceful loop, before pirouetting wildly through 360 degrees on the slick surface of the grass. Kinsella continues.

Thanks to the scuffle Kinsella's line for the next part of the 'S' bend is compromised, too far to the right, he gets well off the throttle, pulling the nose of the DBM back into line. The Spando is alongside him into the right and they share the long left that follows before, momentum lost, Kinsella is passed down the straight, first by a flash of red and white, then by a flash of blue that he recognises as a Prost.

Kinsella wiggled the steering a little down the short straight, watching the cityscape of Sao Paulo dance along the lip of his little windshield. No damage – as far as he could tell. The Prost had some lengths on him, while he in turn was some four lengths in front of a Sauber – more drama at the start behind him, no doubt. The sky in front of him seemed heavy with brightness and he narrowed his eyes a little to find his turning in point for the next corner, hidden somewhere in a band of liquid heat haze. A small rivulet of sweat burst from his collar and ran down his back. Time to settle it down Kinsella, time to find the groove... It's gonna be a long race.

One lap down and he had done the damage. Part of his strength that, the ability to pull a quick lap out of the bag right from the very start. Slam in a hot one when everyone else was either overcautious on tyres not yet as hot – as grippy – as they might have liked, or over-wild in the scramble to make up for bad grid positions. Not for Chico though, never wasted a first lap, never wasted a pole – not Chico. Get the start just right and bang in a quick one, always the way – don't even look in the mirrors, bang in a quick one and demoralise the rest. That's the way the greats had always done it: Fangio, Clark, Senna... Fraser would tell him the gap when he needed to know, when he had settled into a rhythm, broken the tow, found the comfort zone. And only then.

One-hundred-and-ninety mph. There was nothing in the cockpit to tell him, a speedometer superfluous, but he had carried the revs, had the speed – as good as it could have been on full tanks down the main pit straight. The lead DBM traced the edge of the track, then Chico was hard on the brakes, stabbing at a button on the steering boss that jumped the down-change, sixth to second – much quicker than you could say it... All the while the pads bite: carbon fibre pads to carbon fibre discs, capable of slowing the car from 200 mph to 50 mph in 50 metres, operating at 1000 degrees centigrade – so that in the murk of a wet afternoon the discs would glow cherry red through the wheels. The snappers loved that.

A late turn in for *Curva One* to narrow the line – he noted the beached Jordan in the gravel trap – he was still braking hard with his left foot, bleeding off the braking force into cornering force until that delicious moment where the car is on the limit, floating on the edge of adhesion through the steep downhill turn. And then he stabbed at the throttle, inducing a kick of a tail-slide, correcting it with a touch of opposite lock that almost becomes the first movement into the next sequence of the circuit, *Senna's S*. Since the great man's death in 1994 every track seemed to have one of those, here in Brazil the name fitted, for here the man had been a god, just like Chico back home. He lifted, then balanced the car on the throttle as he turned in to the 'S'. There was another moment when the DBM was right on the edge of adhesion, floating through the apex of the turn almost, and then he was through. Perfection. Out of it cleanly, winding the DBM through the gears as the car drifted to the right of the track coming out of the second part of the 'S', *Curva do Sol*... Tugging at the paddle behind the wheel with the middle finger of his right hand, each computer controlled full throttle up-shift taking just 35 milliseconds... Not a slice of time that can even be talked about – thought about – sensibly.

Along the back straight there was a chance to check the instruments, look for clouds in the clear white afternoon, register the skyscraper crammed horizon as he crests a rise – and the deep green of the grass at track fringe which seemed to mirror the field of the Brazilian flag.

Descida do Lago: down to third – just 10 milliseconds on the down-shift as the computer has to blip the throttle to match the revs – careful on the gas mid corner, treacherous camber, keep it straight, for the next left, up to fourth for *Ferradura*: Chico's favourite, a technical piece of tarmac, double apex, the second of which was blind: calls for commitment, letting the car float across the blind brow... Big balls motoring – that's what Fraser had called it – letting it drift to the very edge... Then it's back on the heat for a scruffy little right, thumping right across the brightly-striped corrugated curbing to the inside with a judder and a jolt that rattled Chico's spine every lap. Untidy, yes, but necessary, narrowing the angle, letting him get on the power as early as possible: fast out, that's the secret see, carry the speed – carry the speed to *Bico de Pato*. It's all about traction now, no use wasting time scrabbling about in the slow first gear right hander, and you need to careful here, the speed is down, the wings less effective – they like a slab of quick air on them, anything beneath 70 mph is pretty much ineffective, it's easy to spin the wheels here... Then down the hill through a fast sweeper of a left at *Mergulho*, into *Juncao*. Vital to get it turned in, and then for some long moments the engine sounds tinny as he's off the gas, tinny like a two stroke, and it's all so tempting to flatten the noise with a great burst of revs, but patience, patience. Must get the power on cleanly, mustn't scrub off speed up the hill, the long blast through *Subida dos Boxes*, where Senna dropped it in '94 – always mention that don't they? Just a half spin, but the greats are not allowed mistakes Chico – the greats are not allowed mistakes.

He flicked the paddles up through the gears as the DBM ate up the long curve that led up the hill onto the start-finish straight. Travelling at close to 170mph now, the downforce generated from the wings made him feel like he was being sucked down into the floorpan of the DBM while his eyeballs were shaken in their sockets by the bumps of the Interlagos track. Yet still he thought he could pick out the blurred form of Fraser on the other side of the pit wall, ear protectors clamped to his head, up close to the computer under the mini silver and blue DBM rostrum and awning attached to the pit wall. And then he was gone in a smear of colour, the spectral image replaced by his static laced voice over the radio:

"*Nice one Chico...*" an electronic crackle, "*pit plus thirty... Out.*"

Lap twenty. The sponsor's name on the back of the Prost would be tattooed on Kinsella's consciousness for all time. He was sure of it, he would see it when he fell asleep, he would see it when he awoke – Christ, he might even start to have cravings for the things, become a 40 a day man... But give it one more go Kinsella, give it one more go. The dirty air was the problem, second hand air, air that had done its work over and under the Prost's upside-down aeroplane wings, air pressing the thing to the road. The sort of hard worked air – downforce they called it – that could theoretically increase the dead weight of the car by two. And even at 1:1 the car could, they said, be driven on the ceiling – though as yet no one has tried. Hard work then: tired air, dirty air, turbulent air; slapping around Kinsella's head, spilling about the wings, a part-spent force, making the DBM a handful – but he had to stay in there, hoping for the chance, waiting for the mistake from the man in the deep blue Prost.

For it had become apparent that a mistake from the driver of the Prost would be Kinsella's only chance. In those early laps he had watched as the Spando, which was hanging on to the tail of the group chasing the leading runners – chasing Chico – had gradually eased away. But all he could do was sit there. Yes, he had the legs on the Prost. Yes, he had the grunt up the straight. But it was the age old problem: in this sport of racing actual racing was bloody difficult – if you took racing to mean one car passing another and so on. Aerodynamics – that's the curse you see, all that dirty air means the car behind is slowed, scrabbling about in the turns so that it loses its momentum onto the straights, loses its speed for the passing places, under braking for the corners.

And then there were the brakes. Outbraking. The art of the greats. What it had all been about: you and him, side by side, approaching the corner: chicken at 200mph – who'll be first to clamp on those anchors. Thing is, with the carbon brakes and the ultra light cars, braking distances could be measured in feet, in heartbeats, leaving no room for heroics, no room for creativity. Indeed, with 4G under braking at some circuits it was as much as some drivers could manage to keep their heads on their shoulders.

But Kinsella could hope. Give it one last try, and if that fails? Well then he would have to pit early, give himself some track space for the quick laps, at least there was still the chance of a world championship point or two.

A good run into *Juncao* was the secret, a slow turn, where the aerodynamics are not so critical. But running under the wing of the

Prost for twenty laps had caused its own problems, the front tyres had worn and the car was understeering, the front wheels sliding first, scrabbling for grip into the turns. Could probably live with it in the clean air, he thought, but not here. Still, one last go.

For the last five laps Kinsella had lifted through the left hander leading into the tight *Juncao*, lifted as the front end had gone light and floated aimlessly over a bump in the road – the sort of bump which plagued the Interlagos track and the sort of bump that had jellified Kinsella's peripheral vision into a goldfish life of scuffed up artist's pallet. But this time he has to keep his boot in, more balls over mind than mind over matter. One big breath as the car floats over the bump, hold it... hold it... the front of the car is drifting towards the edge of the track, the steered wheel pointing slightly to the left of the direction of the car – no more big blue wing for a moment, just the jungle of Sao Paulo high-rise – then his heart punches his ribcage, his buttocks clench against the moulded racing seat: too much speed, going off...

For a moment physics was personified, as if an invisible force was tugging at the car, a giant hand intent on tossing it away like a toy, and it floated there, no weight through the steering as the outside wheels ran along the bumpy grass verge. Kinsella jinked the wheel left a little... Then grip. He rode it out, a cloud of dust in the little mirror, and then that wing big and blue – bigger and bluer – ahead of him. Keep it clean through *Juncao* Kinsella, tuck yourself up tight to him, squeeze on the power when he does – there, you have it, a little wiggle of the rear as you put on the power, but he's done the same. Nothing lost. Up close through *Subido do Boxes*, closer still through the long, long left hander that leads onto the straight...

Kinsella jinked right, then left, but the driver of the Prost was not about to be sold the dummy. So it was right again, forcing the blue car in left for the turn, the more acute angle, but still the favoured line in an outbraking battle – more scope for taking the road. Kinsella was a nose ahead and just inches from the Prost when they both jumped on the brakes. But it wasn't enough and, front tyres worn, the DBM just drifted to the outside of the turn. Scrubbing off speed, while the Prost did likewise, taking up the asphalt that Kinsella had wanted to make his own, getting on the power while Kinsella was still sorting out his understeer. The Prost pulled out a few more lengths into Senna. He wouldn't get far, Kinsella knew that, had the legs on the French car, no doubt about it – but passing...

There was the crackle in his helmet, then the static laced voice of Burgess over the radio: *"Pit plus two... Pit plus two... Out."*

Two more laps behind the blue wing, and then, as they entered the pit straight for the 24th time, Kinsella jinked left into the pitlane – here the time can be made up, if you're quick enough, if the crew's quick enough. Make the time here, and on the first few laps out of the pits, and then comes the Prost's turn to pit – and then you will have him Kinsella. Up to the white line and it's hard on the brakes: pit lane speed limit, press the button for the limiter – who was that? Helen or Katie, which one had thought that funny, a speed limit in Formula One? Just another of the rules to make the game a little safer.... Flick at the switch that opens the re-fuelling flap. Find the slot, Kinsella, look for the silver and blue suited mechanics, the spaceman with the lollipop, guiding you in, jink left: and here's the scam to make up the time, the time found in the detail. On the white line, precise, that way the mechanics can get straight to work: jacked up, air guns to wheel nuts, fuel line to filler nozzle – pumping it in at 12 litres per second. Brakes on so the wheels don't spin when the mechanics turn the nuts, careful not to blip the throttle – must not shake the car, got to make this as easy for them as possible – and with that comes the time, the second or two to put him ahead of the Prost.

As the long seconds of lost motion pass the well-choreographed crew are centre stage: jack-men, wheel-men, fuel-men, men who now had their own special part in the drama of the race. Wheels changed first, then more long, long seconds as the last of the fuel made its painfully slow progress through the corrugated, elephantine, hose. The lollipop man in front of him flipped his sign from brake to in gear, someone wiped his visor clean – wet cloth, dry cloth – his fingers flicked the gear selector into first and he buzzed the throttle just as the DBM was dropped from the jacks front and rear. Eight seconds. Just eight seconds. Power, jink right, wheelspin, the tail kicking right as he straightened the DBM, mirrors filled with his tyre smoke, correct the power slide, careful there... check the limiter, just 120 kph through the pits. Patience Kinsella. Patience. A frustrating trundle along the pitlane: then you floor the thing, put the hot laps in, use the new rubber, use the clean air.

Lap 69. Three to go. Twenty-five wins. He should not let himself think it, he knew that, but a little satisfaction after a long race, a tough race, why not? A tough race? Well, okay, Chico had led from the front, start to finish, built up a gap in the early stages, kept it after the sort out of the stops: 10 seconds. Not bad – but hardly domination. Nothing on Melbourne for sure. And they were still there, ten or eleven seconds behind, both the Sultans circling as one, the chase forgotten perhaps – but still too close for comfort, too close for Chico's comfort. There would be plenty of work before Imola. For sure. But for now to stroke it home, keep the gap constant, try to ignore the little noises: singing rivets, nagging squeaks. The sort of noises that tease the imagination: is that engine note a little flatter, was that a misfire, and the way it squatted, out of *Juncao*, the beginnings of a puncture? It was always the way, Chico knew it, the comfort zone could be a mighty uncomfortable place when all there was to do was watch the gap, nurse the car home.

It wasn't surprising really, this late race paranoia. After all, a Formula One car is hardly built to last, just the one race will do for many of the components. Tolerances on parts – like everything in F1 – are taken to the very limit, so that a part worth thousands is often thrown out with the trash after just one outing. Indeed, should the car last the year without being written off there would be very little chance that it would actually *be* the same car, such is the turnover of parts. And for individual races it was the age old balance between the lightness of the components and durability – just enough durability to get the car to the flag, that's all that was needed.

Just enough durability to get the car to the flag then and then it's twenty-five wins. Puts him up there with the greats: up alongside Jimmy Clark on the winners' list. Statistics, satisfying statistics. Measure yourself against the clock, measure yourself against the record book. And then there was Kinsella.

It was the first sight that Chico had had of the other DBM all race. A quick, cautionary, glance at his instrument panel and then there it was, as Chico looked up, in profile against the cityscape, turning into *Curva do Sol*, the length of the back straight away. Too far away to catch. Good, thought Chico. Kinsella had suffered since the Melbourne shunt, however cool he played it – anyone would suffer after that, suffer in the head. It wouldn't help to lap him, rub it in, scuff away a little more of the confidence. Wouldn't help Kinsella, wouldn't help the team.

He gave the DBM its head through the turn, just eight-tenths now, letting the car run with the corner, keeping the loading low on the race-stressed components and the tyres. Coming out of the corner he fed in the power, catching another glimpse of his team-mate's DBM as he did so, closer. Up to *Ferradura* and the other DBM grew bigger, almost as if someone was pumping air into it – must be slowing. Hard on the brakes for the first gear turn, the slowest part of the track, and now he was with Kinsella. The other DBM driver kept to the line, clouting the kerb with the underside of the car, and powering away from the turn. No problem there thought Chico, seems to be handling okay, accelerating okay for sure... Transmission?

Into the next tight turn they were as one, Kinsella certainly carrying the speed. Chico noted that the other DBM slid wide, a little too much understeer – perhaps the rubber was suffering, but that wouldn't explain the sudden drop off in speed? Whatever, he was with him, and had an advantage on him through *Mergulho* and into the tight *Juncao* corner that, ultimately, set the speed for the pit straight.

Kinsella was through clean enough, but Chico was quicker: he should let him by now, Kinsella should let him through now. Ignominy for the Englishman? A little, perhaps – but the Sultans were too close for games.

Chico stabbed at the little comms button on the steering wheel:

"I'm with Egg – has he seen me?" Of course he had, but caution is king at this stage of a race, when every noise is there to taunt you, when every rattle is the harbinger of doom and gloom: the doom and gloom of a grenaded motor.

"Don't know... been on their blower..." The rest of Fraser's words were lost as Chico wound the DBM through the gears, up towards the funnel of grandstands and pit complex, until, within easy range of the pits:

"Comms down... we think..."

Chico had jinked right, to go the long way around Kinsella. As he did so he caught a glimpse of his pit-board, hung over the wall by one of the silver-suited mechanics, last lap's info', of course, still *+10 Solé*, but the Sultans would have gained over the last part of the lap. For sure. Time to get past, put in a flyer, re-stamp his authority on the race.

He was almost alongside Kinsella. As he'd moved out to pass he thought that he had caught a glimpse of the other DBM driver's eyes in the mirror of the car in front – surely he must have seen him...

Towards the braking point for *Curva One* track marshals waved blue flags to tell Kinsella he was about to be lapped by a quicker car: lapped by a car that had done one more 2.6 mile lap in the same 90 minute period. Lapped by his team-mate – the measure of Kinsella's worth.

He knew he was there, of course he did. Had spotted his pit-board, two laps earlier, out alongside Kinsella's in readiness for the race leader. Hadn't thought it through really, just slowed. He was secure in sixth after all – lucky in that after he had taken track position off the Prost others had retired. No threat then, well up on the Minardi now in seventh, well down on the Ferrari in fifth. Just bring it home Kinsella. That's all you have to do...

Yes, they would know that there had been problems, but then again: problems, excuses... what's the bloody difference in this crazy game? Why not show them now? And so he had let Chico catch him... And now came the time to play the game. Just a burst of speed to leave his mark on the race that's all, show them he has the measure of Chico, show them all when the cameras are on the leader. Fraser had been on the radio, hysterical, telling him to get out of the way. Kinsella had ignored it, switched off the intercom: 'must have knocked it by mistake' he would say. And the other DBM so big in his mirrors for half a lap? Thought it was the Minardi, they look alike...

Just half a lap to keep the fight alive, that's all he needed. And so he shared the braking zone with Chico, ignoring the furiously waved flags, a shouted semaphore that said: move over, a faster car is lapping you, should be passing. He had gone in deep, the front sliding because of the understeer still plaguing the DBM. Chico had tried to go round the outside, but had backed off at the last moment. Now to put in some fast corners: through *Senna*, along the back straight, the other silver car tucked up close behind him. More waved blues. Chico with his hand out of the cockpit gesticulating. Just match him through *Curva do Sol*, then wave him through Kinsella...

Chico's hand was violently whipped back by the slipstream, but he steadied it and clenched his fist – motor racing for let me through, you're being lapped. At about the same time the radio crackled into life again:

"Take him Chico... gap's down to seven..."

This had happened before. The impossible. Just when the race was comfortably in his pocket – screwed, thrown away. He looked into his mirror. Sure enough, just coming onto the straight were two tiny orange specks. He allowed himself a curse at this turn of misfortune as his eyes locked onto the ever-swelling orange blobs in the mirror... And that was the first and last mistake that Chico made that afternoon: the corner was on him from nowhere, Kinsella almost at the apex by the time Chico put his foot to the brake. Both front wheels locked as the silver car speared onto the grass, grass that he could hear brushing against the underside of the car as it slid wildly. He massaged the brake pedal to bleed off speed, all the time blipping the throttle with his right foot to keep the engine alive. Then he was off the brake, using the generous run-off to coax the car back onto the tarmac, little jabs at the throttle to bring the rear end around, one big slide, a bump over which the DBM scraped its floorpan... And then he was back on track, fishing for a lower gear – the thundering train of the two Sultans bearing down on him.

Accelerating away in second, up to third, they had the momentum. But he was lucky, into *Ferradura*, Chico was gathering speed all the time, into the first gear *Pinheirinho*, keeping his line as tight as possible, making them try to go round the outside. But there was no room there, only bad track, bad track for the run down to the next right-hander. They dropped back a length and Chico was back in control.

By the time that Kinsella took the flag Chico was half way round his triumphant slowing down lap. By the time he had parked up, Chico was on the rostrum, flanked by the two orange-overalled Sultan drivers. While by the time that the podium finishers had sprayed their champagne over each other to *The March* from *Carmen* Kinsella was walking back to the motor-home for debriefing. Walking past the photographers rushing to the rostrum for pictures of the celebrations. Walking past the small knots of mechanics – losing teams – who were already crating their equipment for the long flight home. And walking past the still-packed stands, where small bands played Samba, the one clue that this was another foreign country, not just that place they call Formula One.

Once in the motor-home behind the pits he peeled off his white and blue race suit. They were lucky for this privacy here, the Interlagos paddock was crammed to say the least, but K-Corp had a presence – it was a sponsor of the race too – and DBM was glad of its little haven on wheels.

So, one point. Not good, but something. There would be trouble though, from Fraser, from Kessler, from the clerk of the course maybe, a fine perhaps for ignoring the blue flag, couple of thousand: peanuts. And trouble from Chico? Not sure there... But he was sure of one thing, Chico had panicked. He had played with the superstar, teased him, panicked him into a mistake – almost threw the race away when it was in his pocket. Chico had done it before, silly things like that, always when ahead, but by not quite enough for comfort – that was the place to get him then, get close and make him do the rest himself. Another something Kinsella could lock away, lock away for the game.

He pulled off the sweat-soaked T-shirt he wore under the three-layered fire-retardant overalls. Through the one-way glass of the motor-home he could see the activity behind the DBM pit. Could see

Kessler, receiving the plaudits, could see Fraser, arguing with Burgess. Zola, the Sultan team boss, was clapping Kessler on the back, a show of sportsmanship that was perverse enough to be hugely comical – Zola: one part accountant, one part hood (or so some whispered) but surely never sportsman?

It would take a little time before the post race TV interviews were over and Chico and the others – Kessler, Fraser and Burgess – would join him for the debrief. It was sure to be rough. Fraser in particular would not have enjoyed those last couple of laps. But Kinsella would see it through, it was early season and he had a few lives left yet – and at least the sponsors liked him, for if nothing else Eoghan 'Egg' Kinsella generated more than his fair share of column inches. He smiled at the logos on the sweat-soaked racesuit which lay in a crumpled heap on the deep shag of the motor-home floor. Then he reached through to the shower unit and turned on the tap. It was a hired motor-home – the team's own buses and trucks only used when the circus was in Europe – and it took him a little while to get the water temperature just right. He stepped in, washing the fatigue of the race from him, washing away the sweat. He had suffered out there, understeered like a pig it had, bloody hard work – something many on the outside do not understand, the sheer physical effort of driving an F1 car. The effort of driving a car which increases in weight by 1.25 tonnes at 150 mph thanks to the downforce. A car which generates lateral loads of up to 30 kg on the driver's neck through fast corners. A car which subjects that neck to the snapping surges of space ship acceleration, and the high G turning of a fighter plane on wheels. And what about the office, the cockpit, the place where Kinsella did the business? Hardly room to swing a monkey wrench in there, so a bumpy track like Interlagos always left him with plenty of souvenirs in just two colours: black and blue. Right now he was beginning to feel them as the gushing jets of the shower found the sore spots, found the little cuts and rubs where the tight belts had dug in.

After he had finished in the shower he slipped into a robe and took on some fluids as he waited for the others, waited for the flak to fly. He drank deeply from a chilled plastic bottle, the re-hydration mixture that had been prepared by the team physician and trainer – and while Kinsella might have preferred to have been sipping at the victory champagne, for the moment this was just the job. He remembered the doc' telling him that up to two litres of fluid could be lost by a driver during a race – and by Christ he could believe it – he felt as if he had been sucked dry by that pig of a car on this hot Brazilian afternoon.

The door of the motor-home swung open and Kinsella steeled himself: plead ignorance Egg mate... that's the way. But it wasn't Kessler, nor Fraser, nor Chico... not even Burgess.

"I'm sorry..." She looked confused, and also, perhaps, a bit disappointed, "I didn't know you were here..."

"No problem," he said, before adding: "I thought you'd be joining in with the celebrations?"

"I have a headache." She was already turning to leave, her hand on the door handle. Kinsella moved to stop her:

"Hey, don't mind me, I'm about done anyway. Besides, if you've got a headache you don't want to go out there, believe me, they're about to play that bloody awful national anthem of yours."

The joke missed, missed by some way – he should have known, it was the same with Chico, joking about the Republic never went down well. But she had turned, turned quickly, a flash of attitude in those eyes, bringing that face to life at last. And Christ, it was beautiful. Even more so now, without the marble demeanour, the solidity of purpose, the *being* beautiful, which had made the DBM pit the place for all the photographers that weekend. It hardly mattered that the attitude was loaded against him, loaded and aimed against him – and ten to one that wasn't just because of his dig at the national anthem...

He hadn't really talked to her since Friday practice, when Chico – no, not Chico he remembered, it was the PR twat – had introduced her. She'd sat there all the time, with the watches – no point really, what with all the computerised timing gear the team carted around. Just decorous. And boy the snappers loved it. There had even been a few sessions with her and Chico for various magazines, and the papers and tele' of their home country, him looking the hero, her looking sophisticated, not Kinsella's type, he had thought then. No, sophisticat was certainly not Kinsella's sort of pussy. But sophisticat with an attitude...?

"There may be some aspirin." He started to rummage about in one of the overhead lockers, tossing aside a spare helmet and a pair of driving boots. He found the pills and he gave her his drinks bottle to wash one down with.

"It takes a little getting used to."

"Yes, it's very sweet," she said.

"No – I mean the noise... your headache?"

"Yes, of course." She finally decided on a seat in the cavernous motor-home, a leather padded swivel chair, some way from where Kinsella sat – as far away as possible in fact, some four metres distant, close to the driver's seat. All of a sudden she let her shoulders sag with a sigh, stretching out those long legs. Kinsella noticed that her deep tan, born of a life in the tropics, almost merged with the brown leather of the seat, though the shine set it apart right enough: polished walnut, Kinsella thought, like the Jag' back home, made for luxury. Her hair was tied up in an ebony knot, with little strands that showed copper-bronze as the low light that flooded through the motor-home's windscreen played through it. Kinsella was glad of the light from the cab, it gave him the excuse to reach for his shades, the excuse to hide behind them. And, of course, the camouflage to study her properly, study the packaging: white top: backless, armless, like the upper part of a bathing costume, truncated at midriff by the belt of white stretch pants. Perfect, cleanly packaged perfection: Polaroid fodder: the stuff of the circus, but still a danger to decorum when all you have to cover your modesty is a little towelling robe. Kinsella crossed his legs.

"This your first race?" he asked, best to change the subject, save all that for Maria – or was it Dolores?

She nodded, curling a strand of loose hair about her finger, seeming to note its shine against the equal lustre of her skin with studied professionalism, but hardly jumping at Kinsella's offer of conversation.

"And?"

"And nothing." She peered out of the smoke glass window, jinking her head a little from side to side as if searching through a crowd, searching for something, searching for Chico perhaps?

"In other words you had no idea what was going on," he said.

He hadn't meant it to sound harsh, maybe it wouldn't have, elsewhere, with someone else. But at least it had attracted her attention. From outside there was the unmistakable thrubber-thrub of a helicopter taking off. Then she said:

"It was not a problem. I could see Chico win, what else is there?"

"It takes more than one man to make a race."

"And to ruin a race Mr Kinsella?"

He laughed, and was awarded with a little smile, a wry smile – the smile of a protagonist. Then she seemed to relax a little more, perhaps happy in landing a solid blow? She continued: "At first, okay: one lap, two lap. But then Chico is gone, far ahead, and then they come in for more wheels, and then...?" She shrugged, raising the palms of her hands to the sky, a submission, "but it didn't matter, I only needed to see Chico."

"You would have been better off watching from the garage, on the TV."

"It was not possible. They wanted more pictures, of me in the pits – it helps Chico, the man said..."

"Of course it does," he said, shaking his head, "of course it does..."

She seemed confused, perhaps even a little troubled? He changed the subject, changed to his favourite subject: Eoghan 'Egg' Kinsella.

"So how was I?" He beamed her a grin as he said it.

"Not good I think. I saw you race the blue car – why did you not just drive past him?"

"Oh," he shrugged, "just a little fun."

"And then with Chico – do you play games with him too Mr Kinsella?"

He just grinned at her, but it didn't help.

"Is it not dangerous to play games Mr Kinsella?"

He was about to ask her what sort of games she had in mind, but somehow he thought it would do his cause no good:

"It was nothing, a misunderstanding, that's all – and anyway, he still won didn't he?"

"Yes – but I think you are a dangerous man Kinsella."

She had dropped the Mr, he was about to ask her to anyway, about to suggest 'Egg', it seemed to do for the rest of them. But he let it slip.

"I wouldn't worry about it if I was you, these things happen you know, you'll get used to it all," he said.

"Perhaps. But the Englishman, Fraser?"

"Yes?"

"He is very angry with you."

"It's his problem – he's an angry man."

"A serious man, yes?"

"Yeah, pretty serious." Kinsella could imagine that Fraser would not have been too keen to have her about the place, not one for distractions Fraser.

"I hope he made you feel at home?" he said.

She just shrugged, seemed to think about saying something, then seemed to think better of it. Then the door of the motor home swung open once again and Chico almost burst in, a few hands clutching little tape recorders following him through the door, some shouts: *Chico, Chico – one more picture please*...And then he had slammed the door, snapping fast the latch.

He turned, and his big brown eyes widened, taking in the scene of Kinsella and Teresa – what was this?

She registered his confusion quickly: "I have a headache – I'm sorry...." He nodded at her, smiled mechanically, then slumped down into one of the armchairs.

Chico looked around the motor-home, running his hand through hair made sticky by the champagne shower the Sultan drivers had given him on the podium.

"You mind?" He looked at Kinsella, reaching out for the drinks bottle.

Kinsella nodded. And tossed it over to Chico, who caught it one-handed, lifting its nozzle to his lips in the same fluid movement. He drank deeply then expelled air in satisfaction before bringing his eyes to Kinsella's.

"So..." The South American's stare was stone: so focussed, so intent, that it was almost frightening. This was Chico with a mission, Kinsella thought, "*what was all that about...*" This was Chico as he was in the cockpit... all attention on the job at hand, talking slowly, that strange sort of accent – like a Frenchman's bad impression of an American Kinsella sometimes thought, but with the lilting cadence of the Latin playing in the background. Kinsella noticed that Teresa had gone into the little galley at the back of the motor-home, he hadn't noticed her stand up, neither had Chico it seemed. Kinsella mustered what remorse he could and explained: "*was about to let him through, could have been the Minardi...*"

Chico let it go, shot him a smile – easy to be magnanimous in victory, yes. But still Kinsella couldn't but help half-liking the guy – pity he would have to beat him, pity he would have to push him out of the comfort zone, push him until he made the mistakes – but then the game went on.

"I almost threw it away anyway," Chico said, "pissed with myself... stupid mistake."

Kinsella nodded: "What did Kessler say?"

"You'll have to watch out, he's not happy, and neither is Gordi'. But," he added, smiling, "he has more to worry about now. Did you see the girl, in the car in Melbourne, the girl with the camera?"

Kinsella nodded, a memory filled with mammary for a second or two, she would take some forgetting.

"It seems, " Chico went on, "that she is Solé's sister... sent to spy on us..."

Kinsella laughed out loud. Yes, that was sure to put the puss' among the pigeons.

Chapter Four

Stubbs sucked the froth off the top of the pint, re-positioning his aching buttocks on the barstool as he did so. It had been a hard night, sitting on the cold stone wall, waiting for the case to come out. Then, when he had – the arrogant little shit – he'd just waved to Stubbs, and off on his way to work. Just a day. All over that one, no point to it at all. It hardly mattered... Sarah would understand when she got wind of this job.

For the hundredth time that day he wished that she had been there when the call came through. Not just to share in the thrill – some real work at last – but also so that she might have helped tidy the office, pull it into some sort of shape... But then again, it was never right, meeting a client there, the front room of a ground floor flat. Granted, he had done the Sam Spade bit with the frosted glass panel in the door. But otherwise it wasn't quite professional enough: the always dormant computer, the empty filing cabinets, the extra desk crammed into a corner – for Sarah, when she sorted through the messages, what little mail there was, just twice a week. And, of course, the sofa, where he had her, now and then – more then than now though. Yes, the Sarah thing had certainly tailed off since the jobs had dried up. The proper jobs.

But a bloody shame she wasn't there this morning, to answer the phone with that over-affected telephone manner – so many words, as if she tried to hide her Essex accent behind them: *"Justin Stubbs: Private and Industrial Investigations, how might I be of assistance to you sir...?"*. Yes, it made him cringe, but still, she would have loved it. The guy from the racing team – Jesus, surely even she must have heard of them, of DBM – that would have got her panties nice and moist. Because there was one thing he knew for certain about Sarah: as long as the cash kept on coming she would be happy, happy with her two mornings a week, happy with her Justin Stubbs.

But she hadn't been there, and the place was the scene of some awful accident he didn't even remember having. So this pub was a better bet, a nice place – all smoked glass and aluminium tubing, palm trees and the bold colours of Matisse prints – just on the fringe of the City. Outside a girl walked across a concrete piazza, struggling with the cellophane of a triangular pack of sandwiches. High above her, in the offices that ringed the square, Stubbs imagined business-men playing computer games with numbers – numbers with noughts: drop a few here, some factory closes, find a few there, a hol-iday bonus. He had told the guy from DBM he would slot him in, made a noisy show of flicking through his diary, holding it close to the phone as he noticed that it was Sarah's birthday next week. Nothing else to mark the pages though... told the guy he could fit him in between Linklaters and PricewaterhouseCoopers – if they were quick.

It had to be the second best suit, not her fault, the wine stain, and it could wait – he had told her. He thought that he might take her somewhere special, when the first of the DBM cheques come through. Late that morning he had found some things to fill his brief-case with, an electricity bill, a notepad, just bits and pieces, bits and pieces to rummage through if he had to play for time, mull over an offer. He put a couple of the gold embossed leaflets in his inside jack-et pocket too, not so many of them left now, and they had been deli-ciously expensive to print, two years ago, when things had been bet-ter. In his wallet there was the last tenner: enough to get him out of the plain Kent suburbs and into London, enough for a pint or two – he had to hope that the DBM man would fork out for the rest, maybe for lunch too.

At the station he had killed a couple of minutes at the magazine rack, high-speed research: *Autosport, Motoring News*... Pages full of news from the San Marino Grand Prix which, he gathered, had taken place the weekend before at Imola, somewhere in Italy. The cover of Autosport was filled with a picture of an orange Formula One car, its high nose – ugly that, Stubbs thought – glinting in the sunlight. The driver had one arm out of the cockpit, punching the air in triumph, while a man stood at the edge of the track, waving a chequered flag. A picture tells... But not enough for Stubbs. And inside he read more: Guido Solé wins for Sultan, Bobby Drake Jnr comes in a 'remarkable' second in the Spando and Eoghan Kinsella is third in the DBM. A dull race, the writer wrote, but, he had added, at least the Sultans were carrying the fight to the DBM team. He looked for news of Chico, the man with the goddess for a wife, the man with a private beach, the man with the talent – the man who searched for the comfort zone. He found it in a results table at the foot of the text: *Retired: lap 14: gearbox.*

A sleekly silver DBM was pictured at the foot of the first page of the report, the number eight car, Kinsella's car. A caption: *Early season woes now behind him Kinsella put in a mature drive to third.* He thought the DBM a prettier car than the Sultan, more raked and racy, rather than angular and efficient. It spoke of speed: from its low pointed nose which curved scimitar-like to the cockpit, to the angled rake of the engine cover, curving back down beautifully to a point at the rear of the car. Then a block – in profile, a block – the rear wing, familiar, what a racing car has, but somehow intrusive to the line of the machine: as if it were the hilt of the silver sword: cut through the air, then stop the air with the hilt. He had thought he could see how it all worked then, the balance of the game: speed and downforce, that's what they called it didn't they: downforce? He had put his hand over part of the picture, blanking off the profile of the wing: better like that he had thought. Then, on taking his hand away he had noticed the little sponsor's logo at the foot of the wing end-plate, one of many on the car: *Option Semiconductors.*

One mystery solved then. One of his better jobs that one, they must have put DBM on to him. He glanced at his watch, still some minutes before the guy would be with him. He took another swig from the tall and tapering, vase-like, pint glass, gasping at the pleasure of the coldness in his throat. The bar was beginning to fill, a few early lunchers – suits, all of them. He let the memory play: yes, Option Semiconductors, definitely one of the better jobs that. Wangling a job on the night shift of the rival, a Korean place up in Scotland. They'd told him where he would find the computer, with the drawings – in the quality control lab. The auditor was asleep – Stubbs couldn't blame him, why bother taking it seriously, the pay was shit. He had downloaded the stuff, completed the job within the week. They had loved him for it. Paid handsomely for it too. Then there was more work, other industrial espionage jobs, and for a while his reputation grew. Except that there were a couple of failures too, one made the papers – a corporate image dragged through the courts – and the big firms dropped him. And then it was back to the dirty streets: repossessions, divorce work... But at least Option, it seemed, still remembered him for the Scottish job, still had faith in him.

"Justin Stubbs?"

He jumped at the sudden appearance of the man's face, filling the mirror behind the bar.

"Yes?"

"Fraser, Gordon Fraser – from DBM." The man offered a hand as Stubbs turned to face him. Stubbs inspected him in the same way he would inspect an employee suspected of embezzlement, sniffing out the cash. The hand the man offered was long and delicate, the hand of an artist, wrists bisected by the impossibly white, precisely straight, cuff of a crisp shirt. Golden cufflinks – expensive – a watch with more buttons on it than Stubbs's TV: 12.30pm – on the dot for the appointment. His arm was slender, sleeved in Hugo Boss. No tie, the shirt open at the collar: suntan, the leathering of early forties – a decade or two in the sun – clean shaven, not a mark on the face, eyes the pale blue of an atlas sea, teeth white – stainless – peeping through an unsmiling mouth. Serious this Fraser. Serious business...

Fraser took control, motioning towards a low table by the window, well out of earshot of the suits. They sank into low leather sofas, facing each other, Fraser awkwardly folding his long slender frame into the seat, crossing his legs at the knee, a Trussardi shoe pointing at Stubbs, eye level, floating before him it seemed, quivering to the man's pulse. Stubbs reached into his pocket for one of the leaflets – a well worn introduction, well worn card, well worn details of a life to the left of the fold, well worn promises: *instant results, full and confidential service*, to the right.

"A drink?"

Fraser shook his head. He seemed ill at ease, not his scene this, Stubbs guessed. Fraser looked at his watch, then switched attention to the leaflet – the sort of total attention that reminded Stubbs of a championship chess player.

He read it out aloud, never looking at Stubbs. His soft voice – Stubbs thought there was a little west country in there – was lowered to a point at which Stubbs had to lean forward, almost to the tip of the gleaming shoe, to hear him. It hardly mattered really, he knew these words off-by-heart.

"... A background in military intelligence, served in the Gulf..." Translation: Royal Corps of Signals, bloody raining in the desert – could hardly believe it – a loose and live wire, dropped from the tailgate of a Landrover into a puddle... before the fighting even started... zap goes Stubbs. Watched the war on TV from a bed in Riyadh, then from a bed in Dorset. But he had the scars – bloody hero...

"... Metropolitan Police Force, three years... technician, communications, surveillance..." Translation: he had helped them fix the bloody radios...

"...Stag's Head Security, industrial espionage expert..."

Translation: the best of the lot this one, night shift at the toilet roll warehouse, then the one break, following the cheating husband – a new venture for Stag's Head – and Christ, the bloody cowboys: it really was run from the *Stag's Head*...

"And you set up on your own, what, three years ago?"

"Yes, that's right." True enough. Private dick first, then the lucky contact, the Options man, and the industrial espionage deal. The good times, for a while.

Fraser ran through the list of past clients, some of which were for real, then, all too suddenly, he sat up and bent towards Stubbs, who was still leaning forward to catch the near whispers, so that their foreheads almost touched.

"Impressive Mr Stubbs. Options told us you were good." His breath smelt of mouthwash, a menthol, antiseptic smell which was undercut by the man's scent, something exotic, something that spoke of flying off to foreign lands. Stubbs allowed himself a smile at the compliment, and Fraser continued:

"I will get straight to the point shall I Mr Stubbs?"

"Justin, please." It didn't seem to register, it had become quickly apparent that they were not about to become bosom pals, and as Fraser continued Stubbs found himself fingering the little scar under his nose, his little war wound.

"I don't know how much you know about DBM or me, but let's assume you are new to all this shall we?"

Stubbs nodded.

"Right. Well I am the technical director at DBM, which basically means that I am in charge of the development of the car, or rather, in charge of the team that develops the car. Although I also double up as the race engineer for Chico – you have heard of Chico, of course?"

"Yes, of course." Stubbs remembered the interview in the magazine, remembered the lucky bastard with the goddess for a wife, remembered the name then: Fraser – always in touch, how they worked together to sort the car, find the comfort zone...

"Anyway, let me tell you about the way we work at DBM. It is simple enough: if we have a problem with the aerodynamics we hire a top aerodynamicist, if the crew need feeding we hire a top chef..."

"And me?"

"Well... I was coming to that?"

Stubbs allowed himself a wry little smile then he picked up the leaflet, putting it back into the inside pocket of his jacket – not enough of them left to be giving them away.

"You see," Fraser went on, "we think we may have a little problem."

"Yes?"

"In a word, Sultan." Stubbs remembered the ugly orange car on the cover of *Autosport*, the car that had won the last Grand Prix.

"It's a competitive business, you see, Formula One. And the competition starts a long time before the lights flick out to start the race – a long, long time before. Indeed, the development of the car takes place all year round – we have even started working on next year's car already...

"And part of this behind the scenes race, if that's what you want to call it, is making sure you have the right people in place, in place in the design team – the right specialists, suspension men, aerodynamicists, whatever. And there is great competition to get the best of the personnel available, and not a little poaching from other teams as I am sure you can imagine..."

Stubbs nodded and took a long draught from his lager as Fraser continued. He was surprised that the other man was doing all the talking. At first he had him marked as the taciturn type, but now Fraser was on his subject it was obvious there would be no stopping him...

"...And as a result, on occasion, we are able to pick someone up from the other team, and from that someone we are also able to pick up some morsel of information that is, shall we say, useful. For instance, we have recently taken on a young aerodynamicist from Sultan, head-hunted him. It cost plenty, that's true, but it's worth it. He's a bright boy. But more than that, he came with baggage, with information. It seems that Sultan are developing a system for its car. A system, which, not to put too fine a point on it, contravenes the spirit – and perhaps the letter – of the rulebook."

"You mean they are cheating?"

"Well... *Cheating* is not a word we use. Let's just say that we think they are interpreting the rule book rather loosely." He allowed himself a little smile at that and continued: "Or at least we believe they are about to."

"How?"

"It seems they have found a way of using some form of traction control that cannot be detected."

"Traction control?"

"Yes, of course – this is not your territory is it? We will have to steer you through the technicalities of the game as and when we come to them." So Fraser explained traction control, explained how the boffins had eroded the driver's art in the early 1990s. He explained how they had found the philosopher's stone: maximum traction from the turns, not a hint of wheelspin. Electronics were the key, sensors in the wheels picking up the first hint of slip, blanking off a cylinder in the engine. It sounded bloody awful he said – with a wince – but it meant that the driver could just floor it out of the corners without the worry of losing the back end. Floor it in the knowledge that he would get the maximum traction, and hence the maximum speed onto the straight. Great for the wet, great for low speed circuits, he said, and good for rocket-ship starts. But by the time everybody was getting it, even the little teams, it was banned.

Making a mockery of the sport many said. Driver aids: electronics controlling the throttle, electronics controlling the suspension, electronics controlling the brakes... And there had even been talk of an automatic steering correction system, which meant that the driver would not need to apply opposite lock in a skid, could just hold on, point the thing in the general direction. A passenger, more or less.

"... We had just gone too far, people were beginning to laugh at us. It had to be stopped, and so it was banned. But there's a problem in that the ban on the electronic aids has been so difficult to police, the ban on traction control in particular. And just about any time a team has an advantage the suspicions are voiced, often with good reason.

"You see a big part of this sport is concerned with interpreting the regulations, finding the loopholes – it's the part that few are aware of but it's the part that often finds the time in the car. Sometimes it's a little more blatant, and yes, sometimes it's downright cheating. Not so long ago, for instance, one team – which shall remain nameless – was able to run a light car by fitting a set of water filled tyres whenever it was weighed, changing them for normal boots when it was time to hit the track. While another team found a similar benefit from fitting a specially weighted rear wing whenever the car was anywhere near a weigh-bridge – suspicions were only raised when someone noticed it took three mechanics to fit it. Those days have gone now though, thanks to the introduction of random weighing, but there are other ways to beat the scales. These days the drivers are weighed too, and the minimum weight is a total of car and driver – and suffice to say that when the drivers are weighed at the start of the season there have been mutterings... You know the sort of thing, ballast in helmets, lead plates sewn between the layers of Nomex overalls....

"But mostly the tricks are played on the computer keyboard now. And between you and me we all do it to some extent, *interpreting*. Finding the time in the wording of a sentence in a rulebook, hiding some trick in the software that can give us some degree of traction control, or whatever. It may not work in quite the same way, we wouldn't blank off a cylinder to stop wheelspin now, too obvious – but you might influence the way the diffs work on the rear wheels, has the same sort of effect. And if you have found a way, well then it's easy enough to hide – especially if you only activate it during periods when the scrutineers cannot get plugged into the car."

He paused for a little while, as if to check that Stubbs was still with him, and then: "And according to our aerodynamicist friend – our defector – Sultan have found just such a way."

"And I take it that this is where I come in?"

"Yes," said Fraser, "If it works Sultan will be in the clear for a race or two. Granted, the other teams, teams with something to lose, will kick up a stink, leak their suspicions to the press. But there's sod all they can really do about it without proof: a disk downloaded from somewhere would be ideal, proof that they have such a system at least. With that we could threaten them, get them to take it off – or we could go straight to the top, get them banned. We will protest them as soon as we suspect they are using it anyway, but it's nothing without proof.

"How you do it is up to you, and you are on your own from day one – we have never heard of you. That is perfectly clear, yes?"

That last chilled him a little, always the same with these sort of jobs, of course, but still, the way Fraser had said it – a serious game this, no doubt about it. He nodded.

"And I take it the other teams are up to the same tricks?" he asked, professional curiosity getting the better of him, the chance of tapping into a lucrative market beckoning.

Fraser just shrugged: "Who knows, we can never take the chance that they are not and it will be the same with Sultan, you can bet on it. There's always somebody trying to take a peek at what you have in the car. We had a trick braking system discovered after one of the cars retired out on the far side of a circuit a couple of years ago. A photographer from one of the magazines was out on the track, poked his camera into the cockpit, and found himself a nice little scoop.

"You just can't be too careful, and Sultan aren't above pulling a few stunts believe you me. In Australia this year we think they gave a sister of one of their drivers a camera so that she could have a good snoop about while everybody in our pit was busy gawping at her tits, busy making it easy for her." He curled his lip, as if the episode disgusted him a little, then continued:

"It's nothing new though. Most of the teams take someone from the drawing office to the races, armed with a camera, just to keep an eye on rivals' developments. One team manager even went to the trouble of attaching a scale to the bottom of his trouser leg, so photographs of him standing alongside the car of a rival could be easier interpreted back home. There have even been accusations of teams tapping into rivals' radio messages during a race, to get a fix on tactics. The Cold War, it never ended you know, it just moved to F1." He allowed himself a smile at his little joke, then continued: "It's that sort of game you see, Formula One. It is like a little planet all of its own. Nothing touches it from the outside, nothing from the real world – all we take is its money and its sex and its intrigue. Nothing else bothers us much, we were just about the last sport out of South Africa and I wouldn't be surprised if we keep the fag sponsorship for a good few years yet. No, Formula One is different from any other businesses you have worked in before."

The tense of it jarred, the arrogance of the man, Stubbs wasn't sold yet. However different it bloody well was he would still need a fee – he was far from sold yet...

"Well hold on there a minute – I haven't even decided I'm going to take the job," he said.

Fraser made a show of placing his wafer thin briefcase onto the low table and then taking a chequebook out of it. Its cover bore the DBM logo, the letters – white on dark grey – underlined twice in pale blue. His pen was charcoal-coloured. Stubbs noticed that the light picked out a weave in its construction, some hi-tech plaid like carbon fibre – a pen that could withstand a 200mph crash, useful eh... Expensive? You bet.

"Name your price," he said. He really did. And how many times had Stubbs dreamt of this – '*name your price*' – the start of the best fantasies sitting in the flat-come-office waiting for the phone to ring. Christ, he should know how to go from here – just name your price man...

"I see... You're unconvinced,"

Had he paused so long? Had his chin dropped? Was he a picture of scepticism? Whichever, Fraser was on numbers. And some.

"Consider this Stubbs..." 'Mr' forgotten now, Justin? Perhaps he hadn't heard? "...In this country this little business of ours is some seven times bigger than the film industry and its balance of payments surplus exceeds that for steel and agriculture. It's big money stuff, very big. At DBM we have an annual budget of about $70m. We spend $15m on the half-a-second a lap that is Chico – $2m on the debatable talents of Egg Kinsella. So, if you can help us retain any advantage you will be worth your weight in gold, believe me."

Stubbs thought of a number, then doubled it... Then added 50 per cent – then panicked and dropped the total by £5,000.

"£15,000." He looked for Fraser's eyes, searching for a sign of response. But they were down, following the silent scribble of the expensive nib against the cheque. He was already wishing that he had asked for more. Yet had hadn't dared hope for anything near this when he left the flat that morning.

"£7,500 now, the rest later," Fraser said, folding the cheque between thumb and forefinger and passing it to Stubbs.

"It's the way we work at DBM, all of us. You get more money when the results come in. Agreed?"

"Of course..." said Stubbs; £7,500 virtually in his pocket. This would make Sarah sit up and take notice...

"Of course, there will be no contract, I'm afraid we will just have to trust each other." Fraser looked at his watch, said he had to be somewhere else soon, looked like he wanted to be somewhere else soon. There was no handshake. He left.

Stubbs unfolded the cheque and stared at it. He should have been ecstatic, but there was something else clouding his happiness, a strange feeling that he might have jumped in just a little over his head here – too many bloody noughts for comfort, he supposed. He ordered another beer to help chase away the doubt.

Chapter Five

She had been at the apartment for a couple of days, her first time at the Monaco residence, her first time in Monaco. It was drably clean and airy. Although it was never used now – except for the week of the race – Chico had a cleaner visit once a week to keep it spotless.

There was nothing of her in the apartment. Nothing of Teresa, Señora Perez – a title that still did not sit comfortably with her, it hardly helped that half the paddock insisted on calling her 'Mrs Chico'. That morning she had annoyed him by bringing the subject up, his real name, calling him José – it always got him down, reminded him of something. Silly, she thought, and yes, silly of her to remind him. But that, at least, was the one way she could get his attention. Now, he paced the room in front of her, the telephone clamped to his ear. He was talking to the PR man – him – how she hated him. The way he had put his arm round her, talked to her like a child, told her she would be helping Chico, just a few minutes for the photographers...

Chico was animated as he spoke, not quite angry – but getting as close to it as she had seen. The sheets of a British tabloid newspaper were strewn over the floor. There had been a story in it, something about Kinsella, saying that Chico was getting preferential treatment in the team, all the best bits for the car. It had upset him. Chico had felt betrayed, or so it seemed to her – he hadn't said. But now the PR man seemed to be calming him, seemed to be explaining that it was nothing to do with Kinsella, just the man from *The Brit*, making things up, they all do it – she could imagine him saying it. Had he checked with Kinsella? Chico asked, then nodded as the PR man seemed to answer in the affirmative. Then he demanded that the journalist should be banned from the pit, and the PR man was left with the task of balancing the needs of the DBM star driver with the needs of the DBM star sponsors... the call would drag on she was sure.

She half sat, half lay, on a low sofa, facing a dormant TV. She was still in a white bikini from the morning worship, just an old dress shirt of Chico's over it, tails tied in a large knot beneath her breasts. To her left was the big window onto Monte Carlo: a view of sun slapped blue – sea and sky – and skyscrapers, blocked intermittently by the pacing Chico. Every now and then the smear of noise that was a racing car passing five storeys below – qualifying for one of the support races – reverberated through the room. The smell of the air was the smell that she knew would always, now, be Monaco to her. However often she visited, at whatever time: a mix of burning rubber, well worked brakes, petrol fumes... and suntan lotion. The ivory tinged painted walls of the flat were bare except for some pictures of Chico in various cars, pictures she had not seen before, but still obviously him: the tricolour stripes of the Republic on his helmet clashing garishly with the corporate paint schemes of the cars. Cars he had raced before they had met at the President's ball just eighteen months previous.

Eighteen months a princess... she giggled to herself. Everything a girl could want. Theirs was the perfect match the papers had said: her the beauty queen, him the national hero. Ten months later millions had watched the wedding ceremony on TV, more than had watched the football final, if the PR man was to be believed – and she wasn't sure if he was. She had loved Chico then, as she loved him now, as she would always love him she supposed. But then that was just the problem: she had loved him then as she loved him now. No change. Loved him to the same nth as when they married, almost to the same nth as when they met. She couldn't even feel she knew him better, she even sometimes felt that she was just one of the thousands that loved him – just another girl from the Republic in love with the hero. They were intimate of course, there was that difference – and he had been the first, something that she suspected not even her mother believed. But how often? Too busy now, the racing, developing the car – but then when does it stop? The last race, and then there is next season... And Chico always looks for more from his car, always more from the car, and Fraser, and the team.

She could complain, and she had tried to talk to him. But then he had given her more than she had ever wanted, more money than she could ever spend, more homes than a twenty-three year old former beauty queen could ever know what to do with. Homes like this apartment which, she guessed, cost as much as a hacienda with hundreds of hectares at home – someone had told her that even the smallest of flats could cost somewhere in the region of half a million dollars here. So, she only needed to look around her to feel guilty – to feel guilty if she wasn't happy...

Chico was still on the phone. She thought for a moment about going down to the pool again, until qualifying. But there was only an hour or so, it was hardly worth it. Better to choose something to wear, Chico – and the PR man – had told her that the photographers would go crazy for her at Monaco, and they had been right. But it hadn't been so much of a hardship at first, on the Thursday evening.

She had arrived a day after Chico. At Monaco the race is run through the streets, Chico had explained to her that it was the last of its kind, a throwback to the days when all races were on public roads rather than specially constructed autodromes. And these were working streets – as much as anyone really worked in Monaco. So it was that first practice was held on the Thursday and Friday was a free day, a respite for the Monegasques, those who stayed put for the race, time to see to business, air the Bentley, walk the poodle...

With Friday free, Thursday had become party night, or as near as Teresa had come to any partying in Formula One. It had been something like she had long ago expected, hoped for. Walking through the gardens with Chico in the evening sun, dawdling amidst the palms and ferns, the jacaranda and magnolia – a riot of colour that was too much a backdrop for some of the photographers to resist. Chico shrugged it off, just part of the job, he had said. They had eaten at the Hotel de Paris. An extravagant building with hints of rococo that was everything Teresa had hoped for of Monte Carlo – an antidote to the disappointing pastel washed, bar-graph high-rise that seemed to be crammed between the hills and the sea – drowning what survived of the pink belle époque villas in sickly concrete. She had craned her neck there, at the hotel, between courses, looking for the beautiful people and the film stars, who – they said – moved along the coast from the Cannes Film Festival, moved along the coast to the next place to be seen. Others, she noticed, craned their necks too – to catch a glimpse of her and Chico. It made her slightly uncomfortable, as if she was just acting a part, a charlatan.

Later, as they walked across the Place du Casino to the Casino itself, Teresa had an insight into Chico's world. He had dropped her arm as they approached the temporary steel barrier, erected overnight earlier in the week for the Grand Prix. She followed him as he passed through a gap in the barrier, taking her first look at the track. It surprised her, as narrow and bumpy as a street in a

47

Mediterranean town could be expected to be, with the marks of everyday life: a broad white line to demarcate a parking area, even a zebra crossing further up the road. Chico walked to the centre of the road. There was some traffic but it was slow – cruising supercars, and stretched limos off-loading at the casino. He had crouched in the centre of the street and Teresa had watched with wonder as he reached down to the asphalt, touching it, stroking it. Some young men in a passing Fiat had recognised him, shouting their good lucks for the weekend, and he had replied with a wave. Then he had walked back to trackside and Teresa had grasped for his hand again.

"Is it alright darling?" she had asked.

"Saturday..." he had said, "on Saturday I will drive through this little funnel of tarmac at close to 155 kph – isn't that crazy?"

"I'm not sure... Is it?" she had said.

"No – it's beautiful..." He had laughed at that, and then led her to the tables.

K-Corp has hired a large room in the Casino for the DBM party, attended by the sponsors and some selected members of the press, plus a few B list celebrities. Kinsella had been there too, playing a table, as reckless at the roulette wheel as he was at the steering wheel it seemed – where Chico placed $500 on black, Kinsella placed $5,000 on number eight. Both lost, both laughed – low stakes, she thought, for those two. All evening Chico had looked uncomfortably uncomfortable in a dinner suit, most others were casual – Kinsella had apologised, a misunderstanding, he said, him telling Chico it was black tie earlier in the day. Chico had taken it well, laughed it off, saying it was good to dress like James Bond in the Casino, but Teresa could tell that it had annoyed him – and for her part she could not help wondering whether Kinsella had done it on purpose... Though why he should she could not think.

Something in Chico's manner on the telephone brought her back to the now. She noticed he was smiling, and he had stopped pacing, perching himself on a stool on the balcony, where the high decibel wake of the support race cars hung in sheets between the high rise buildings. Not that he seemed to mind, sorting through a problem with Fraser – it had to be him – to the music they loved, the music they shared.

She looked at her watch, still time to kill, then reached down for a page from the British newspaper – but picked up a magazine instead. It wasn't to read, just to hold. So she opened it, recognising it as the glossy that had run the feature on Chico. It had been cold that day, but the photographer had insisted on taking a picture on the beach.

Chico hadn't minded, he had to swim anyway, part of the never-ending fitness regime – but she had shivered as the photographer looked for the light, looked for the way to show the best of her.

She flicked through the pages of this month's edition. She could hear Chico laughing with Fraser, laughing at something she knew she would not understand, could not share. She wished that she could like the Englishman – for Chico's sake – but there was so much coldness there. To Fraser – she felt sure – she was just the PR man's toy, nothing that could make the car go faster, nothing that could help in any way. And she had tried to like him, for Chico's sake...

There was Kinsella. Over a full page. She smiled, still fun to recognise someone in a magazine, still the little girl in that respect. Despite herself she had grown fond of her little spats with him. At first it was something to relieve the boredom. She had never expected to need that – but with nothing to do but look pretty all day, nothing to do but wait for Chico to finish at the track, it was welcome. She had not expected the loneliness either, and Kinsella helped there too. Not that there weren't other people to talk to. Just that there were few who saw her as Teresa, rather than Mrs Chico – a thing to be gawped at. Besides, most, it seemed, were too scared to approach her, and shy as she was she felt it easier to keep her distance. She wondered if they thought her aloof, cool and aloof? Maybe. But at least Kinsella didn't seem to care, teasing her as if he played a game with her, trying to tease her into biting, his little digs at Chico, better jokes at the expense of Fraser. Despite herself she had to admit, he was fun to be with. Although she should never let on how much fun. No, that would spoil it.

There was more too, after their traditionally frosty openings they had often really talked. And he had explained things to her in a way that was different from the others, different from the PR man, different from Chico she supposed – in some little way. For Kinsella she was more than just something to be photographed she felt, more than just a butt to place the K-Corp logo. Yes he was, as her mother might have said, a wicked man, always a new girl on his arm. Yet she sensed that he played up to it, played his part in the show just like her Chico. Her husband the serious one, the genius, Kinsella the playboy, the risk-taker, the one without a care in the world other than to finish the race and get on with the party. But yes, sometimes she wondered about him...

The close up of Kinsella over one whole page was, for the most part, unflattering. But then, as she knew, no skin could survive that close a lens job, not even hers as she had discovered after a shoot for a French magazine two weeks before: she shuddered at the memory of the little valleys the picture had shown. She had had to beg them not to use it. And on this face there was more than little valleys, much more. The marks of a life – 34 years of a life. The face was set upon a thick, muscled neck, like Chico's, she thought, a mark of the trade. The face was unsmiling, cool, how the photographer would have wanted him: his dimpled chin resting in the palm of a hand, thick fingers, nails cut short: bitten? She doubted that. The forehead, a sand sea of a brow, as though it was alive with thought. A little scar, old and white against the tan, marked the extent of his short cropped black hair, some little flecks of white in there, one or two – she wouldn't have caught them without such a close shot she was sure. And then the nose, signs of hard living – perhaps – around the nostril flares, a tangle of broken red veins, refusing to blend with the tan. Further up it was a little crooked, perhaps he had broken it at sometime? Then there was the broad bridge and the white skin: panda eyes, that's what she thought. Not surprising really, how often had she seen him without those wrap-around sunglasses of his? Rarely.

So here was an opportunity to dwell, the best bit. Those eyes. The long shadow of the photographer clouded the little pupils, then there was an explosion of green – through a dark jade and lighter at the fringes, almost a lime. Flecks of red zapped in the white of the eye, dancing electrically from the green: red and green, the colour of the poisonous – danger. But then the way they looked up at her, from the page, the way they shone bright against their panda fringes, there was something else too, there was fun, and not a little warmth. Told her what she knew already, she thought, a complicated fellow this Kinsella, like they all are in this game.

She glanced at the facing page, the profile was entitled Joker in the Pack. She read. It wasn't so unusual, she told herself – after all she had been swatting up on the sport for two months. Swatting up for Chico, for her, for her to be able to talk to him about it, a little like Fraser did. But there was a long way to go yet, plenty more study. She read...

There's an Englishman, a Welshman and an Irishman, only they are all one and the same person... Sounds like a bad joke, right? Well maybe, only I had the feeling that Eoghan 'Egg' Kinsella's not quite in the mood for laughing at the moment.

Why? Well this year Kinsella's gone head to head with the best in the World and, whichever way he chooses to dress it up, to the rest of the world he's coming a very poor second best. But more on that later, first of all, what about that bad joke Egg?

"Yeah, it confuses me sometimes too. It goes back a while I guess, back to the early years doing Formula Ford in Britain. I was doing okay but there was never really enough cash. I suppose it was the same for all of us, the budgets were just getting bigger and bigger. At the time I was desperate to move up into Formula Three but even then it was about £150,000 a season – so I had to get my name about. My mother's Welsh, so the Welsh papers and TV were interested – they were short on racing drivers. I got a lot of publicity, and a big sponsor as a result of it."

Which is why the helmet that pokes out of the number eight DBM is red, white and green. But as for the rest of the joke – simple: English upbringing and an Irish family name. And, it must be said, all of this is typical of the man – nothing is straightforward with Egg Kinsella.

"Mind you, it's only when I do well that they argue over me," he added with a flash of a smile.

And over these past few years there has probably been quite a lot of tri-national bickering over just where 'our' Eoghan hails from. Sometimes to laud him, hug him close to the bosom of his motherland, but on others to disown him unconditionally. For this has already been one hell of a career.

Think on it: First Grand Prix. Qualifies the unfancied Bianchi ninth, then causes a huge shunt at the first corner, taking out the then world champion in the process. But he did enough to attract the attention of a bigger team and he was soon on the move to Spando – all of which resulted in a bitter battle over the terms of his contract in the courts.

Later that year he causes another shunt and is banned for two races. But by this time he has consolidated his position in the team: beating his team mate – the once highly rated Mario Negri – 9-4 in the qualifying shoot-out throughout the season. Negri? Last heard of pottering about in the German Touring Car Championship.

For Kinsella's second year in Formula One he is joined at the then flourishing Spando team by Graham Patterson. After the first four races, where the veteran had the upper hand, Kinsella is consistently quicker than his illustrious team mate. Patterson quits the team and the sport by season's end. Kinsella has a handful of podium finishes, including a brace of impressive second places, but there are still more crashes.

Then Jordan. Wins were expected, but no – just two more careers consigned to the scrap-heap as Kinsella makes himself the undisputed number one: Jacobsen – Champcars now – and Facti – back to the *ignomony of trying to qualify the Bianchi this year.*

And now the 'career wrecker' – as one media wag christened him last year – is at DBM, facing the sort of drubbing that he has meted out to team-mates over these past seasons. For one man has not read the script, and that man is unquestionably the quickest, sharpest, most complete racing driver on this planet today: Chico.

"Chico's good, no question about it..." He says it absent-mindedly, attention riveted on the lightly wrapped slither of sex who brings us coffee – we are, incidentally, speaking on the after deck of Kinsella's yacht, *Akrasia*, a 60 ft Technomarine ocean cruiser, bought, he tells me, with the bulk of his DBM retainer.

"...But I think I can match him. Then beat him." I must look as unconvinced as I am, and to be honest I wonder if he's joking. You never can tell with the man, those dark glasses always hiding the nuances in his eyes – it took all the persuasive skills of our photographer to prise them off for the portrait later in the day.

"The only advantage that Chico has over me," he continues, " is that he's used to the machine. Pure and simple, give me a couple of races and I'll be with him, I promise you."

Others will need more than a promise though, they will – quite rightly – point to the facts: consistently half a second off in testing, half a second down at Melbourne, and some 1.5 seconds off Chico's pace at Interlagos. Granted, he had clawed back some of the time at Imola, coming within 0.3 seconds of his illustrious teamster and finishing a laudable – if lucky – third. But is the die already cast? Most think so, and there are mutterings coming out of DBM that the management are far from impressed with Kinsella's showings thus far, particularly at Interlagos when he was less than co-operative when Chico tried to lap him at the end of the race.

"That's all bollocks – the Brazil thing was just a misunderstanding," he said, suddenly very serious, "while as far as the speed is concerned, I know what I am capable of. And I know that all things being equal I will beat Chico. I know that I can – will – beat Chico, simple as that."

All things being equal? Was he suggesting a certain lack of parity as far as equipment is concerned? He thought for a moment or two before replying: "No. I Just know that I will beat him, I am sure of it."

It's the sort of unwavering confidence that is a mark of the man, yet is also in marked contrast to the slightly nervous young Egg Kinsella that many of us knew in Formula Three some years ago. The young man euphoric at securing his first chance to prove himself big-time. Perhaps he's grown – racing professionally in Japan and then four *years of F1 is sure to bolster confidence after all. Question is, which Egg Kinsella do we prefer?*

Whichever, you have to say his is an admirable attitude for a racing driver to possess. And despite his bluster you also have to admit that there is much else to Kinsella to be admired – anyone who witnessed the way he shrugged off the incident with the Bianchi in Melbourne will testify to that. But come on, confidence is one thing – but beating Chico. Now that is a joke...

Teresa looked at the other pictures of Kinsella dotted across the feature, him on his boat – a nice craft, half the size of theirs she guessed, moored here at Monaco the caption said. In all the pictures, other than the main portrait, his eyes were shaded. There were one or two of him in racing cars too, one of which was a blue Formula Ford, or so the caption said – a lovely little thing Teresa thought, sleek and uncluttered, no wings to spoil the lines of the car.

"We will have to go soon, I need to go over some telemetry with Gordi."

She nodded and put the magazine onto the coffee table, leaving it open, folded against the spine.

It was when they left for the pit lane that she could see the sense in him keeping hold of the apartment. She had thought that Interlagos was crowded: but here there was room for nothing, and nothing more. They rode a silver and blue Piagio scooter, just the thing for the narrow streets that wound their way from the apartment to the pit lane area on Boulevard Albert 1er. Just the thing to dodge around a phalanx of tifosi – the Ferrari fans who swell the principality's population each May – just the thing for her to get close to Chico, hug him tightly around the waist. And all the way their progress was marked with the whisper of the camera shutter and the whirr of the motor-winds – and shouts of *Chi-co, Chi-co, Chi-co...*

It had always amazed her how much his fame transcended national boundaries, how the devotion – for it was devotion, she had seen the piles of letters the PR man had to deal with – was almost as strong across the world as it was in the Republic. She pressed her cheek to his shoulder blade, feeling the patter of the little wheels on the asphalt through the hard muscle of his back. She loved to be with him when he drove: one of the Ferraris, the boat – even this. The delicacy of his touch was something to be marvelled at, a maestro at work. Earlier in the year he had taken her for a ride in a Ferrari F355 road car, around a track, somewhere in France, Nogaro, she remembered.

It was quick, obvious that, sometimes she looked at the speedometer to check, while at others she seemed to be looking down the track through the side windows. But him, there was nothing. Just an ease, everything flowing smoothly, slowly, light little moves of the wheel, a little dance on the pedals, and the stroking of the gear stick through its metal gate. Rather like now: swinging the scooter through a turn and into an impossibly narrow gap between the Safety Car and the Medical Car, effortless – as though the wheels were part of him. Right, she didn't know much about evolution, but she did think to herself that if they ever had children it would be no surprise to her if they came out with wheels on. Children? Oh, Mamma's nag still rung in her ears. 'Plenty of time,' she had said.

Chico parked up the scooter alongside Kinsella's similar machine, both had been personalised with name and racing number on the windshield, neither as big as the K-Corp logo, but prominent all the same. He told her to wait for him and then disappeared into the pit area. In the garage she could see the two DBMs up on their stands, sans wheels and wings, without much of their bodywork, naked and functionally ugly. Yet so, so clean. A picture of contrast jumped into her head, Papa and the tractor in the barn, cursing as he shears yet another rusty bolt.

"Penny for them?"

It was Kinsella, he had come from nowhere, startled her.

"Oh, hello... Eoghan." She had never called him by his given name before, nobody did it seemed, but she gave it a go, tried it for size.

"*Owen*. But you were close enough." He was laughing.

"I'm sorry." She had thought she had got it right, copying the commentator on Channel Two. She felt herself flush at the throat, foolish, and to blush... How stupid, and had he noticed behind those mirrors?

"So how are you enjoying Monaco?"

"It's fine, but many people, too many people. I am glad we have the apartment. Where do you stay, on your boat?"

"No, it's too noisy this week. Just a hotel, as usual. They are all the same you know, I sometimes wake up and forget which country I am in."

She nodded and smiled with him.

"And what of this crazy sport of ours? Got to the bottom of it yet?"

She was glad of that, an opportunity to confront, attack him through his trade in a way she wouldn't dare with Chico. He sat himself on some tyres, still new and glossed black, unscrubbed as Chico had said once.

"I am learning all the time," she said, "but there is still much that I do not understand."

"Well fire away, we're here to help."

"Okay." She sat herself down on a tyre too, just the one, so, with her long legs folded she could rest her hands on her knees and her chin on the backs of her hands.

"Okay... First, it is a race... yes?"

"So they say." The sunlight caught the silver frame of his shades, so it appeared that he had said it with a twinkle.

"Yet you line up one behind the other, Chico, then the Sultans, then you..."

"Ouch!"

"Oh, I'm sorry, just an example."

"I forgive you, but there is the first race first you know – the qualifying race, the one against the clock."

"Yes. I understand that, but the real show is the Sunday yes?"

He nodded.

"And on the Sunday what happens?" She didn't wait for a reply, into her stride now, "There is a lot of noise and some things might happen at the start, cars pass each other, and they weave and dodge – but then nothing." She shrugged, "The cars just seem to go around in one long line for an hour and a half."

"Well you seem to have grasped the basics anyway..."

"And even if a car does get close enough to pass," she wasn't about to finish quite yet, "it can't because the car in front make too much mess of the air, so they cannot get close – right?"

"Right," he was smiling. "But some of us see that as the challenge."

"But you would rather it the old way, yes? Chico says that even the tracks are wrong for racing now, this is why he builds the Chicodrome."

"It could certainly be more fun, but this is Formula One, the pinnacle of all motor sport: if you want to see cars passing each other three times a lap go to a Formula Ford race – this has to be very difficult."

He hardly seemed convinced himself, she thought, or was he just tired of the same old questions? Whatever, she could not stop herself now, starved of conversation: save for the inanities of the PR man and the photographers, and the long distance crackle of the family back in the Republic.

"But the thing I really do not understand is that this is called a sport at all. I mean if it were a pole vault competition would it be right if one man had a longer pole than another?"

He laughed: "Well in this game it's more to do with the size of your balls than the length of your pole to be honest."

"Sorry?"

"Oh, nothing, an English joke."

"But you see what I mean. The man in the pretty car, the Bianchi, he has no chance against Chico and yourself in the DBM. The only race is with you and Chico in the same car and..." She tailed off, afraid that in drawing the comparison with her husband it might hurt him, hurt his pride. For she knew the hurt of these men, of her Chico, when the comfort zone disappeared, when he was beaten. But Kinsella hardly seemed to notice anyway.

"I have been looking for you." It was Chico, appearing from nowhere. He carried his helmet by its chin-guard. The words were directed at Kinsella, but all the same he had glanced at her as he spoke them. There was something in the way he looked at her, some recognition for sure – for a moment she hoped that it was jealousy, but she somehow knew that was not it. Chico wanted to talk to Kinsella about the press reports, and so she left them to it, walking away to find a patch of unshaded paddock, to sit in the sun until the start of qualifying.

Chapter Six

He laughed into his helmet as he strapped it in place. Chico had been a pussy-cat: they'll write any old shit, Kinsella had told him. Called in Mossup's favour – that's what he hadn't told him. Just propaganda, just part of the game, let them think the British guy is getting a raw deal. But there was something more to the encounter he was sure, something of an awkwardness between Chico and Teresa, something which interested Kinsella. Was Chico peeved, just a little maybe? Peeved that Kinsella had been getting on with Mrs Chico so famously? Christ, he should have been – getting on famously is never good when you know what Kinsella is famous for.

And that one had rumbled the game quick enough hadn't she? Smart cookie. At first he had thought she was just the usual, just the tits and the smile for the camera. But there was more after all. And was that a blush? Oh you rogue, don't even think it. Just file it away in the dossier Kinsella...

He remembered his conversation with her. Normally, he thought, he would have argued more, tried to stick up for the sport just a little bit – the least he could do, after all it had bought him *Akrasia* and maybe soon would buy him his jet. But not here, not here in Monaco. She was right anyway, it was nothing but a bloody circus – and this is where they send in the clowns. You see, Kinsella had done the sums. He could act fearless for the cameras, for the game: if you go off these days chances are that you'll end up in the kitty litter after all, not so much of a risk really. Okay, you can never be 100 per cent sure, as the tickets say: *Motor racing is dangerous*, and look at Melbourne, there's always the chance of a freak shunt like that. Yet the odds were usually stacked in his favour. Except here – at Monaco. Here it just didn't bloody well add up...

Here's the equation see. You have a town and you race through the streets of that town. Pure, the way it always was. *Was* is the word though – by rights this place should have gone out with the front-engined roadsters and flying helmets. Christ, some of the roads they were expected to race on had been laid before the car had been invented. If anyone dreamt up such a race now, took it to the little-big-man for approval, they'd be told where to go for sure, Kinsella thought. Either that or the man at the top would start looking for the candid cameras.

Yeah cameras. That's what it's really all about. Viewing figures, top three events: Olympics, World Cup – then the bloody Monaco Grand Prix. And because of that the sponsors loved it, and if the sponsors love it the teams will find something to love about it. Such is the way of things. But what a poor showcase it made, passing in F1 is all but impossible at the best of times, all but impossible at Silverstone, at Hockenheim. But here? Insanity: streets as narrow as... well, streets... and corners as tight as Kessler at contract time – at the Grand Hotel hairpin the DBM didn't even have enough steering lock to make the turn, he had to kick the tail round on the throttle. Someone had once told Kinsella that in the first fifteen seconds of the race the gearbox goes through fifteen changes here, he hadn't counted but could well believe it, it was a place where everything – and everyone – was worked to the limit. On top of that there was hardly a hint at straightness along its two-mile course, nowhere to take a breather, just the ever-twisting funnel of Armco barrier. As one former world champion once put it: driving around Monaco is a little like trying to ride a bicycle round your living room.

Kinsella had never really gone well here. Always a little wary, that split second of caution on the brakes, that split second of hesitancy on the throttle. Wouldn't do to hit the wall here, wouldn't know where you might end up – even in the harbour, like Alberto Ascari did in 1955. But more than that, much more than that... There was the thing – his thing. Always, since the Jap' was killed at Sugo, flipping the Formula 3000, landing on the barrier, on his head. Kinsella had been first on the scene and it had hit him hard. At the time, and ever since, blasé was the only way through it and some had hated him for it. But here – where the barriers are but inches from you – the act was all the more difficult. So Kinsella never went well at Monaco. It hadn't mattered so much before though, by this stage of the season, round five of the championship most years, he would have had stamped his authority on the team, beaten the confidence and the cockiness out of his team-mate. Right, they might be closer here, and one year he had been out-qualified, the year with Patterson. But then that's playing the percentages. And what's the first rule of the game Kinsella? Right, don't get yourself killed.

But then there are times when you need to bend the rules. Times when you are three-nil down in the qualifying stakes, most of the team's attention is squarely on your team mate, and nobody believes you can beat him. Yes, sometimes you have to bend the rules, ignore the calculations – sometimes you've just got to put your imagination to bed for the afternoon and get on with the job, sometimes you just have to go to work Kinsella.

He lifted a leg over the sidepod and stepped into the car, so that he stood on the seat. Then, grasping the edge of the cockpit, he slid himself down into the thimble-tight slot. His legs were stretched out before him, angled slightly upwards – but not so much as they would be in a Sultan or one of the other high-nosed cars, like sitting in a bath with your legs on the taps in those. He felt for the pedals, brake and throttle, and squirmed himself down tight into the seat. He remembered how, before the start of the season, he had sat in a bin liner full of warm liquid foam for half an hour until it had solidified to mirror every contour of back and bum precisely. A tight fitting seat then, and it had to be, anything less and Kinsella would be black and blue after a lap, for there's hardly any suspension on one of these things, nothing to soak up the bumps. And it was tight with the straps too. A mechanic reached in to tighten them, two crotch, two lap, and two shoulder belts, tongues connecting into a boss at his lap. Kinsella winced as the straps were tightened, yet he asked for another tug all the same; tighten till it hurts and then one more tug, that's the unwritten rule.

In the office: gripping the chamois covered, butterfly shaped wheel at a quarter to three, eye-line a foot or two off the ground, just above the lip of the cockpit and a row of warning lights – hydraulic pressure, oil pressure, coolant temperature, upshift, rev limiter and neutral. The knees of the mechanics scurry past as they busy themselves with removing the electric blankets from the tyres – blankets that bring the rubber up to within 20°C of usable temperature. Stood just beyond the nose of the DBM Burgess nods and Kinsella raises his left hand. With one finger he stirs at the air, the signal for the mechanic to insert the electric starter into the rear of the car. The motor is turned while an engine man monitors its health on a laptop computer plugged into the car. All is well and it's fired up, the engine man breathing the motor once or twice with the remote trigger before letting Kinsella pick it up on the accelerator. Kinsella holds the engine at 4,000 rpm, just enough to keep the hydraulic pressure up.

He checks the warning lights, checks the switches, then with his left middle finger he pulls at the lower paddle under the steering wheel. The orange light just below his eye-line glows, telling him there is enough hydraulic pressure to select a gear. He flicks it into first, feeling a slight kick as it goes into gear, then he eases the rpm up to 6,000, lets out the clutch lever and cautiously trundles out of the pit garage. Time to go to work Kinsella...

The qualifying session was into the fortieth of its sixty minutes. Chico had used up half of his 12 laps: just two quick ones and the two 'out' and 'in' laps. A couple of flyers to go then, but not now, for now is the time to watch and wait. Kinsella had just taken to the track for his fourth run, he was closer than usual to Chico, but Chico felt there was a little to spare in the lead DBM, perhaps as much as a tenth through *Casino*, and maybe a bit more time through the swimming pool complex. He was still strapped tightly into his car, two wafer thin TV monitors pulled down level with his eye-line. On one monitor there was the list of the qualifying times thus far. Every now and then a row of figures would turn green, to indicate that someone had beaten their best through a sector, while a blip of the screen would mark someone moving up the grid, which in turn would mean someone moving down the grid. But at the top it was stalemate, just as Chico had expected. He was top – just – Kinsella right behind, and the Sultan of Guido Solé was breathing down their necks.

Solé's pace was a worry. Fraser had told him that Sultan had something in the pipeline, but he had not expected them to claw back the advantage that DBM had on them so soon. But then Solé's confidence would be stratospheric after his Imola win and that counted for so much here. And as for Kinsella? He was close, yes – but there was still that tenth at *Casino*... Normally, it should not be a problem...

On the other monitor, showing the television feed pictures, the director had left the on-track action for a while. For a moment Chico could see himself, then past himself he could see the cameraman, focussing in on his eyes, the only part of the racer you really see when he's at the office, and only then when he has the visor up. Then the cameraman moved down the pitlane, panning as he did so, and the picture switched again, to the Sultan pit this time, next door. Guido Solé was out of the car, helmet and fire-retardant balaclava in hand, his boyish, toothy grin big and white on the screen, he walked quickly to the back of the garage where Zola ruffled his hair in a show of affection rare from the team boss. Solé took a deep swig from his drinks bottle and the cameraman switched his attention to the other

Sultan, where the veteran, Thierry Michel, sat strapped up and ready to go, waiting for the time when the track was clear enough for his next lap. His next chance to try to shave the 0.7 seconds his team-mate had on him. The camera zoomed in on the eyes again, eyes fringed with the ingrained experience of ten hard seasons in Formula One, and the eyes that told a story – to Chico at least – of worry. Michel was struggling to match his young protégé, was becoming the Sultan number two, and he had so hoped to end his career on a high. Poor Thierry.

Chico was wondering if his eyes had betrayed something of him too, when the camera had rested on them. Had it told the world that all was not well, that something was amiss? Not a superstitious type Chico, not like many of the drivers: the ones who would wear the odd coloured boots or lucky underpants because of one good result in strange circumstances, or the ones who would insist on always stepping into the cockpit from the same side of the car. No, not superstitious like that. But he believed in a God, in a destiny, in his right to be the fastest racing driver in the world. And if he had wronged this God, this destiny – this gift – would it disappear, be taken from him...?

Stupid, of course, he told himself. But it nagged at him all the same. So that all that went wrong seemed to be inextricably interwoven with it. Little things at first: Kinsella's Melbourne shunt shocking him, then there had been that nonsense in the press – the English press mostly – about him feeling the pressure at Interlagos, almost throwing the race away. And once they have their teeth into you those dogs they never let go. And this latest thing. Just because his engineer doubles as the team's technical chief, why would that mean he would get the best parts, development parts, better parts than Kinsella – can't they see it's a team sport, do they really think that K-Corp would allow that?

Nonsense, of course, but they had quoted an unnamed source at the team, making it sound like it could be Kinsella. The PR man had put him straight, Kinsella had put him straight. But still, there was something about the Englishman, something deeper than the internecine rivalry that was part of the sport, something that made him wonder about that obstructing lap at Interlagos, about the mix up with the dinner suit – had he been playing with him?

Teresa seemed to like him though... something of her drifted into Chico's consciousness, a part of her image which he tried to trap, solidify... but it drifted away. The poor girl, a mistake, and only she could suffer. Then the guilt washed through him once more, so he closed his eyes tight to fill his head with a picture of *Casino Square*, where he could find the extra tenth, some sort of bearable reality, something less confusing. When he opened his eyes again the TV director had switched his attention to the other DBM, starting its fast lap, the last of its fast laps.

The sheet of noise that trailed behind the DBM hung in the air as the number eight car rushed along the pit straight down towards *Ste Devote*. It hung in the air so that Chico's TV pictures were supplemented by the booming surround-sound of the passing car just metres over the pit wall. A noise with no escape route this, hemmed in by the high-rise buildings of Monte Carlo, bouncing amongst the balconies and the balustrades, only spent by beating itself in a thunderstorm frenzy against an eardrum.

Chico watched as on the screen his team-mate's DBM flicked through *Ste Devote* almost nudging the barrier on the exit of the right-hander as he drifted wide out of the turn. It was precise, and he had lost no time – Chico had to give him that. Kinsella had the grip for the all important drag up the hill to *Massanet* and *Casino Square*, threading through the eye of the needle now, threading through the eye of the needle at 160 mph. Blind into the corner, the car going light over the crest, sometimes all four wheels off the deck, but the TV never picked that up. The car looked settled into the turn, then it ran a little loose, the back stepping out – that could cost him.

The back was out at *Mirabeau* too, it looked scruffy, spectacular yes – the fans would like it – but scruffy all the same. But then the split time: *Kinsella* – 0.2, and on the timing screen the numbers flashed magenta – quickest. It seemed to hit him in the chest first, the shock of it, but he calmed himself... early in the lap yet. And look, Kinsella's locked up the front into the *Grand Hotel hairpin*. The DBM ran a little wide at the painfully slow hairpin, just scrabbling through as Kinsella kicked out the tail of the car with a jab of power, setting it up in time for *Portier*, the corner where Senna crashed in '88... They had given him a hard time for that. The greats – Chico reminded himself – were not allowed mistakes...

But Kinsella was, and my God was he getting away with them, was he lucky. The tail of the DBM nudged the barrier out of *Portier* and Kinsella slotted it aggressively through the tunnel, a long curve right that passed beneath an hotel, the silver of the DBM darkening gunmetal grey for some seconds before bursting once more into the sunlight, its nose kissing the tarmac as Kinsella tried to scrub off the speed for the fiddly chicane alongside the harbour. It was late braking, and again there was the tell-tale smoke of a man in a hurry, a man on the limit, a man so, so close to over-driving. Yet, once again he had made it through the turn, this time scraping the underside of the DBM on the high kerbing as he let the car run over it. Power on for *Tabac* and the time was there again, Chico had almost missed it, engrossed in his Team-mate's efforts to keep the DBM straight: but there it was for all to see: -0.2. He had held the gap. Fraser had seen it too, had signalled to Chico to get ready, time to respond.

Chico tried to pinpoint this emotion, this new emotion. Alright, he had had the fight brought to him before by a team-mate in qualifying, even been beaten once or twice. But so, what's that, a minor annoyance – beat the guy next lap, or beat the guy next race. Simple. For sure. But this was different, this time he felt as if this lap of Kinsella's was more than just some very ugly, very lucky, very quick lap. It was somehow malicious – it was taunting him: *go on Chico, have you the balls to match this...*

And then there was that image of the other DBM at Interlagos, that image of himself overdressed at the casino... My God, he would show him.

The number eight car seemed to clatter through the swimming pool complex of corners, the rear left tyre smearing one of the barriers black as it ran a little too wide on the exit. That should slow him, Chico thought, but somehow he knew that it hadn't. And the fact that Fraser, who was hunched over one of the timing computers, still looked grim, told him that the lap was still quick. Would still have to be beaten, be beaten comfortably... be demolished, be pulverised. Chico was ready for the lap of his life, if ever there was a time for the perfect lap then this was it, and why not? If Kinsella could carry that speed with an untidy – an ugly – lap, the speed must be in the car... He crossed himself as the mechanics started up the engine of his DBM with the portable starter. Just then Kinsella crossed the start-finish line, his time for the lap flashing magenta while the number one flashed onto the screen: -0.01. A nothing, a fraction of a nothing, he had it in him he knew, through *Casino Square* he could make it up and more, and there were tenths to grab at the swimming pool. He could easily be half a second up on him, comfortably in front, should be – by God, he would be.

Chico was out of the pits, working the tyres to get them up to heat. By the time he reached the top of the hill at *Massanet* he could see the tail of the other DBM, Kinsella on his slowing down lap, Chico on his winding up lap. Kinsella should have let him through immediately, but Chico was glued to the tail of the other silver and blue car all the way through *Mirabeau*, the hairpin and into the tunnel. He could see the red, green and white bands of Kinsella's helmet reflected in the

63

number eight car's mirrors. He could imagine him grinning as he pulled out of his slipstream on the way down to the chicane. He could imagine him laughing as Chico locked a tyre in his quest for the space, the space for his run-up for that lap – the lap that would knock the grin off Kinsella's face.

A fast lap, or the fastest of fast laps, always starts some way before the lap actually starts. In that some of the work has to be done there, you need to have the speed onto the straight, and to have this you need to have the speed out of the last corner of the previous lap. And Chico had it: clean and quick through *Rascasse* and *Anthony Noghes*, Fraser's excited voice over the comms, telling him the track ahead was clear. The DBM ate up the pit straight and was into *St Devote*. It clipped close to the barriers left then right as the track funnelled into the turn. Then Chico took it neatly through the right-hander, using all the road to the nearest centimetre, powering the DBM up the hill, towards *Massanet* and the section that runs past the Casino: the section where he could take a bite out of Kinsella's lap. For sure.

An extra gram on the scales, that's all it takes. He thought it was there: gears down to third, massaging the brake pedal with his left foot, in blind, the car light as it crests the rise, tip-toeing on the limit of its suspension. Then it is floating through the turn as he nudges at the wheel to keep it left of the track, a rub with the left foot again, and the squirt with the right, and the car is drifting, but well placed for the plunge right into *Casino*, where he can make up the time... Just let it drift a little longer as it plunges through the right hander at close to 100 mph, just let it drift a little wider on the exit and there's your tenth...

It might just kiss the Armco barrier, but he thought that he had it, had it perfect. There was a flash of a grinning Kinsella in his head, and then there was the crunch, and before he knew it his horizon was shifting at a giddying pace and the steering wheel was whipped from his hands.

Kinsella had just pulled off his helmet and his sweat-soaked Nomex balaclava. He felt as if he wanted to throw up. One of the mechanics offered him a hand in congratulation, but he turned away, digging the ear plugs out of his ears, just to keep his hands busy, in the hope that no one would notice just how much he was shaking. Everyone else in the pits had their eyes fixed firmly on the TV monitor, on Chico's lap. Kinsella looked up just as the other DBM was turning into *Casino* on the brakes. A lovely controlled drift, beautiful to watch, perfect. Almost. Drifting towards the barrier the tail of the car kicked out slightly over a big bump. It was lovely car control, Kinsella conceded, but Chico had run out of road. At first Kinsella thought he would get away with it, just a brush with the Armco, but for whatever reason – perhaps a protruding bolt or a kink in the steel – the rear of the DBM hit hard and ricocheted off the barrier. Then it spun at high speed in the opposite direction to the turn. Much of the first impact was missed by the cameraman, who was panning to follow the DBM through the corner, but then the camera jerked back and the DBM filled the screen once more, spinning through 180 degrees once. Spinning twice, three times, shedding bits of bodywork as it did so, before coming to a rest half way around its fourth revolution.

For some long seconds Chico sat motionless in the cockpit. Kinsella turned to see where Teresa was. Was she watching this, was she still learning about motor racing, learning the hardest lesson? There was Fraser too, he noticed, face as white as the pristine floor on which they all stood stock still, waiting for something to happen, waiting for some sign of movement from the DBM cockpit. Teresa was at the back of the pit garage, sitting on a tool locker, her head buried in her hands. Someone said they thought he had moved, Chico had moved, and Kinsella found himself looking at the screen once more. The car had lost its rear wing, and much of the bodywork down the left side. One of its wheels had been torn from its safety tether and in the background Kinsella could see it roll to a stop against the barrier. The track marshals reached the car. Kinsella could hear Fraser, talking now on the comms. No, he thought, not so much talking: pleading, praying almost:

"Chico... Chico, are you alright... Chico... Please be alright."

And then, on the screen, Chico raised his hand high, waved it about a bit. And a collective sigh, like a wave breaking against the shore, seemed to issue from the pit lane. Chico climbed out of the stricken car, hobbling a little, and then Kinsella allowed himself his little smile – his little smile of victory. He noticed that the shaking had stopped, and he noticed that his name still topped the time sheet. He had gambled, and he had won. He climbed out of his car and moved to the back of the pit, time to offer Teresa a shoulder to cry on...

Chapter Seven

More than a month doing nothing much. That's how it had been. A good lump of the money gone: bills, a treat or two for Sarah, a new car – or rather a new old car, a beaten up Sierra which had made worrying noises on the long four hour drive west. More than a month doing nothing on much except for keeping an eye on everything Formula One. Swatting up at the library, surfing the Internet, and keeping up to date with all the magazines – Christ, had Stubbs bought the anorak. He just hadn't known what to do with the bloody thing. But then background research is vital, and he had watched with interest along with everyone else as the season had unfolded. He had watched as Chico won at Monaco despite a big shunt in qualifying. He had watched as Chico then took Spain, his team-mate 10 seconds behind as they crossed the line. Then he had watched Montreal: Kinsella outqualifying Chico for the second time, both DBMs retiring from the race with technical problems, the Ferraris coming one-two – and Solé 0.2 of a second to the good on pole before crashing out. Yes, Solé was beginning to look a threat. No wonder Fraser was getting rattled: on the blower, asking him what the bloody hell he had been up to this past month...

He had been glad of his lucky break then alright. It's always difficult with these out of town operations, finding the watering hole. But there had been a pub on the fringe of the Bicester industrial estate where Sultan was based. He had sat there, at the bar, three nights running. Then there was the mouthy one – there's always one who wants to tell the world how important he is – part of the test team he had told the barmaid, off to Wales on the Thursday morning, off to Pembrey for some development testing.

The *Canolfan Rasio Modur Cymru*, as far as the M4 reaches, tucked away behind Llanelli, flat and featureless, an old Spitfire base, used for club racing mainly, but a good test venue. It's narrow, but there's a tight hairpin and a good range of corners. He had picked up the details from a motor racing handbook, the rest he had to work out for himself the night before: the lane through the adjacent country park, the hiding place for the Sierra – out of sight – the wood that reached to within 20 metres of the trackside. And now the field work: it almost always seemed to come down to this, cold and wet and up to his elbows in mud.

Stubbs lay under a bush, just the long lens of the camera breaking the line of the tangle of vegetation in front of him. The deserted pit area was some 100 metres down the track to his left, made remote by the ribbon of dark asphalt that was the start-finish straight. Water dripped onto him from the canopy of the wood above him. Wales, mid June: it had rained all bloody night. He stole a glance at his watch: 9.00am. He had been in place for three hours already and there was still no sign of the Sultan truck, still no sign of anything. Not that he had any idea of what he was supposed to do when they got there – after all anybody could take a picture of the bloody thing at the races... But at least he felt that he was doing something.

It occurred to Stubbs as he waited that this was his first visit to a racing circuit of any description. There was, he thought, something strangely eerie about the place. Or rather, something strangely eerie about the place being empty, being quiet. It was a small track, with little in the way of infrastructure, just a race control tower, and a couple of buildings. There were no grandstands, but on the far side of the circuit he could make out the big grass covered berm that he guessed must serve as spectator banking.

He waited for another hour. Then, finally, when his patience and the level of the coffee in the vacuum flask was running low, the huge Sultan orange articulated truck arrived, easily recognisable with the silhouette of the high nosed racer etched in black on its flanks. The well drilled crew, each in orange coats against the unseasonal biting wind, unloaded the pristine Sultan in next to no time, housing it in a canvas awning that folded out of the side of the truck's trailer. For the next hour or so there was nothing. Then, momentarily, a racing engine burst into life, a solitary roar, and cough, then quiet. A little time later a mechanic disappeared into the back of the truck, returning in five minutes with a tray of coffees.

Then more waiting. It was almost midday when the helicopter finally arrived, landing in the infield some way from the pits. With his binoculars pressed tight to his face Stubbs could make out the small figure of Guido Solé, attaché case in hand, mobile phone pressed to his ear. Alongside him, ducking in the wash of the slowing rotor, was Zola, a cigarette clamped in his teeth. Stubbs shifted his weight a little to help the circulation, scratching at the little scar under his nose, then he took the stopwatch from his pocket. The Sultan's engine was fired up again, and he conceded it was something special: more mechanical scream than roar, with a musical cadence as the mechanic blipped at the throttle. Then there were peaks of it, great gobs of power, the noise – he had read – that had been likened to the million times magnified sound of tearing silk.

Stubbs was sure he would never forget that first *live* sight of a Formula One car flat out. The first few laps – to warm the machine up – had been exhilarating enough, but by now Solé was obviously pressing on, winding through the gears up the back straight then carrying unbelievable speed through the right hand kink. It was an instant change of direction, almost as if the Sultan had bounced off a force-field. Just incredible that he could turn at that speed, almost unbelievable that the car did not keep on going – keep on going all the way to Carmarthen, just like Newton would say it should. It was like nothing he had ever seen, certainly like nothing he had seen on TV, and at once it meant more to him. Into the long right-hander where Stubbs hid, Solé stood on the brakes and worked it down through the gears in a matter of yards, the brake discs glowing cherry red through the wheels. The blipping engine – machine-gun quick on the downchange – peppering at Stubbs's eardrums while wafts of well-worked car smells were carried to Stubbs' nostrils by the gusting wind. Sensory overload, that's what it was. Yet Stubbs craved for more, craned for more, poking his head out of the cover of the bush on each lap to watch as one of the world's finest drivers drove the turn. Watch as the rear wheels tagged the fringe of the track, kicking up cement dust from the kerb as Solé powered it out and down the straight... The Sultan diminishing to a dot in the blink of a wide eye. Stubbs had the stopwatch on it, but the figures meant nothing to him really – just numbers, information to please Fraser, that's all.

Solé pounded round the little track for twenty laps before stopping briefly. Then there were two more, slightly slower, laps before he brought the Sultan in again. Solé was then out of the car and talking to his engineer, Zola looking on. There was some animated chat, could be an argument, could be a joke, could be a discussion on wing angles – Italians. Then Solé looked at the sky, darkening behind him Stubbs noticed, maybe rain coming off the sea. The little Italian climbed into the car, stepping on the seat before easing himself low into the monocoque. Some mechanics busied themselves around the rear of the car and then it burst into life once more, the noise tearing through the fabric of wind-laced quietude that hung about the circuit. Solé took to the track again.

A pattern developed. Solé would complete some laps then pit, and Stubbs once again congratulated himself on the choice of his hide, looking straight down into the pit lane. The cloud grew thicker, blacker, then drooped heavy and low over the circuit. Finally the tarmac began to darken with the rain and the canopy of the wood began to sing a song of drenching, not unlike the sound of sizzling bacon Stubbs thought.

Despite the downpour there was a longer stint, some thirty laps or so, every now and then the slick surface pitched the car into a lurid tailslide, while huge rooster tails of spray marked the Sultan's progress right around the circuit. It was a progress that was much slower than earlier in the test – the watch told Stubbs – but a progress that was almost hypnotic. So much so that by the time Stubbs took another glance into the pitlane the mechanics, now with their anorak hoods pulled up tight over their heads, had erected all the framework and paraphernalia of the pit-stop. All the familiar equipment he had seen put to good use during those vital seconds counted down digitally in the corner of the TV screen – the air guns, the refuelling rig and the jacks.

Then there was the burble of a down-change and the Sultan was steered into the wide pit lane apron. The mechanics poured over the machine, each knowing his job: the wheel-men, the fuel-men, the jack-men... And then the man with the shock of shaggy blond hair, crouched up close to the car, a large orange Sultan golfing umbrella protecting his laptop from the elements, an umbilical from the laptop plugged into the sidepod of the racing car. Then unplugged. And the car falls from the jacks and it's away.

The clock is on again. First lap: out lap, second lap... Stop the clock. No, must have pressed the button at the wrong time, Stubbs thought. But then... the way the car left the turn, not even a hint of a wiggle from the rear end – yet the rooster tail was as high as ever, the rain as hard as ever. Stubbs pressed the little button on the stopwatch again. Next lap: two seconds quicker. The next lap: the same. The next lap: two and a half seconds. He looked at the sky, then looked at the puddles forming at trackside. He listened to the beat of the rain in the branches above him – if anything it was raining even harder. And even through the rain, even past the hoods of the anoraks, even under the orange umbrellas, he could see that the Sultan crew were smiling, laughing, clapping each other on the back – having a bloody ball.

Solé stopped five more times, and each time the Sultan crew tried to disguise the process of plugging the computer umbilical into the side of the car. Finally, it was given to one of the wheel-men to handle – a quick enough job, after he had let the used wheel fall away while he was still crouched behind the Sultan. Yes, quick enough, and certainly well hidden in the confusion of your average pit-stop.

This was enough, for now. Stubbs crawled backwards from under the bush, wincing at the muddy mess smearing the length of his jeans. He collected his equipment: camera, flask, binoculars, watch and pad, and made his way back to the Sierra. This should do for Fraser, he thought, he would get on to him in the morning – and how about *Gianclaudio's* for dinner tonight? Sarah would like that...

Chapter Eight

She put her hand over one of the lovely little breasts and then lifted the hand away, cupping it about two inches in front of her chest: "About here."

Kinsella nodded, and turned his attention back to the newspaper.

"Kim says no, but I am bored with them – and a little bigger will be better, no... No?"

He looked at her again, gleaming yellow-bronzed in the Mediterranean sunshine. Christ, 24 hours previously he would have been bursting at the sight of it: all the pleasures of the orient neatly packaged in nothing much, nothing much but a tiny pair of white knickers. White knickers small on her now, but microscopic on the cabin floor last night. What a bundle of fun she had been, always the same – the rich wives – too bloody bored, and when they get their teeth into a slice of Kinsella – well, then there was no telling what might happen. He winced as he felt the raw, fresh scratches on his back rub against the fabric of the sun lounger, winced again when he saw those lethal nails, playing with the dark, hard nipple, as she still talked about the operation. The operation her husband didn't want her to have, the operation her husband would eventually pay for, frittering away the money earned in her absence as he cultivated an ulcer in the boardrooms of the world, the face of K-Corp in the City, on Wall Street. Poor sod.

He wondered how the mighty Kim had snared her. Must have been the money, surely. And Christ he hated to think what she had been up to before that. Little Kobe, Hong Kong Chinese, the essence of raw sex, and as dangerous as Eau Rouge on a hot lap in the wet... yes, a slippery little minx.

Until the morning that is, then it's the normal: bloody talk, just another piece of fluff to get rid of, somehow. He found himself drifting as she continued, her almost American accent loud against the gentle lap of the sea at the hull of Akrasia. The sun was already high, they had slept in. Well, not slept. He looked at his watch. He would have to train soon, a swim and some weights. Perhaps that would make an excuse to be rid of her?

Kinsella smiled at Kobe then picked up the tabloid newspaper again. The Brit, a day old. Pablo – who looked after *Akrasia* – collected it for him every morning, from one of Monte Carlo's hotels. Had to have his *Brit*, had to keep an eye on Mossup, keep an eye on the story – keep an eye on his story. Especially now, after France.

At last he had raced him, raced Chico. They had crossed the line as one, almost. Kinsella even managed to poke his nose alongside into the tight final corner. And yes, how many times had Chico bottled it? Three at least. Kinsella there, big in the great man's mirror – okay he had been lucky with the stops – but still, he had been there, taking the fight to him. And Kessler hadn't liked it, bloody Fraser hadn't liked it – almost close to tears – and they had warned him there and then, play the team game or don't play at all, Chico's ahead in the championship, you're just there to back him up, not to race him... Arseholes. But they had made it clear, anymore games and Eoghan Egg Kinsella would be down the job centre.

Still, good old Mossup and his mates were not hanging back, just the thing to up the ante on the run-up to the British Grand Prix. And this was good stuff indeed...

What comes first – the Chico or the Egg?

South American Speed sensation Chico is in the pits...
   That's the word coming out of the DBM racing team, where the pace of our very own race ace Egg Kinsella has left the twice world champ' hot under the fireproof collar.
   While in the lead up to next week's big race Chico is in a spin after a series of Grand Prix gaffs.
   Blunder one: it's Brazil nuts for Chico as he almost throws away the race within sight of the chequered flag.
   Blunder two: It's Monte Carlo and bust as Chico is lucky to survive a frightening crash at the Monaco Grand Prix.
   Blunder three: He's given a French lesson as he is pushed to the flag by the underrated Kinsella at Magny Cours...

And so it continued. Yes, a job well done, and Chico would not be able to hide from it. The other papers might tone it down a bit, but the questions had been asked of him, and even if Chico never saw a bloody newspaper again the questions would continue to be asked, over and over again, at the conferences... in the man's head.

"You fancy something... a coffee, a juice?" he asked Kobe.

"Champagne?"

Yeah, that would be good. But sadly those days were gone, even coffee is a crime for the modern Formula One driver in the lead up to a race. Still, ever hospitable... he thought he had a bottle somewhere. To get to the galley of the cruiser he had to make his way to the stern and climb the stairs to the bridge. There was a fax machine there and he picked up a sheaf of correspondence. The first was a questionnaire from a journalist, one of the specialists, asking him the usual stuff, asking him about Chico, asking him about Sole's Sultan and its suspicious turn of speed out of the *Adelaide* hairpin at Magny Cours. He would see to it later. The next was from Mossup, thanking him for the lead, then there was a letter from the garage about the E-Type, which was ready. He pictured a familiar road and the long scarlet snout of the old Jag stretching out before him, eating up the empty tarmac. It would be fun to get back to that.

Something made him glance behind, through the storm glass of the bridge, where the stern of the boat stretched to the quayside, almost kissing the jetty. It was moored between two other boats, separated by the wood-slatted access piers. One belonged to a banker and the other to a writer. Both were a little bigger than *Akrasia*– bigger holes in the water to pour money into. Each a reminder of why he had to find the time, just a tenth or so now. For then his market value would go up – Christ, after Magny Cours he had already had one team boss on the phone about next year.

On the quayside a knot of tourists were taking pictures of the boats, dwarfed by the bar-graph backdrop of Monaco, or Manhattan-Sur-Mer, as someone had called it. There was a Daytona yellow Ferrari F360 parking up there too, two a penny in Monte, but then you never lose the eye for a beautiful car. Nor a beautiful woman come to that, and when he saw her he suddenly remembered the invitation: *"I'll be moored in Monte... drop in if you're in the neighbourhood."* Never thought she would of course, but here she was, flicking the hair back over her shoulders, the sunlight catching the red in it, burnished bright, as she slammed shut the low door of the Ferrari –all eyes now on her. And then the recognition, the wave, and she was coming down the steps to the jetty.

"Kobe – shit!"

Kinsella rushed to the door at the rear of the bridge, letting the sheaf of faxes spill onto the floor, like a sailor at battle stations he slid down the rails of the stairway, his hands hot with the friction of the well-polished brass, then raced around to the bow. Kobe had shades on, face to the sun, lying outstretched on the long lounger. There was no time for explanations. Just time to grab her around the shoulders, under the knees, feel her nakedness against his bare chest again, feel those lovely, hard little breasts again, feel the snap of the knicker elastic as it ruffled against the belt of his shorts. And then he spun her once and let go. For one delicious moment the all-but-naked chief executive's wife was panic-stricken against a sky of corporate blue, her black hair trailing stiffly like the bristles of a paintbrush as the action seemed to freeze around her moment of panic. And then she splashed down into the harbour. Kinsella looked behind him, down onto the companionway. Teresa was shouting something, waving to him again. Then there was Kobe shouting too – could she swim? He rushed to the bow rail again, and there she was, that same look in her dark eyes as when he had taken her the night before: anger, passion, one and the same in this one.

"Quiet, you idiot – it's your husband!"

"Kim... But he's in New York?" She swallowed a good mouthful of Mediterranean.

He found her clothes lying by the lounger. The shoes landed with a plop and sank to the bottom of the Med. The dress was an ivory silk number, sheer, light and very expensive – it seemed to believe its own publicity, floating in disbelief before landing in the harbour like a butterfly down to drink. By the time he had thrown her champagne glass from the night before over the side Teresa was there.

"Are you okay – I hope I haven't come at a bad time."

"No... No," he slapped a grin to his face, "someone's just thrown a woman over the side, that's all."

She went to look but he took her by the shoulder and led her to one of the sumptuous white leather seats that flanked the two sun loungers. There was no resistance, just a shrug, and she sat on the edge of the seat, balancing her face on upstretched palms, rounding it, making it as sorrowful as a moon, he thought.

Kobe would be alright, find a friendly port on one of the other boats, somewhere to dock for the afternoon, and what a way to get rid of them eh? Only thing was, he couldn't quite see why he had done it – what's it to Teresa?

Then, what's it to Kinsella? All the same, fun to have your fun, then throw them over the side...

She smiled at Kinsella, a little smile, then eased her long body back into the chair, crossing her legs, which were clad in white stretch pants again just like that first time they had talked at Interlagos.

Kinsella offered her a drink, she said yes, just a juice, and he disappeared into the galley, taking care to put the faxes in a safe place on his way through the bridge.

The short time it took for him to prepare the juices gave him the breathing space. Of course he had said drop in, as a friend – they had talked more and more after all, but he had never expected it, quietly hoped maybe, yes – certainly, he had hoped. But now she was there, and if nothing else the game would go on. He took the juices back to the fore-deck.

There was an eternity of small talk – five minutes of it, before he couldn't help himself.

"I'm surprised you came."

"I was bored," she shrugged.

"Bored?"

"Yes, Chico's away testing for Silverstone, he wanted me to stay in the flat."

Testing, yeah, Kinsella hadn't seen a lot of that since his naughtiness at Interlagos, less still since beating Chico here in Monte in qualifying. But he could take it as a plus, take it as part of the game, Chico using his clout as the superstar to keep him away from the car, keep him from honing his ability in the car. If so that would work in Kinsella's advantage – if Chico is this defensive, this wary, he will make mistakes, no doubt about that.

"... He did not want me there... Or perhaps it is Fraser who did not want me there," her eyes seemed to light a little at that thought, "they have had their pictures and..." She shrugged again then sipped delicately at the orange juice.

"So what have you been doing with yourself, we have missed you, you know." He said it with a certain amount of truth, for the DBM pit had been a dismal place to be in Canada and France, what with Chico's mood, Fraser's backbiting – a bit of beauty would have done the lads a power of good, would have done him a power of good.

"Oh, I have been in Switzerland, in the chalet, but there is no snow and I know no one... So I came here."

"You have friends here?"

"No... But the sun, and you said I could drop by... I have."

"Yes, of course." How sad it seemed, one of the most beautiful women in the world, but she seemed to have nobody. Nobody except Chico.

"Why not go home for a while... I mean, if you are lonely, not that

75

I'm trying to get rid of you, you understand."

She laughed, and then:

"I would like to go home, how much I would like to go home. But it is so difficult now, you cannot understand how things are there Eoghan... Did I get it right?"

He smiled and nodded, allowing himself the flash-fantasy that she had been practising pronouncing his name.

"You see at home Chico is more than just a sportsman, more than just a celebrity. He is like a god, just like a god. But because he is a god he is not allowed the mistakes of mortals.

"But, as you know Eoghan, Chico has not been himself lately, he has made mistakes and at home they cannot understand this, they cry for him, and some – the newspapers – criticise, say something is wrong. Some even say it's my fault."

"Your fault?"

"It's the way they think, he was okay last year, what's different this year?"

"Well there's me for a start," Kinsella said, more indignant than he had meant.

"Yes, I know that, Chico surely knows – but we are talking about a god, Chico cannot be beaten they say. I think some who read the papers put it down to me, I am the evil influence."

"No, come on, you must be joking?"

She shrugged: "I don't know. But whatever, I cannot go home yet, not while things are bad for Chico. They would see it as a betrayal, the PR man says I should stay as close to him as possible."

"But he's at Silverstone, you're..."

"Yes – have you something a little stronger?" She held up the glass, flicking her wrist so that the pool of juice shone like a wobbly yoke in the sunlight.

"There may be some champagne, some gin... some whisky?"

"Just a little whisky then, I have the Ferrari."

He found a bottle in one of the cabins and poured a generous measure into a tumbler, she asked for no ice, no water – beauty to spare and a taste for Scotch, Grandad Kinsella would have liked this one, he thought. She took the first sip with a gasp, and he thought he saw the ghost of a flush reddening its way up her throat beneath the tan.

"So," he asked, "why aren't you at Silverstone?"

"I have told you, they did not need me."

"And...?"

"*And*... they did not need me." She let the whisky roll around in the bowl of the tumbler for a while, trying – it seemed to him – to peer past her reflection in the mirrors of his shades. Then, her hand suddenly still, she seemed to make a decision, sitting up straighter, bending slightly towards him:

"It is not only that..." Five words, slowly, five words that were the easing open of a heavy old door of restraint, the creaking of the hinges before it swung freely towards him, oiled by just that little splash of whisky – sometimes it needs so very little.

"I know I am being selfish, Chico has given me everything, there is not a girl in the Republic who would not wish to be in my position. But they do not see it, Papa and Mamma do not see it, nobody can see it, how this sport eats up everything."

"Maybe, but you knew that didn't you, the time it would take up, all that?"

"Yes, of course, I was warned. But this is much more than time. It is everything – *everything*. I should not say this I know, and you should say nothing... Agreed?"

"Agreed."

"He has hardly touched me since our wedding night, all it has been is the car, and the track, his track – the Chicodrome. I know it's bad of me, but I need some attention, and now it is so much worse, with the problems – and he doesn't even want me with him, says I am a distraction..."

Well he has a point there, Kinsella thought, tracing the bulge of the stretched white cotton over her breasts through the shield of his glasses.

"...I just have to hope that things will be different at the end of the season."

Fat chance there love, he thought – then there's the testing for next season, the endless round of sponsorship functions and prize-giving dinners. And if he wins the championship, well kiss goodbye to wedded bliss Señora.

"Well, you can hope I suppose," he said.

"You are not much help, I had hoped you would lie to me, cheer me up." She smiled a little as she said it.

"I would help if I could," he said, flashing his best smile of sympathy in return.

She seemed lost in her thoughts for a moment, sipping at the whisky and keeping it in her mouth for a while, slowly sluicing it about before swallowing with a slight grimace.

"You could help," she said.

Despite himself his imagination ran away with him: Christ, yes he could help, he could make up for all that loneliness, one good tumble in the bunk, a nice thought to keep there for a while, watching it melt away as she talked of things oh so familiar – idiot. He should have seen it coming, but had Chico really drawn her into the game? Not so sure there, not yet...

"You know Chico has a problem with you. He doesn't understand why you are against him. It is new for him. Always he works for perfection, a perfect car, a perfect lap, a perfect team. But now he has someone there, someone who is in the team who is against him."

"I'm not against Chico, I'm just racing – it's what we do."

"Chico thinks you do more, you play with him."

"Does he now?"

"Yes. It is new for him, always before his team-mate helps him, but not you. Why?"

Yes, that had been the way hadn't it? But then they were not Eoghan Kinsella – no shame in being beaten by Chico they would say, most at the end of a career, testimonial seasons. And what if they show better once or twice, or come close? Look good alongside a great you'll find the second best of seats for next year. But not Eoghan Kinsella.

"I help him as much as I have to, we are both out to win you know?"

"Yes, I know. But could you try... Try to understand him, talk to him... For me?"

He thought for a while, he could see that she was peering deeply into the lenses of his glasses again. Then she gave him more, the poor, lovely fool.

"He says you are very quick you know, one of the quickest... He must have great respect for you, do you not think?"

Kinsella nodded.

"Once he could not sleep, all night – after qualifying here. He did not understand where you found the time. He was very angry, angry at someone... no, himself – angry with himself, it was strange. As though he had been punished...

"He said it was an ugly lap, your lap... yes, that was it: an ugly lap but a great lap."

"That's good of him, perhaps I should thank him?" As he said it he whipped the glasses from his face, so that she could see the mischief, see the light of fun in the green.

"No," she said, "please don't say anything about me coming here, I'm not sure he would like it, not the way things are between you two."

His smiling eyes seemed to have unsettled her, they had that effect on the ladies he had often noticed, and she drained the dregs of the whisky and, a little flustered, she stood up unsteadily and glanced at her watch, in that – the wrong – order.

He smiled at her again as she made her excuses, saying she would see herself off the boat. A few minutes later he heard the lovely full-throated roar of the Ferrari as it coughed into life. He had plenty to do, his workout at the gym for one, but he was sorry that she had left. Why sorry? Good for the game, of course, silly girl that she was. But more than that, and it surprised him, he quite liked her being there. And more, he almost wanted to help her. Careful Kinsella... Careful.

He took her empty glass back through to the galley, stopping on his way through to use the satellite telephone, which sat alongside the ornate walnut wheel. He dialled that familiar London number. What would Mossup make of it all?

Chapter Nine

It was the PR man's idea, who else? But Kessler and the K-Corp people had rubber stamped it, and who the hell was he to argue with them? The naughty boy of the team that's who – no doubt about it. Chico and Fraser had been busy these past two weeks for sure, using all their clout with the sponsors, with Kessler. And why not? Just the game, and who would they rather lose: him or Chico? No contest: two world championships, an adoring public, and K-Corp sales down on the year in South America. And Kinsella? Just the bad boy, bring him into line, get the boss to show him who's *boss*.

And this was part of it, part of the reconciliation – not that any bust-up had been admitted, not even to Kinsella, never mind the press. This was how it stood now: Chico has the most points, leading the championship by some margin. The Sultans are getting close – and we have word they have a huge development in the pipeline – you *must* back him up for the championship.

Team orders. As it ever was. As it ever will be. And there would be no excuses, he'd messed up the once, at Interlagos, had his warning from the boss. Kessler's patience was wearing thin – never one for the old game, they never are, the bosses – their picture is much too big for the real drama of the show. The picture the bosses were interested in was the one to show to the public. This one, the stunt. Kinsella and Chico training together, running the Silverstone circuit together, comrades united before the next attack, before the next skirmish in the war against Sultan and the rest. The PR man's idea – it sucked.

It was the Friday morning, early, but there were still quite a few spectators pouring into the circuit – many of them would camp outside the fences for the entire four days of the meeting. Friday is free practice day, the times not relevant, not for the grid, just good to show where you are in relation to the others, to show if you have gone the right way on set-up. But there was still the buzz of anticipation in the Formula One paddock, the little village of priceless, smoked glass motor homes from which all but the privileged few are excluded – all but the team members, the media, the rich and the famous...

They had both kitted up in their personal restrooms, each of which took up a large part of the silver and blue articulated motor-home. Other rooms were put aside for debriefings and entertaining the more important of the sponsors – earlier that morning Kinsella had tipped Kobe a wink as she and her husband sat with Kessler, discussing a K-Corp promotion for the Chicodrome race at the end of the season. She had smiled at him provocatively, the Monte Carlo dunking seemingly forgotten. The motor-home opened up into an area with a collapsible wooden floor which reached across to another motor-home – catering and the PR office, and more office space. The area between the two motor-homes was enclosed in grey aluminium and partially smoked glass, and its raised wooden floor was dotted with an archipelago of tables and chairs. It was, in effect, a fully enclosed and fully portable building, where K-Corp guests and team members sipped at coffee and nibbled at croissants – and watched the two DBM drivers warming up for their run.

They were both dressed identically: blue K-Corp T-shirts and white running shorts with the DBM logo on the right leg. Chico's trainers were about the best that money could buy – a career's worth of shop lifting for some inner city kid. Not that he had bought them though. No, a shoe deal – has the stripe on the race boots: joins the basketball player, the soccer star, and the Olympic sprinter in the corporation's hall of fame.

Kinsella strapped his equally useful, but paid for, shoes to his feet. Chico was stretching, going through his pre-run ritual, warming up the muscles in his legs and shoulders as meticulously and diligently as he would warm up the engine, gearbox, brakes and tyres of the DBM on an installation lap. The camera shutters were already chattering, the PR man nodded to Kinsella, in a way that was supposed to be private, but was as obvious as a Bianchi in a gravel trap. Time to start the show.

"Nice shoes."

"Thanks."

Well, it was conversation, what more did the twat want? Kinsella's eyes did a clever trick – those shades again – of looking past the PR man, looking past his panic and through the open door to the paddock, where Kessler and Fraser were having a furtive conversation with a man he had never seen before. A slightly flabby sort of fellow, gut straining at the waistband of a grubby pair of jeans, scuffed leather jacket draped loosely over an olive drab sweatshirt. Not a Formula One type, that was certain, not at ease in the paddock, not the right kit. He was flicking through a fan of photographs, showing them to the DBM men. Fraser spotted Kinsella's interest and pulled the man to one side, out of sight, but not before Kinsella had taken a good look at the man's face: the greasy hair, stubble, and the angry looking scar under his nose – the scar he kept fingering with a podgy digit.

"Right, you two ready?"

"Yeah – let's get it over with."

"Yes."

It took Chico longer then he had expected to get into his stride, he was just not used to running alongside others. That's all. He had tried before, even ran out with Fraser once or twice, but although the engineer was fit it was a lot to ask for someone to keep pace with a modern Formula One driver. Kinsella though, he might have hoped for more from him.

Okay, there were the stories: the parties, the drink, the women. But nobody really believed them did they? Except perhaps the part about the women. It wasn't possible these days after all, the playboy lifestyle. Even people on the outside were beginning to see Grand Prix drivers more as athletes – you just have to be. Chico remembered the time when the Republic's Institute of Science had carried out tests on him over a period of three races. He remembered how they had wired him up and recorded his heart rate. How they had been astounded at the sheer work that was asked of the organ: 170 beats a minute for the entire race, peaking at 210 when he had a moment, or when he was lining up to outbrake someone. As the doctor had pointed out, the maximum the heart can cope with is 220 – and yet the heart of a Grand Prix driver plays perilously close to this territory for the entire race.

Easy to see why the training is vital then, perhaps more so than many other sports. And Chico had grasped this early, so that now he was considered one of the fittest – if not the fittest – on the Formula One grid. And it was a matter of some pride to him that after a bout of very serious training indeed a maximum heart rate of 198 would fall to 46 in just five minutes, just six beats over his resting pulse of 40. Seriously fit. He remembered that time, just a month or so back, when he had trained with the Republic's national football squad, embarrassing them in front of the assembled press corp.

Those in the know were the only ones not surprised that day. Those in the know who had seen what it takes to pilot a modern Formula One car. Those who knew the sort of upper body strength required to withstand 4G in cornering or braking, when the sheer deceleration is like a sledge hammer in the back, and those who had witnessed the sort of punishment Chico, and the other drivers, had to put themselves through. Punishment to the arms, back, stomach and neck. Particularly the neck – Chico had added one and a half inches there in the last few years, through the sheer effort of driving and through the use of a special pulley system he had rigged up, which manipulated weights through wires attached to an old crash helmet. It was the only way, you had to be fit or you couldn't do it.

And Kinsella could still do it, even towards the finish he could still put in the fast laps, as Chico had seen all too clearly a fortnight before in France, had seen at DBM high altitude training in the Swiss Alps before the season started. Yet he seemed to be struggling here, matching him stride for stride yes, but all the same breathing heavier, struggling slightly. In front of them a little hatchback trundled along in first gear, its boot open, the long lenses of two photographers pointing out towards the running drivers. The PR man was at the wheel of the hatchback. Every now and then Chico could catch his worried glance in the rear view mirror. His idea, this show of solidarity. Kessler had agreed, but not Fraser, waste of Chico's energy he had said. And Chico was not certain. He could not be certain about anything when it came to Kinsella.

They had run about one and a half miles, about half of the Silverstone circuit. Neither of them had talked in that time. Dotted along the spectator bankings were little clusters of spectators, the early birds after the best spots. Many carried the Union Jack, and some had banners with Kinsella's name on it. The Englishman waved to them as he passed. Chico looked out for the flag of the Republic, there were usually a few, a loyal band of countrymen – and women – who followed him around the world.

It was strange to see familiar landmarks at this pace, the apex for Club where they now ran, where later that day he would squeeze on the power, having to use all the road on the exit. Now there seemed to be acres of it, acres of the grey. Kinsella was waving to a small knot of fans on the spectator banking beyond the debris fencing. Chico thought he heard him laugh, then he caught sight of a banner with his name on it. They had run past so he had to turn slightly to read it: *Chick, Chick, Chick, Chick Chico, – how about some more Egg on your face?* He wouldn't have understood, only he had seen something similar in an English paper earlier in the week, dwelling on his mistakes. Mistakes? Just two, three maybe? Why had they made such a fuss? He still led the World Championship. Yes, it had upset him. It upset him now too, people wanting him to slip up, wanting it to go wrong – it had all been so different before, even here in Britain, where he had many fans.

He glanced at Kinsella as they ran up towards the left hander at *Abbey*. Yes, the Englishman was suffering, his cheeks red with the effort now, the sweat pouring from his forehead and down behind those omnipresent sunglasses of his. Kinsella suffering, he allowed himself a smile. Good to see it wasn't it? Yes, good. He had not wanted to believe Fraser, Fraser's theory. Fraser's theory of Kinsella – working the press, poisoning it, working to undermine Chico's position as number one in the team. But he had to admit much of it added up, all the little things – like the way he would say: go easy through there Chico, it's a mother and there's oil down. And where was the oil? No oil by the time Chico was there, for sure. Yes, it all added up, but it didn't matter now. They had clipped that one's wings, in Kessler's office. Fraser had done it in the end, told him that Chico was threatening to quit if the Englishman was not put in his place.

So, right or wrong, it was over. If Kinsella had played games the game was over. Time now to concentrate on the championship, concentrate on beating the Sultans. He glanced at Kinsella again. The July sun was higher and the sweat was flowing, even Chico was beginning to feel it now, but the pace was comfortable, and this was nothing on training in the crippling humidity of the Republic.

So he thought he could beat me did he? Chico allowed a silent little laugh to bounce inside his skull, and then he lengthened his stride a little. Pulling ahead by a metre almost instantly. It's the one thing he lacked, they said – they wrote. The ruthless streak. And, they said – they wrote: greatness demands it...

The cameras in the back of the car snapped happily to the change in the symmetry of the picture. He sensed Kinsella's head snap up from its lolling, jogging motion, and then he heard the quicker slap of the Englishman's trainers against the asphalt as he pulled level again. A quicker stride now, pulling alongside the little hatchback, one of the photographers craning around the edge of the rear quarter panel, snapping away at the K-Corp emblazoned form of Chico overtaking the little car. The PR man looked aghast as Chico drew level with the open driver's window. He mouthed at Chico to slow down, then – panic writ large across his face – he stole a glance in the rear view mirror, obviously looking for his other charge. But Kinsella was already alongside Chico, his facial topography giving Chico the lie of the land instantly: no chance mate, you've a race on your hands...

Hell, everybody knew that Chico was the fittest Formula One driver on the grid – so what in the name of holy shite was he trying to prove? Wasn't it enough that he had beaten him at the game, pulled in his corporate muscle, gotten old Kinsella to play ball or risk losing the DBM dosh? Wasn't that enough? And now here they were, trying to show the world what great chums they were and Chico wanted to run off into the distance, make a fool of him. Christ, what's a guy supposed to do?

Chico had set off at a quick enough a pace, a bit too quick for a race weekend Kinsella thought, but now, into *Abbey* the guy had kicked, then kicked again. Kinsella had matched him, thinking that he caught the trace of a smile at the corner of his team mate's mouth – knowing that he had caught the full impact of the PR man's look of horror. Not that it was his fault, if Chico wanted a race, so be it – at least there were no team orders here.

The PR man had passed them again, the photographers in the back shooting off roll after roll of film, all-seeing long lenses catching every nuance in the strained faces of the drivers. At *Bridge* Chico had two metres on Kinsella, but the Englishman had found a stride now, a thump-thump of the heart to the slap-slap of the rubber sole of the shoe. His blood was pumping freely and with the extra surge of adrenaline from competition – always the real buzz for Kinsella – the run now seemed easier, even though the pace was well up. As they turned left into the loop at *Priory* Chico glanced over his left shoulder, and the clear look of surprise when he saw Kinsella so close was a boost. But then Chico kicked once more, and Kinsella watched as those hardly soiled soles flashed before him in an ever faster piston progress. Watched as the K-Corp logo on the T-shirt grew too small, as the gap between them stretched. How could he do it, where did he find the extra strength, the extra will?

They were in the stadium section of the circuit now and the grandstands were already beginning to fill for the first of the Formula One action later in the day. He had managed to claw back a little of the gap, but the easy pace of his team mate in front contrasted sharply with the heaviness he was beginning to feel in his legs and the tightness at his chest. It was bloody stupid, practice later in the day, a Grand Prix that weekend and he was playing stupid buggers in a pair of daps. He would have stopped there, folded himself and filled his lungs, and yes, he should have stopped there. But then he heard it.

A few shouts at first, unusual, almost creepy. No engine sounds to drown them, that was it. Nor were they muffled by the usual press of people in the grandstands, just one or two isolated individuals or groups, patiently waiting for the day's action, glad of the welcome diversion: two of the world's fastest racing drivers head to head at Silverstone – without their cars.

"*Go on Egg my son…*"

"*C'mon Egg, you can take him…*"

"*Go on Egg…*"

The home crowd's always a lift, any driver will tell you that. But never had Kinsella felt this immediacy of support. Alright, he had shared their joy – or was it them sharing his joy? – when he had come second here the year before. But this was different, now he could feel the will of them, for the first time. It wouldn't matter if he won or lost, not this race, but to hear his name – and now many more were shouting – made him realise that it was him they had come to see. The banners were there too, plenty of them, all with his name on. And the union flags, the Welsh flags, it was all there for him. In that one panting, lung bursting moment it suddenly dawned on him that the game was so much bigger than him and Chico, so much more than an extra few noughts on his pay cheque.

It was the sort of extra burst, the supercharge of energy, that mothers get in times of crisis – they say – lifting a piano off a toddler, that sort of thing. He could never say where it had come from, but it was similar in a way to the burst of will that had seen him through that hairy, scary lap at Monaco. The PR man had sped off down the pit lane now, but not before the two photographers had jumped out of the back of the car. Other snappers were there too, running alongside them, while the noise from the grandstand just grew and grew, nothing organised, just "*C'mon Egg…*"

He was close to Chico's heels as they took to the pit lane entry road, close enough to see that his team mate was really sweating now. Alerted by the noise from the grandstands many of the mechanics and team personnel had gathered at the pit entrance. Here the support was not so partisan, most was for Chico – Kinsella's style had made him few friends down the pit lane he was the first to admit. But the noise from there had nothing on the shouts from the grandstand anyway, and by the time they entered the pit lane proper they were neck and neck as the massed ranks of pit crews, journalists and track workers parted in front of them like the Red Sea.

The DBM pit garage in sight – Kessler's frown already all too visible – Kinsella tried to sprint the last hundred metres, but there was nothing there, nothing left. He waited for Chico to sprint but there was nothing there either – and they came to the DBM pit garage together. There was still the cheering, the boys had loved it, the crowd had loved it, and a TV crew was ready to suck in the sight: Chico cool, already talking to Fraser about a set up idea for the afternoon. Kinsella exhausted, leaning against the garage wall, taking in deep draughts of fuel-fume laden air. Kessler just looking at him, shaking his head.

Chapter Ten

She hadn't really thought about the mini bar until she'd seen the tail plane, just the tail visible from the first floor suite, just the tail with the colours of the Republic, the flag of home a carnival of colour against the grey English sky. Just the tail taxiing shark-like outside the sealed window of the airport hotel room. And then she had thought of the mini bar, and of home: in many ways just a short taxi ride away, into Heathrow proper, find the desk, buy a ticket. If only it were that simple.

She had called Mamma and Papa, they had told her about the newspapermen, they had told her about the lies – how they had written that Chico had lost his edge, had lost his edge since she had come on the scene. How they had written that she did not support him: after all, where was she in France, where was she in Canada? Sunning it up in Monte Carlo, there had even been a picture Mamma said, but from the description of the bathing suit it must have been taken during the Grand Prix weekend. Mamma sounded upset, Teresa sensed she was choking back the tears – she missed her so. And then the line went dead. Trouble that end, of course, the government's priorities: tanks and attack helicopters first, the crumbling telephone system, the crumbling water system, the crumbling spirit of the people... Always second. Which was why Chico was so important to them, something good, a winner: the flag fluttering proudly over the rostrum when he sprayed the victory champagne. She had put down the telephone receiver and without really thinking about it she had fished into the mini bar, pulling out a selection of miniatures.

So she had come. Come to Britain. He had not wanted it but in the end he agreed. He had seemed upset, apologising about the way of it at home over and over again – but it wasn't his fault, she told him. And then there was no car that morning, no car to take her to the heliport, from where she would fly to Silverstone. It had taken all morning to contact him, in the end she had had to ring the PR man on his mobile first, and at that stage Chico was out on the track for the morning warm up, checking his race set up. The PR man made some promises, promises to do his best, hurrying her off the line – 300 guests of K-Corp to entertain in the hospitality marquee he had said. And then Chico had rung, he seemed sorry, really sorry. Fraser had said he would arrange it he explained: the driver, the helicopter, the passes for the race, everything. He may have forgotten – they had been very busy. She felt like slamming the phone down on him, but he was like a little boy in so many ways, playing with his cars and there was much to do he explained. The Sultans were getting closer – even quicker than DBM in the rain on Friday afternoon – he had told her, and there had been more trouble with the planning office over the Chicodrome...

They arranged to meet after the race, at the hotel. There was little chance of her catching a chopper now – for this one afternoon Silverstone becomes the busiest airport in the world and flights are booked solid, he had said, and the traffic outside the circuit would be unbearable, he had said. But at least they talked, he talked – as she sipped her way through a tiny bottle of whisky, a tiny bottle of vodka.

With the weight of her disappointment – another lonely day ahead – it was a while before it hit her that Chico had been in such a good mood, despite his worries about Sultan and the Chicodrome. A mood like that which wrapped him after the first two test sessions of the season: up on the Sultans and quicker than Kinsella – always that name in there somewhere...

Perhaps now he could forget him. Even if the Englishman out-qualified Chico it should not matter, he would have to let Chico through. Knowing that had helped him, he'd said, and yesterday he had taken pole, 0.3 seconds up on Kinsella at his home circuit – yes, things were back to where they should be, he had told her.

She was glad that he was happy again, perhaps now they could get back to normal – whatever that was. She cracked open another little bottle and poured its contents into a tumbler. But poor Eoghan, was it fair? No. But too important. Too important for everyone... And him? She sighed to herself. How often she had asked herself why. Why she had chosen him as a friend – if that was what he was. Why she had chosen him of all people?

But that was not to dwell on now. And so there had been new plans for the lonely day, a trip into London for some shopping, some sights, and with that – her mood a little lighter – she opened a half bottle of champagne. Half an hour later it was drained. A pile of clothes lay on the bed, dresses, slacks, pants and blouses. None seemed to suit the English grey and it was a difficult choice, with only beers left in the mini bar to ease her creativity. She rang down for a bottle of champagne, and some more miniatures. Room service, a boy, late teens, eyes on stalks, skin shining like a polished red apple – she had forgotten, just the tiny knickers, with the little silk slip hung loosely over her breasts. Well at least she had enlivened one Englishman's grey day, she thought.

In the end it was a straight fight: Harrods and Big Ben v the bottle: no contest. Teresa swept the clothes from the bed into a tangled pile on the floor, then she stretched out on the big mattress – all too big today, all too big for a lonely day. The remote control can have a double action, especially for the lonely, and without even knowing why, she had picked it up, aiming it at the big box in the corner of the suite. Why did she kid herself? Okay, she really had seen the movie, the one with the woman in China, the long line of kids, alright she didn't understand cricket – what was going on there? But this, hadn't she promised herself? Hadn't she congratulated herself on seeing through the whole charade of this *sport*, a *race* in which – mechanical maladies and rain aside – today only Chico could win?

But still, there they were big on the screen, the drab of the day soaking into the colour schemes of the DBMs, so that the silver was robbed of its glint, two little grey torpedo boats at the head of a long convoy of riotous colour. The grid girls shivered to a gust of wind in their skimpy little outfits, protruding nipples strangely punctuating *Sultan* with little half umlauts, white hands tightly gripping the poles with the banners atop them, one for each driver: Chico, Kinsella, Solé, Drake, Michel... Stretching back down the grid. The poor girls, she thought. B-list glamour, faces caked in make-up, a forgotten hint of sexiness amidst the precisely organised chaos which was the build-up to the start.

The TV director seemed to tire of a cameraman's fascination with the miserable looking grid girls and switched the shot to one of Chico, who was already strapped tightly into the cockpit of the DBM. Fraser was crouched by the side of the car. He was talking to Chico through an intercom system plugged into the driver's helmet. Under the lifted visor of his helmet Teresa caught a glimpse of his eyes, rapt, staring out at Fraser, as if he hung on every word – every word: *two stopping, soft compound, might rain...* Or the state of his roses, tube strike, he has an itch... It could be anything for all she knew. The painful thing was that her man was listening, and listening in a way that he seldom

– if ever – listened to her. Again she felt it, her with the looks, with the life any girl in the Republic would kill for, she felt it. Pure, unadulterated, magnificently irrational... jealousy. If it wasn't for the drink she would have felt stupid, of course she would. But now all she could find in herself was a somehow delicious hatred: hatred for the man that could give her husband all that he needed – a car that could beat the Sultans, a car that could beat Kinsella.

As if on cue the camera switched to the number eight DBM. Kinsella was standing alongside the car, his helmet hanging from its chin guard in his right hand. A man in headphones beckoned for the cameraman to come closer, then thrust a black foam microphone up close to Kinsella's face, the cameraman reflected clearly in the lenses of those familiar fly-eyed sunglasses.

Teresa once again remotely reached for the remote, turning up the volume.

"Egg Kinsella, second on the grid, just your team mate in front – what's the strategy?"

"Just the usual – go like hell..."

"What about the Sultans, the forecast is 50-50 for light showers and they went well in the wet on Friday...?"

"No," he sniffed at the air, "I don't think it's going to rain, they're not a problem."

"And team orders, they say that you have to defer to Chico now – what about that?"

"First I've heard of it."

"Well, that's the buzz in the paddock."

"Fine, if you know why are you asking me?"

The reporter laughed nervously, and his next question was cut off by the wail of a siren, the signal for the mechanics, grid girls, press and hangers-on to clear the grid. Kinsella flashed the camera a smile then whipped off his shades just as the cameraman zoomed in on his face. For a moment, a fraction of a moment, she thought he was looking straight at her. And at that moment, that fraction of a moment, something travelled through her, from the chest, then tight at the stomach and tense, almost solid, at the groin – so that she gave out a gasp.

When the picture went long again she was herself, save for the heat at her throat, at her cheeks. She tried to douse it with the chilled champagne, trying not to think about the reaction – best to concentrate on the race.

The start, as always, was something to savour. After all the time waiting as the cars sit on the grid, then complete their warm up lap, the start is always a release to all concerned: drivers, pit crew, wives and viewers. Of course there is the excitement of it, the thrill of all that pent up energy and power unleashed at once, one seething mass of colour hurtling down to the first corner. And then, in many ways, this was also the race itself: drivers off the racing line, faster or slower starts: opportunities – perhaps the only opportunities in the race. So, there was usually some fun. This time Bobby Drake Jnr – who had been bogged down with too much wheel-spin at the take off – was punted from behind by a fast starting Bianchi, the same Bianchi with which Kinsella's car had been over-familiar with at Melbourne. Both cars pirouetted as one, coming to rest axle deep in the gravel trap – momentum arrested before they hit the barriers – beached and out of the race.

Then the TV was full of the long multi-coloured snake, straightening itself out of an esse bend, already stretching from the head, the silver-grey head of the two DBMs, nose to tail, with the orange of the Sultan close behind. It stretched along the length of a long straight before reaching the next corner, where the field folded up on itself under braking once more, like the bellows of an accordion.

"Chico, Kinsella, Solé..." shouted the TV commentator, proceeding to list the entire field before he was cut short with his own: *"look at that..!"* as another car failed to make a corner.

And then, after the first lap the race seemed to settle and Teresa was surprised to find that she was sitting on the edge of the bed, surprised because it wasn't really like her to take such an interest. Lately she had tried not to watch, there was always the fear of seeing something bad, something like Chico's accident at Monaco: it had shaken her that one, reminded her – and perhaps reminded them – just what this game is all about. Sometimes, she thought, they needed their reminders, locked in their hermetic world of money, horse-power, money, grip, money, lap-times, money...

She took a long swig from the champagne bottle and then lay back, her head sinking deep into the soft pillow. She closed her eyes, all of a sudden so very weary, the champagne and whisky sloshing through her skull, seeming to soften it from the inside. Then, for the next hour or so she trod the fine line between being asleep and awake, so that her dreams merged with the commentary of the race:

"Kinsella is very close now, but are there team orders...?"

There he was, on his boat, listening to her as she tried to pierce the veil of his shades, listening to her as she tried not to dwell on those wispy little hairs that curled about his chest, and around his navel, disappearing in a long line into the waistband of his shorts...

"You have to ask – has Chico got a problem...?"

Chico, sat in the car, Fraser beside him, a micrometer to hand, they are talking about Teresa, about her breasts, should they be bigger – if they were bigger would she be faster..?

"Chico's in the pits... No, my mistake... It's Kinsella... Kinsella's in... Kinsella's in... I have the watch on it: the car's up on the jacks, all four wheels changed, fuel in – looks like he's one stopping – 8.6 seconds! Faaaantastic stop...!"

He was taking off those glasses, then he reached over, stroked her hair, placed his hand on her breast...

"This is amazing! Chico's stop is slower... and let's see... yes... yes... yes, he's out of the pit lane now and Kinsella is past – Kinsella passes just as Chico returns to the fray – Eoghan 'Egg' Kinsella is leading the British Grand Prix – and the crowd is deeeelighted...."

Mamma and Papa are watching, watching as he has her on the after-deck of his boat. Then there is Chico and Fraser, with stopwatches and the PR man with a camera, the biggest camera ever...

"Team orders or not, Chico can do nothing about the other DBM, Eoghan Kinsella is going to win, Eoghan 'Egg' Kinsella is going to win for Britain and DBM after a superlative performance..."

Eyes wide open. She shot up, just in time to see the two silver cars round the last twiddly section of the circuit. On TV the sun was shining now and the noise from the crowd was incredible, almost drowning out the wail of the engines of the two, obviously hard pressed, DBMs. So, it wasn't a dream then, she thought, the helmet colours clear: the man in red, white and green crossing the line in front of the man in the helmet with the colours of the Republic.

On the slowing down lap Kinsella punched the air and waved to the fans, many of who had now found their way through gaps in the high debris fencing and were streaming onto the circuit. Some were running alongside the victorious DBM clapping Kinsella as they did so. One fan, Teresa noticed, stopped in front of Chico's car, pulling down his shorts and flashing a fat, white British butt at him. Her husband drove around him and accelerated past Kinsella, not glancing to the side to offer a congratulatory wave. So he had won, and she was pleased. It would mean trouble, yes, but perhaps now they were rid of him? She was rid of him?

By the time that Kinsella had reached the far end of the circuit he was travelling at walking pace. And then the press of people – many with union flags tied like capes around their necks, some with the red white and blue painted on their faces, some with the DBM baseball caps, all with smiles of jubilation – that press of people. That press of people stopped the DBM in its tracks, and Kinsella was lifted clear of the cockpit and carried atop the pack of fans while marshals tried to find a way for him to get back to the pits.

His helmet and balaclava off, Kinsella's face was shining with the joy of his first victory, his eyes alight and there for all to see – for Teresa to see as a brave cameraman plunged deep into the mob. For her to see just as they had been in the half dream, her and him. She flushed at the memory and then her hand strayed down towards the base of her hard, flat belly, her fingers finding that gap, the gap her hip bone made between skin and cotton. And she parted her legs a little, closed her eyes tight, and touched – almost hearing the lap of the Med against the hull of his boat as she loved herself to the real noise: the commentator, *The March from Carmen*, the muffled roar of a jet taking off outside – and the quickening of her breathing...

Chapter Eleven

From here Kinsella could see most of the bay. He could see *Akrasia* sitting still in the clear green water so that its white hull seemed to be encased in jade. He could see the few people who knew about this place stretching their whiteness out for the sun on the beach some 100 metres below. He could see the horns of the rocky capes that almost made a fist around this bay. And with the phone that sat on the table in front of him – alongside the oil and the vinegar – he could talk to the world.

Pablo had picked up a small crew in Monte Carlo and sailed *Akrasia* around the long boot of Italy and into the Ionian Sea, to this place, this island, that Kinsella had discovered almost by accident some summers before. Now that he had the boat it was a place which truly came into its own. He had left the phone with Spiro the evening before, when he arrived from the airport with the girl, so that this morning it was just a matter of diving over the stern rail of *Akrasia* and swimming ashore. Then he had showered on the beach and climbed the goat's path through the olive grove to Spiro's Taverna, which clung improbably to the rock-face. A walled platform projected out from the taverna, supported by a couple of concrete pillars which – Kinsella thought – would not bear close inspection. Here he sat, in the sun.

It had taken Kinsella a little while to educate Spiro in the diet of the Formula One driver, but by now the friendly Greek had cut down on the oil, and Kinsella was able to enjoy a late breakfast of fresh fruit and an omelette liberally spiked with olives. Although *enjoy* was a relative term – as there had been very little in the way of true enjoyment since the narcotic thrill of that first win had given way to the sober realisation that Eoghan Egg Kinsella had stuffed up badly. The realisation that Eoghan Egg Kinsella had well and truly pissed on his

95

chips – losing the second best seat in Formula One. He still wasn't quite sure why he had done it, like he wasn't quite sure why he had played with Chico at Interlagos. The game yes, but suicide too – yet in some situations he just couldn't help himself. All who watched supposed he was show-boating, that he would let Chico through on the final lap. And somewhere in his head that was certainly there, the thing he should have done to keep the second best seat in Formula One. Yet when it came to it he just couldn't do it, couldn't let the other man by – it was him against Chico, and him against himself... And there was nothing in him that could let the other man win. Game over.

After breakfast he stayed out on the terrace, in the sunshine, on the phone. So that by now the phone was hot in his hand – hot from use it could be, he thought, if such a thing were possible. Guido Solé's sister still slept on the boat far below. He had found out all that he wanted from her, even discovered that she had thought it innocent, the Melbourne thing, when she had crawled over the DBM, the DBM belonging to what had been his team, just snaps for Zola she had said, as they lay there naked. He laughed now when he remembered the panic the girl had caused, Kessler up in arms, all but ready to declare war on the Sultan team. Christ – the fool – he was better off out of it. Wasn't he?

And Guido Solé's sister had told him more, after they had made love. Had told him all the things that little Guido told her, all the things he suspected. All about the Sultan team, how Guido had played the game, turned everything on its head. How he had become the undisputed number one at the expense of his mentor, Thierry Michel, the old man of Formula One – 38 and 192 Grand Prix under his belt, seven of those finished on the top step of the podium.

She had been helpful and fun in the sack. A bit too hairy really close up for Kinsella's liking though, a Latin thing he thought. Perhaps Teresa was the same he wondered – oh, the wonder of that wonder. Anyway, there was nothing really new in what Guido Solé's sister had to say. After all, the one thing that doesn't lie in Formula One is the stopwatch. And what had it been: a fraction at Melbourne, yes, and just 0.4 at Interlagos. But after that the rot had set in and at Silverstone and Hockenheim Michel was three quarters of a second down on Solé who – to add insult to injury – now lay second in the world championship standings. Then the questions had been asked: was he past it? Had the old fire in the belly been doused? The press was full of it, helped in no small part by Kinsella – through Mossup – it must be said.

That was the one good thing thought Kinsella – along with the win – back in the game straight away. Fired the Monday after Silverstone, the Spando team manager on the phone the day after. Young Bobby Drake snapped up by DBM, the American out of his contract, a big fat cheque from K-Corp helping things along, having his seat fitting that very day – number two at DBM – and make no mistake about that, not like the last guy they had. But the straight swap wasn't on, Spando wasn't for Kinsella now. It was a tidy little chassis right enough, but it lacked the grunt to challenge for wins – a customer engine, bought from a specialist builder, second best of everything. So that wouldn't do, not for a contender with a taste for the winner's champagne. And contender was right – still in with a shout as things stood: 29 points to Chico's 66, with six races to go. Okay, a tall order, yes, but still 60 points on the table: everything to play for. Just no car.

And the only thing that looked like it was on the same planet as the DBM this year had been the Sultan. But Sultan had its drivers, both continentals, Italian and French, both from the countries where the Sultan fags are top selling cancer sticks. It would be a tall order to break into that cosy little set up. But worth a try all the same – the championship's not over just because you've been slung out on your arse after all, there are always ways.

It had taken a week or so for the focus to fall upon Michel. At first the British press, especially *The Brit*, contented itself with venting its fury at the DBM team – how dare they sack the hero of the hour, the conqueror of Silverstone, all because he had the balls to actually race, *race*. Isn't that what it's all about? The DBM team – Korean sponsors, French engines, but British through and through – made the usual noises: the team must come first, Kinsella had been warned, the focus must be on the world championship. And by the end of the week it was old news, and Kinsella's tilt at the world champion's crown looked to be over with for this year.

Privately Mossup had shown little sympathy for Kinsella, as he'd said after the race: "For a guy who doesn't give a shit so long as he's paid you've sure stuffed up this time." Yet much of that was disappointment at the thought of losing his most reliable source of column inches. And with Kinsella's prompting Mossup was the first to run the new story, a chance of Kinsella slipping in beside Solé, and the other papers soon picked it up. Of course, Sultan denied it, but it could not have helped Michel's cause or confidence – indeed, he had a nightmare weekend at Hockenheim for the German Grand Prix. Yes, Mossup and the lads had done a good job, even the Sultan personnel were beginning to believe it – poor Thierry.

And why not? It made sense. Perhaps the one man who can beat Chico in perhaps the one car that could beat the DBM. Solé's sister had told him that little Guido was not too keen on the idea, but then he wouldn't be, and he wasn't flavour of the month with Zola just now anyway. A bit too erratic most said, the speed was there, sure it was – his second stint at Hockenheim had to be seen to be believed, awesome out of the chicanes, stunning in the tricky stadium section, indeed, fast enough to excite the conspiracy theorists, DBM among them. But Guido had dropped it under pressure from Chico towards the end of the race, rejoining to finish third.

As for Chico, well he went very well in Germany, very well indeed. Pressure off now see, Drake content to compare himself with a great for the time being, be there or thereabouts and pick up a number one seat if and when one became available. Kinsella had watched it on the television, watched as his former team mate stretched his lead in the championship, building himself his comfort zone in the points table. He would need to get a seat soon, need to get a seat soon or it would be over for this year. No doubt about it.

And so he had phoned around, asking them if they had heard the rumour, heard the rumour that poor old Thierry was sure to be dropped, had they heard that rumour – that rumour that he had just started by ringing them to ask them whether they had heard it? Yes, the game never stops.

And now it was the waiting time, waiting for the phone to ring, waiting for Zola to get his skinny little Italian arse into gear, waiting for Zola to give him the call: come to us Kinsella, come to us and win the championship. He was thinking about his salary when the phone did ring, thinking about taking a cut, of course he would have to take a cut, hardly in a position of power to negotiate from was he?

He pressed the answer button, ready to act surprised if it was Zola. In the event he was surprised, not Zola though. No, Teresa. Surprised and pleased.

"How are you?"

"I'm fine... fine, and you?"

"Okay."

There was one of those long telephone silences, and then she said: "Are you busy?"

"Busy?"

"Oh... I'm sorry... I didn't mean..."

"Forget it, I'm fine and there's plenty to be getting on with here – what with the garden to do..."

She laughed softly and Kinsella enjoyed one of those rare

moments of his, back in touch with humanity, away from the game.

"They say you are going to drive for Sultan?"

It was a question, and for the briefest of moments Kinsella wondered if Chico or Fraser had put her up to phoning him, after all, they must be itching to know what he was up to. But with her soft laugh still tinkling in his skull he somehow found it difficult to think ill of the girl. Still, he offered nothing, just changing the subject.

"I didn't expect to hear from you again."

A long sigh issued from the phone, at one with the play of the sea against the rocks below, at one with the soft wisp of cotton wool cumulus that marbled the dense blue sky, at one with the warmth of the sun on his chest.

"We can still be friends, can't we?"

"And what would Chico think of that?"

Since Silverstone even the pretence of camaraderie between the two drivers had been abandoned, and Chico had made his feelings about his *treacherous* team mate clear to all. Yes, treacherous was the word he had used, the sort of word the papers in that half-arsed excuse for a banana republic got off on.

"I don't know... I haven't seen him for two weeks, and he never speaks of you now."

"Still busy then is he?"

"Yes."

Does sound have a shadow? Not an echo, a shadow. Kinsella thought it might. There it was, those dark shades of grey wrapped around the girl's *yes*. For a moment he wanted to hold her, hold her close, hold her tight.

"I thought it would be better now with..."

"Me out of the way?"

She said nothing for some aching seconds, Kinsella watched as a gull landed on the low wall of the taverna, watched as it eyed the remnants of his breakfast.

"It's not that," she said, "it's not really you..."

"Is there something you are trying to tell me?"

"No... I'm just a bit lonely, that's all."

It was a cry for help, of course it was. And Eoghan Egg Kinsella was always there for damsels in distress.

"Where are you?"

"Geneva – but I will be in Monte Carlo in a few days time."

"Can we meet... For a chat, a drink." He felt no need to tell her he wasn't actually in Monte Carlo, he could get there, quick enough.

"I would like that – thank you Eoghan."

They arranged the details of time and place and the call was over. He let himself think for a minute or two, think about the girl. Yes, he wanted to have her, of course he did. But what did that mean, Kinsella wanted to have loads of girls, all sorts of girls – and he had most of them. But this seemed more, even more than the game, even more than getting one up on Chico. Christ, there was even the weirdest feeling somewhere inside him... It shouldn't matter that he was going to hurt her, he had got used to that. Yet somehow it did matter.

He picked up the phone again, standing up to pace the terracotta tiles of the taverna, once more down to business and up to something. He rang Mossup at The Brit. Poor Thierry. Poor Teresa.

Chapter Twelve

The Hungarian Grand Prix had been a disaster for DBM and when Stubbs met with Fraser the man was obviously suffering, deep shadows beneath his eyes, coarse stubble at his chin and a tired stoop that seemed to speak of endless hours hunched over the computer keyboard. While Stubbs – Fraser made it clear – had been no help. No help at all.

He had tried to stick up for himself: what about the pictures from Pembrey, what about the data, the times? But that was no good, that was there for all to see now. Just look at the Hungaroring. Chico on pole, young Bobby Drake a fine second. Then the race: both the DBMs pulling away until the first round of stops. Then both Sultans are faster for the second part of the race, even Thierry Michel, almost two seconds a lap quicker at one point. Enough to put Solé in front with some breathing space. Of course, Stubbs had seen all this, but on the TV he had been unable to pick out the wheel-man, plugging in the computer cable at the stop, plugging it in at the second stop to change the software back. DBM, Fraser said, had already voiced its suspicions, gone to the very top – but it needed proof, lap times alone were not enough.

Fraser had told Stubbs that DBM was already working on its own system, can't sit still in Formula One, he had said. But there were better ways, he had added. Why go to the expense, after all, when they were already paying someone – a professional – to get them their proof? Proof that they could take to the men at the top, get it banned – maybe even have the Sultan scores docked – it's a hair-split of an 'interpretation' after all, he had said. In the end he had Stubbs over a barrel, a barrel that Stubbs could not but help think of in a tasty mix of metaphor – loaded with £7,000...

Anyway, it was all fair enough. There had been nothing much

since he had taken them the pictures, at Silverstone, where he had watched the drama unfold without even being able to see the cars. He had stood outside the motor-home as Fraser had done the demanding on Chico's behalf: the straight choice – Chico goes or Kinsella is put in his place. Later, Kinsella's disobedience had been dealt with harshly, too harshly Stubbs thought what with his first Grand Prix win in sight – and his home race at that. And even though Stubbs was far from a fan he felt a certain sympathy for Kinsella that day. What was the guy supposed to do, just let Chico through? It seemed so. No room for sentiment in F1 then, no room for professionals who do not do their job to the letter – no room for the balance of the payment if Stubbs couldn't deliver the goods. No doubt about that.

And Sarah had her heart set on a week or two somewhere hot, it was the least he could do, let her get some sun on all those lovely white bits, the bits she hadn't let him see for a fortnight now. It was the least he could do to find the blonde engineer he had spotted at the Pembrey test too. Follow him home from the Sultan factory, try to pick the spot where he lost sight of the laptop. But no chance. Anyway, there was no guarantee whatsoever that the dirty data would be with him, still on his machine.

In the end there was only one thing for it, to get into the Sultan factory, take a peek at their R&D lab, download what he could. Fraser had helped a little with some intelligence gained from one of the boys in the DBM drawing room – the hot young prospect with a background in aerospace who DBM had poached from Sultan early in the season. The same one that had tipped them off about the traction control system in the first place. Over a coffee Fraser had chatted to the young aerodynamicist, said that they were thinking about redesigning the R&D lab and the design room, he had asked about the layout at the Sultan factory. The young man must have had his suspicions, but then, if you want to be part of a winning team...

When it came to computer passwords there could be no doubt about Fraser's game, but the young man told him what he wanted to know, with the rider that it all might have changed, it had been months after all. But that was a risk that Stubbs would have to take. Other risks? He wasn't sure – it probably wasn't technically breaking in, the way he had it planned, and it would be his disk, so is it theft? But best not dwell on that...

The kit had been easy to come by: shirt, cap and a natty little moleskin jacket from a Formula One merchandise shop. The jacket fitted well, and he was pleased with it, he might have bought it anyway. It was a deep tangerine colour with the Sultan Cigarettes logo, a black scimitar fiery fringed in bright yellow-white, emblazoned on the back. It wasn't quite what the team wore, but it would do, and in a press of people he was confident it would pass muster.

And now there was the waiting, always the waiting in this game. Stubbs often thought that it must be similar to the life of a First World War soldier – except that Stubbs seldom got to go over the top. He waited in the old Sierra. It was raining and he had to peer through the silver trails of the racing raindrops on the windscreen to get a good view of the factory. It was a familiar view now, he had watched it – from a distance – many times. Not that that could really help his cause, he knew. But he had to do something, and watching was what he really knew, and – he congratulated himself – he had managed to pick out the blonde engineer from this very vantage point. But today was the day to go inside. Today was the day to earn the dosh.

The building was sleekly functional, squat and steel and veiled in the darkest of smoked glass, a glass that seemed to suck all the worst of the grey morning into its reflective surface. It was all too easy to imagine all them watchers, in there behind the dark glass, watching the watcher, unwatched. On the roof the angular lines of the structure were broken by an ugly cluster of communications gear: dishes, aerials – magic stuff that could pick up data, telemetry, as the car lapped in the sunshine of some distant land. Stuff bounced through space, magic stuff that cost the earth, Fraser had told him.

There was a low wall and a high diamond mesh fence, topped with barbed wire, around the facility, while CCTV cameras clung to the bevelled edge of the roof. The fleet of Sultan trucks, for transporting the race and test teams, were parked around the side of the building, where – Stubbs could see from the sketch plan Fraser had furnished him with – they had direct access to the workshops. Out front of the building was a large apron of asphalt, a grid of freshly painted white lines formed boxes for cars to park in. Where the building met the asphalt apron a steel and smoked glass salient formed the entrance hall. Alongside this were the better parking spaces, the top brass parking spaces, and the spaces reserved for sponsors or visiting guests. An hour or so earlier he had watched as Zola had arrived in his chauffeur driven Mercedes C Class, the driver deferring to him at the factory entrance, letting the boss through first, furtively looking over his shoulder as the automatic doors whispered shut behind him. There was something in the action, some menace in the man, which caused a shiver to run down Stubbs's spine. That was the thing, everyone had heard the rumours about Zola, about the type that worked for him.

As Stubbs had hoped, his chance came at about 9am. Most of the factory workers started to arrive – almost all with something Sultan wrapped about them to keep out the unseasonal rain. From his research, a well chosen magazine, Stubbs knew that Sultan employed at least 300 people here at any one time. Not all were to do with racing though. A fair proportion worked on the much talked about road car project, while others helped with the R&D for the company's Formula One engine supplier. Others still, mainly locals who could walk to work, helped out in the canteen, or with the running of the building. Those who drove were stopped at the main gate. A security guard, who Stubbs knew was coming to the end of a long night shift, gave their IDs a cursory inspection and waved them through. Stubbs climbed out of the Sierra, pulling the Sultan moleskin jacket around him and zipping it up tight before walking the one hundred metres or so from the car to the gate. He had timed it well, the guard was chatting with one of the arriving staff, leaning into the car. Stubbs just walked past, giving a little wave as he did so, it was a technique that often worked, brazen it out, that was the secret.

It took a nervous age to traverse the big car park but by the time he was at the doorway to the facility others were walking in to start their day at work. Some looked at him, curious – perhaps a new man? But he was into the factory without any trouble. The long steel and smoked glass salient turned out to be the reception foyer. Parked down its length were five gleaming Sultan racing cars, each in the distinctive orange livery of Sultan Tobacco International. Behind the cars, shiny charcoal-coloured tiles gave the room the sort of carbon fibre, hi-tech, feel he had half expected, while the sparkling white marble of the floor spoke of efficiency – or was it excess? But there was no time to dwell on that, no time for sightseeing, he had to get into the heart of the building before someone decided to get friendly, before someone decided to ask him what department he worked in.

He had memorised the little sketch map, but still the labyrinth of corridors foxed him once or twice, and on one occasion he opened a door to find a broom cupboard. Luckily no one was about to see. Then, at last, he found the race shop, somewhere to take his bearings from. There were five Sultans up on the work stands in the waist high white bays, all in various stages of undress. Mechanics were busy around two of the cars, some wearing white coats that looked for all the world like the house coats of hospital doctors. The floor gleamed polar white – ditto the walls – all was spotless, it reminded Stubbs more than anything else had of the semiconductor clean room he had infiltrated two years before.

He knew that the lab lay the far side of the race shop and he found it without further drama. As the aerodynamicist had told Fraser, entrance to the lab was via a coded doorway. Stubbs tapped out the four numbers he had been given into the key pad. But there was just a red light. A shame, but not unexpected. There was a coffee vending machine some metres down the corridor, a lucky excuse to stand there. So he fished into his trouser pockets and took out a handful of change. The coffee was bitter and it burnt his tongue. But it meant that he was there, not so out of place, when the next man came to the lab. Was there to see him key in the figures: 0,9,1,0. Nine and ten, the race numbers of the two Sultans – lazy security, nearly always the way. He might have figured it out anyway.

It was cramped up there but it would do. He had guessed that there would be a suspended ceiling, at least in the office part of the building. Then it was just a matter of finding a toilet, checking each way outside, standing on the wash basin and lifting the ceiling panel. The steel frame supported his weight, just. And then there was the long day, crouched amidst the piping and ventilation shafts, totally dark save for the little slither of light that peeped through the ceiling panels. He dozed a little, but there was always the fear of slipping, crashing through the panels and onto some unfortunate pisser below. Once he heard the roar of an engine, one of the racers being tweaked elsewhere in the building, but otherwise there were just the sounds and smells of the toilets. And the waiting – always that.

They worked late that night, or at least some did. It was approaching 10pm before the square crack of light that had marked the extent of Stubbs's world for the last thirteen hours was finally extinguished. Still, he gave himself half an hour more before finally dislodging the panel, sliding it aside and dropping down onto the floor of the wash room. With the panel back in place he pulled the little pencil torch out of his pocket and opened the door onto the corridor.

There were still noises from other parts of the factory, someone working an all-nighter perhaps, but the office area, and more importantly, the lab, seemed to be empty. Stubbs keyed in the code and walked in. He found the blonde man's desk almost straight away, the beam of his torch illuminating a picture of the man with his wife and kid almost instantly. Some of the computers in the lab still shone a ghostly light, but the blonde man's machine was dormant. Stubbs powered it up, switching off the torch to work in the glow from the screen. As he had expected the damned thing wanted a password. Here the young aerodynamicist had come up trumps: Chico, the cheek of them eh? He found a likely folder, Fraser had told him what to look for. All of the files were clearly labelled, each to do with some part of the car or other, but one was marked with just a number. He opened it. There it was, all figures, nothing much to look at. But it was what Fraser had told him to look for – he could sort it out. Stubbs pulled a Zip disc from the inside pocket of his jacket and slotted it into the computer. Fifteen minutes later he was back in his little place in the toilet ceiling, waiting for the morning, waiting for his chance to slip out.

The flush of a toilet woke him. The lights were back on and there was talk too, two of the Sultan guys analysing the mammary merits of a new girl in accounts as they sprayed merrily away against the urinal. They left and Stubbs waited for a minute or two, checking that the toilet was empty, before lifting the panel again. He dropped down onto the wash basin, reaching back above him to put the panel back in place. The door opened just as he made it to the floor. He turned on the taps and started to wash his hands, hardly acknowledging the hearty good morning of this new arrival. He splashed some of the water over the edges of the porcelain, washing away his dusty footprints as he did so. Time to leave, time to get back to the car, back to Fraser, collect the dosh.

It was always difficult, at this stage of a job, the hard bit out of the way. Always difficult not to rush away, draw attention to himself. But he tried, loitering over a notice board for some long moments and picking up a discarded clipboard before entering the race shop.

It was there that he saw him, in the race shop. He was with Zola and some other Sultan staff, including the chauffeur, the sullen looking man with the bulges in all the wrong places. They were showing him over the car, a photographer in a Sultan shirt snapping happily away. So it was true then. Would this be worth even more, he wondered, what would Fraser give for this information? Kinsella at Sultan...

He was turning dream figures over in his head when Kinsella turned to see him. There seemed to be some kind of puzzled recognition in the former DBM driver's face, but that could not be possible, they had not been introduced. Then Kinsella was talking to Zola again, but still looking in Stubbs's direction. By the time Stubbs had left the race shop with a glance over his shoulder others had joined in the discussion. He could not help but feel their hot stares, square at his Sultan logoed back as he beat a hasty retreat through the corridors, and down past the line of racing cars in the foyer. He crossed the car park and was out of the gate as quick as he could without running, all the time fingering at the shiny scar beneath his nose. There was a shout, the security man he guessed, as if alerted by those inside. But it was too late, he was away. Just find the car, start it – second time, a worry there – swing it through 180 degrees, and drive away.

As he worked the Sierra up through the gears he felt at the hard square of the disc in the inside pocket of his Sultan jacket. Then he let himself enjoy a smile before glancing in the rear view mirror. Getting smaller all the time was Zola's chauffeur, just standing in the middle of the road, getting smaller in the mirror as Stubbs and the Sierra made good the escape.

Chapter Thirteen

Moving *Akrasia* to Greece? Not an issue that had lodged in Kinsella's mind for too long really, just a cool place to be in the heat, he told himself – a place to chill, time to kill. But now, some hours off the plane, back in Monaco and walking up the hill from Ste Devote, he saw the other reason, the one he had hidden from. Back in May he had touched 180 here: and down there, near the mooring, he had shaved the wall on that hairy, scary lap, while on the far side of that wall he had almost lost it trying to avoid a spinning Spando. Yes, just too many bloody reminders, hardly the place for an out of work Formula One driver this. But now it didn't matter. Now that he was back – and some.

He was late for her, but ready to stay true to a promise, ready to stay true to two promises... He had tried to rationalise it, and it fitted well: he wanted her, nothing wrong with that, fits the Kinsella spec': tits, arse and legs, all in the right place. And then there was the game – to win the game, with her help, that would be something. But there was something else too, something deeper that had urged him to return to Monte Carlo, something in her that he would like to find, something that he suspected the mighty Chico hardly guessed at. Or perhaps it was something in him that – he supposed – he hid behind his sunglasses, behind the game, behind just being Eoghan Egg Kinsella?

She had been in the principality for a couple of weeks now. They should have met some days ago, but the call had come from Sultan and he had to make his excuses to her, get to Bicester, then on to Austria and another taste of the victory champagne. Cool, it might have been, to keep Zola waiting – but he had decided that it was best not play with him. Some did... Like the flabby man, the one he had seen in the Sultan race shop before Austria, the one he had recognised from Silverstone: 'Don't I know that guy?' he had said. Maybe he did, but they didn't, none of them, and Zola's minder had clocked the flabby man's number plate as he drove away. Could be press, could be anything when Zola's around. That's the thing with Zola, you see the shadow of his past before you see the man – it's a big shadow. One story. In Formula Three in Italy, all this a long time before he bought into the then struggling Union Shield Formula One team and tied it to Sultan branding, giving it the financial clout to reach the top. No, this was when Zola started out in racing, a hobby, something more savoury than high finance he would say. It was a way to make a steady buck, the drivers found the sponsorship, and just as often Daddy paid for them. Only one tried to pull a fast one, three races down and still the money hadn't come through, the results were not up to much either. Next race and his name was off the entry sheet and someone – so the rumour went – had bumped into him in Bologna. He told them he had had a bad shunt, a bad testing shunt. It must have been bad, they said, to bruise a face so very, very badly. To bruise a face so badly even though it was protected by a crash helmet. Kinsella sucked in some salty Med' air through gritted teeth – for the flabby man's sake he hoped he hadn't been up to mischief. They had his number, and Zola had said something to Kinsella: there are ways, he had said, ways to find people, if you have a car's plate number and the right friends.

But then that wasn't Kinsella's worry. Teresa was his worry. Fine, she wanted to talk. But he would have something else out of it. He would have her or he would have something else out of it for sure – maybe both, that's the way the world works, that's the way Kinsella's world works. Which is why he had rung Mossup, which is why he had not let himself think about it... You see, beating Chico was still the thing.

The entrance to the lime washed block of apartments was via a central courtyard, sun-starved this late in the afternoon and crammed with auto-exotica: two Ferraris, a Bentley and a Lamborghini. The building was the sort of place that was empty for much of the year, the sort of place Kinsella had looked at three years before, when he had inked the Jordan contract, a way to keep the tax man off the hard-earned Kinsella readies. As it turned out he had never got round to it, just kept the flat in London and now the boat – while he was also on the lookout for a place in the country, some-where in the hills, somewhere. As he pressed the button of the inter-com he found himself day dreaming. There was an image in his head as big and bold as the art-deco doorway in front of him. A mental image so naff it made him laugh out loud, yet he held on to it for as long as he could, he held on to it until he heard her voice over the intercom. It was an image of him and her, walking the hills, the wind teasing at her hair... Christ, there was even a Labrador at their side.

He reached the top of the stairs, the door to the flat was open, she shouted that he should come in, she was in the kitchen and he could smell the coffee. Flowers too, so many of them, enough that their scent vied for olfactory supremacy with the strong aroma of the coffee. Like two rooms this one, he thought instantly, a wrestling match of a room: one side of flowers, the other of clean white walls, a racing print or two, some pictures of single-seaters, of Chico. There was an open newspaper on the coffee table. She shouted through from the kitchen

"I have the coffee on, you want one?"

It was him, in the paper, news and comment on the Austrian victory, in French.

"Yes, thanks – black, no sugar."

The picture showed the Sultan coming out of one of the tight turns at the A1 Ring, the tight turns where it had come good in that damp second stint, where he had nailed the throttle to the floor and let the car do the rest. He could see why they asked the questions – the press, the rival teams – but Christ, his job is to drive the thing – that's all – as Zola had reminded him at the debriefing. Besides, with Chico still far ahead in the championship he could use all the help he could get. Best not think on it, best turn the page, concentrate on the job at hand.

All the other flat surfaces in the apartment were piled high with flowers, vases erupting with the things, even the floor, two vases – no, they were trophies he realised, two of Chico's trophies, both capped with heavy, drooping mops of yellow, pink and white magnolias. The glass doors to the balcony were open, and through them a sporadic car horn orchestra of Gallic impatience punctuated the steady hum of the traffic five floors below. The sun was low now, peeping from behind the mass of another tall building, lighting up the inside of the flat in streaks of layered mote. Kinsella let himself sink into the low sofa.

And then there she was. Carrying the coffee pot on a solid mahogany tray, arms slightly crooked, wrists trembling to the weight of the pot and the cups and the plate of cakes with vivid rainbow strata. Her eyes were rooted to the trembling tray and if it had not been for the coffee pot he might have said that her head was dipped in shyness. She crouched in front of him and placed the heavily laden tray onto the coffee table, onto the unfolded page of the newspaper.

Her hair was tied up in a bundle, with little strands of red-brown breaking free from the knot, falling in front of her face, little copper wires floating and gleaming in the sunlight. It was, he thought, one of the most beautiful sights he had ever seen, just the hair, those little pieces of hair, doing their thing electric there. Then she looked up, smiled at him, and poured the coffee. She wore a thin cotton dress, patterned in concentric circles, a mimic of the flowers that filled the room – just a membrane of material. With the right angle of the light he would see through it, no doubt about it. Obvious. He gulped at the thought, then had to shift in the seat, pulling the rucks of his trousers up about his lap. Obvious too. As she stood the dress fell sheer to her knees, seeming to hang vertical from the hard nipples as if they were hooks – again, all too obvious.

They talked. That's what it was about after all. They talked of her family in The Republic – she had been to see them – they talked of Sultan – she was pleased he had the drive, she said, without any great show of enthusiasm. And then the talk dried up. He asked about Chico, just a shrug from her in reply, which was somehow encouraging.

"Have you anything stronger," he asked, sloshing the dregs of the coffee about in the bottom of the cup.

"I thought you were not to drink during the season?"

"Celebrating," he said. This'll loosen her, he thought. She went into the kitchen, he heard something scrape against the floor in there, something like a stool, manoeuvred into place, something to stand on to reach up high.

It's a strange thing about Monte Carlo. The most expensive jumble of real estate in the world yet still a village in many ways, or at least that's what Kinsella had found. Though it might also have been that he kept the company of so many women, so many jealous women, so many bored women with little to fill their lives with other than other peoples' lives. It was them that had told him the stories, poor lonely Mrs Chico, hitting the bottle. It's all he would need to help things along – and who knows, he might get lucky – then the other thing could wait till the morning. He took off his sunglasses and placed them on the table, alongside the empty coffee pot. The last of the sunlight spent itself in the mirrors of the lenses. She switched on a low lamp, just enough light for them to see each other. They drank together.

There was nothing in the way of tonic to help the gin along, just a little ice, but she didn't seem to mind, and while Kinsella took little sips she took deeper and deeper gulps. He knew when he had her, he always knew when he had them. She had poured another big gin into the tumbler, more of her hair had fallen out of place now, and a wedge of it kept falling over her eyes, so that she would flick it back with awkward fly swats of her wrist. She sat down beside him, forsaking the easy chair opposite – where she had sat before, where she had met his eyes. He had thought it would be awkward, like the conversation had been, him making all the running, making all the moves. But he was so wrong. So wrong.

Christ, he'd known it all before – known the hungry, known the famished – the wives of the busy boardroom. Bored. But this... This was animal. The kiss almost cursory, a tiny formality: gin flavoured, gin wet, then gone – wet mouth around his neck, then the searching hand, delicate but firm, finding him.

She stood up, shook off the thin dress, letting it fall softly like petals to the floor. He tried to face her, look her in the eyes, but her nipples – so solid, so dangerous, aimed at him – had him in their spell. She reached down to him, took him by the hand and led him to the bedroom.

Alright, they are all a little different. That's the joy of it, for Kinsella. But this was different again: fun and the game – what more could he ask for? How best to break a man who had lost him the second best seat in Formula One but take his wife, take her there, in his apartment, take her better than she has ever been taken before – him and his perfect lap. Get this for perfection Chico old son...

So he spent longer than normal with the fingers, then with his tongue, longer than normal holding it ready, set to touch the softness. And then, with that first delicious kiss of dampness, she moaned, drew him in, nails digging into his back, and curled those long legs about him. He smelt the gin again, and caught the look of total abandonment in her eyes. They began.

It felt as if she was sucking the very life from him, hardly letting him pull back before she pulled him to her again, then tensed on it. For a while it looked like he would come straight away, he never bothered not to, normally – something that Guido Solé's sister had commented on, the cheeky little cow. But this time it was all about performance, and Kinsella set to tricking himself. Set to thinking of other things: braking points at Silverstone, then the list of champions. Or those he could remember – a big gap in his memory for the 50s, just lots of Fangio, then Jim Clark, Graham Hill in the 60s, more gaps, the seventies, the 80s, the 90s: Fittipaldi, Lauda, Prost, Senna, Schumacher, Hakkinen.... Chico.

Then she gave out a cry of such relief that it startled him, brought him back to the world of now, brought him back to spending himself in long aching spasms, spending himself into the wife of his rival.

Both finished, she lay back on the pillow. Then he had to almost peel himself from her, their skins sticky from the humid Mediterranean night. He lay on his back beside her. He heard her sob beside him, but he let her be – closing his eyes.

Of course he would have waited, the man would have waited. Christ, this was too good to miss, the thing that type fed on. But Kinsella was allowing himself to believe it, believe he might have gone. But he had promised Mossup. It had to be done, too late to pull out – he certainly could not afford to have them against him.

In the intoxicated passion of the night before Teresa had forgotten to draw the curtains and the early morning sunlight had flooded the room, its heavy shaft finding Kinsella first, waking him with a start. She still lay beside him, naked, a band of single white sheet across her, rucked and folded on itself, covering nothing much. She lay on her front, one of her breasts squashed and spilling out from under her torso. Kinsella traced the line of her back with his finger, lightly touching all the little ridges, thrilling to the softness of her skin, skin still cool from the night. She shivered a delicious little shiver, made a little chewing noise, sniffed deeply at the morning air, then came back into the world.

But this was not a world she was happy with and certainly not a world to be naked in. There was a look of sheer panic, the furrowing of that beautiful brow and then the rush to the wardrobe, grabbing at the short white robe.

"Get dressed," she snapped. Then: "Please..."

He found his discarded clothes and stepped back into his trousers while she sat on the edge of the bed, wringing her hands in front of her, rocking slightly. There was little doubt that she wanted him to leave, wanted him to go now – out of there. Well, he thought, if that's the way she wants to play it, if that's all it was, just the night – well fine. The bloody job's as good as done. It was a thought that should serve him well, but he wasn't kidding himself, the doubt was still there. But like that time back in May, when he had put aside his imagination in the search for tenths, now was the time to put aside the doubts for the bigger picture, for the game.

"Doesn't a chap get a cup of coffee here in the morning?"

She looked up at him, something swimming in her eyes, a confusion of sorts:

"I have to go out..."

"It's early," he said, "just the one cup?"

She said nothing, but marched off in the direction of the kitchen.

Kinsella went through to the lounge. The long windows were still open and the breeze tickled against his still bare chest. He could hear her in the kitchen, opening the fridge door and slamming it shut. He thought it through once more: there was nothing he could do, it was all arranged. Then he walked out onto the balcony, taking a deep breath of the early morning air. The sun was shining in his eyes, it would help.

When she had finished making the coffee she shouted through to him, but he stayed put. Then he said:

"Come here Teresa, I have something to show you."

"I have not the time."

"Please..."

She huffed, then walked out onto the balcony, shielding her eyes from the strong sun. He put his bare arm about her shoulders, she moved away from him a little – but not enough. Then he pointed towards a knot of lightly bobbing boats moored down in a corner of the harbour.

"See that one, the black and silver boat?"

She didn't reply.

"It belongs to the lead singer of *Puberty*... or so they tell me."

She gave him a puzzled look, then shrugged his arm from about her shoulder.

"I have to go out – please, you must leave..."

Chapter Fourteen

Again he found himself reaching for the scar, rubbing it. Then he turned to the rear view mirror. It was full of one thing, and one thing only: the big and bulbous Audi A6, the big and bulbous Audi A6 which had filled his mirror for the last hour, had filled his mirrors since he had left the flat-come-office. The Audi which had been on his tail since he left Sarah to tidy up, tidy up the mess they had left – those who had broken in the night before, ransacking the place, stealing his computer.

Being followed was bad enough: him, the follower, followed – too bad. But there was so much more to it, something so sinister, so out of the Stubbs way of things, that it made him as scared as he had ever been. So scared, in fact, that at one set of lights he had wound down the window, leaned out and thrown up his breakfast. They had smiled at that, those in the Audi. But made no move, just sitting on his tail as he let out the clutch to the green light. He could see that they wanted him to know they were following him, wanted him to see them, them in their dark suits, their expensive car – right there, big and bulbous in the mirror all the time.

He had tried to shake them. But the big Audi could turn on the speed when it wanted to, no doubt about that. The needle of the petrol gauge was beginning to nudge the red now, he would have to stop soon. Perhaps he should stop anyway, have it out with them? But there was menace aplenty there, he could feel it, the way they hovered without striking, the way they played with him. Besides, he had no idea where he was now, except that it was somewhere to the southeast of the city, down from Crystal Palace, among the suburban rows with their well kept gardens. Ahead was a junction to the right, into a side street, with the red disc and white bar of *No Entry*. They were running at 30mph, still nose to tail, but slow. Stubbs thought he could make the turn without slowing, it was a gamble but with any luck they would over-shoot the turn and then he would have the chance to put some distance between them – and maybe they wouldn't even risk driving the wrong way down a one way street? He doubted that, but all the same it was a chance.

He wrenched the wheel to the right, provoking an instant squeal from the front tyres. The Sierra wanted to go straight on, no doubt about that, but Stubbs somehow made the turn, although he had to use much of the pavement in the no-entry street to do so. Then the Sierra crashed down off the kerb, narrowly missing a parked car and Stubbs trod on the gas, gripping the wheel tightly and hunching forward in the seat, all attention on the road ahead, all attention on stretching the gap between him and the Audi. It wasn't a particularly hot day, but still the sweat ran off him, ran into his eyes, soaked his hands; hands wetly clamped to the now slippery wheel. He took a peek in the mirror. The Audi had overshot, that was good. But its driver had reversed back to the junction and was now turning it down the one-way street, chasing.

Stubbs was lucky in that no one was coming the other way, the right way. But unlucky in that this was not the street for speed, built up brick platforms, inches high, every 50 metres, traffic calming measures they called them – but they did little to calm Stubbs. He hit the first without even seeing it, and the Sierra was launched into the air, its steering wheel spinning from his hands with the impact. The car landed some metres later with a spine-jarring thump of fully compressed springs. Stubbs was at the wheel again, but too late to stop the offside of the Sierra scraping down the side of a parked-up Renault Clio before rebounding back into the middle of the road. Then, in the mirror, the Audi had reached the little ramp, ready to wake the sleeping policeman. Stubbs watched as it hit, flew, two or three feet high, and landed with a little bounce, hardly unsettled. Stubbs hit the next ramp with as much force as the first, though this time he was ready, as was the driver of the Audi – ever nearer. Both cars flew, one after the other, the first crunching against the bump stops of its suspension on landing, the second coming off the jump with all the assured poise of a three-day-eventer. There was one final ramp before the street reached a junction and Stubbs readied himself for the impact, gripping the steering wheel even tighter, pressing his spine into the back of the seat, tensing his shoulders – a glimpse in the mirror, it's there again, big – and then...

From nowhere, like some *Star Trek* trick, the little boy, on the little red tractor, peddling out into the road, mouthing the words of a nursery rhyme: eyes big in surprise, then fear... Middle pedal... The nose of the Sierra dips under heavy braking, bowing at the child, smoke pouring from the locked-up wheels, animal scream of rubber on asphalt. And stop... Then crash, a shower of glass as the rear window explodes and the Sierra is punted a foot or two further down the road as the Audi hits it up the rear.

The little boy is up, the tractor abandoned, he is running towards one of the houses. Stubbs is shaking, he can hardly move, hands gripping the wheel so tight his knuckles are alabaster white. In the mirror two men climb out of the back of the Audi, both inspect the front of the car, one shakes his head. Stubbs recognises him as Zola's driver. Stubbs leans out of the window and is sick again.

The man wasn't Italian, as Stubbs had assumed, but was a Scot. A softly spoken Scot. He had been polite, but in a way that suggested there was no room for negotiation. Of course he would join them, if they could prise his fingers from the steering wheel. One of the others had followed in the battered Sierra, while he sat in the back of the Audi with the Scot. He was offered a cigarette, he accepted. Sarah would kill him if she knew. It was a Sultan, he recognised the flavour, had smoked them in the Army. He told himself that it was because he didn't want to offend, why he had accepted. But he knew he wanted it, for the first time in four years he wanted it, desperately so. There was little talk in the car. He asked where they were going but the Scot just smiled, and then the driver – crew-cut and dark glasses – switched on the radio, turning it up loud so that talking was just about out of the question. Stubbs felt sick again, but held it down – it wouldn't do to mess up the Audi.

They drove north. Every now and then the Scot would smile at him, but there was nothing in that smile to comfort Stubbs. Finally they turned off the arterial route and into a mesh of streets that the big Audi gobbled up in long surges of effortless acceleration. Then they arrived at a little industrial estate, a run-down little industrial estate, one of the units derelict, three quiet, one busy. This last one was some kind of engineering company, its roller shutter doors wide open to the day. The Audi was parked up beside the doors, then they all climbed out. Stubbs felt some relief when his car arrived too, a minute or so behind them.

In the little unit a few men worked on vertical lathes. Silver candy-floss shavings littered the dirty floor, sparkling amidst the grease stains while the washed-out blue of the walls was enlivened by a couple of Miss Augusts, fleshly shining, white smiles, huge breasts. The place smelt of grease and the burn of well worked metal, while a radio tried to make itself heard through the constant shrill of cutting and drilling. Some of the workers peered through their safety goggles at him, a momentary curiosity, before shifting their concentration back to their work.

Stubbs thought of running, there and then, what could they do, with the witnesses? But something stopped him, something lead in his legs, a heaviness that stretched to the base of his belly, a sluggish heaviness that seemed at odds with the high speed hammering at his ribcage. The Scot showed him though to a back office, completely sealed off from the rest of the unit but with the same background noise, the same smells, and the same Miss August pinned to the wall. The only illumination came from a flickering strip light above them, which pinged and buzzed in spasms of strobe and seemed on the point of failing completely. The Scot sat on the desk, moving a telephone and a spike of papers aside to make room for himself. He motioned to Stubbs, a make yourself comfortable motion. Stubbs found a plastic chair in the corner of the office and sat. Another man, the one who had driven the Audi, stood in the corner. No one spoke. The Scot played with the spike, first flicking through the papers in the sheaf then running his fingers along the length of the naked steel at the top. Stubbs found his eyes drawn to it, its point gleaming in the flickering light. Then the Scot pulled the papers from it, letting them fall to the desk top in an untidy muddle, before examining the heavy wooden base, feeling its weight, bouncing it up and down close to his face. He seemed to notice Stubbs's interest.

"It's an evil looking thing eh?" There was a gleam in his eyes as he said it, and he turned to his colleague, offering the other man half a smile.

Stubbs nodded, then cleared his throat. He tried to say something, to agree, to disagree, anything. But nothing would come, his mouth moved but no words, just a chewing on the stale air of the office.

Both the men laughed, and the Scot continued, his voice as soft and low as ever: "Dare say you could do some damage with this... No?" He pressed his index finger onto the point, Stubbs noticed the skin of it turn white with the pressure.

"You know," he had turned to his colleague in the corner now, "this would be just the thing to deal with a snooping little bastard eh?"

The other man laughed, but Stubbs failed to see the joke. The Scot pressed down harder on the point of the spike, until a little bead of blood appeared, a tiny bead of blood, so round, so perfect, so bright... And for the longest moment of Stubbs's existence that bead of blood filled his life, while the pump for his own blood had all but stopped. He felt his mouth sag open, and all he could do was watch... watch as the scarlet bead grew, watch as it seemed to burst its tight meniscus, watch as the little trickle of blood made its way down the spike...

"Ah, Mr Stubbs..."

It was such a shock that he literally jumped some three inches off the chair, and it took some long seconds to regain his composure, some long seconds before he recognised the man who had just walked into the office. There was Zola, through the door already, offering his hand, a face splitting grin strapped to his head:

"Ah, Mr Stubbs..."

The Scot had found a handkerchief and was dabbing the red from his finger with it, offering his boss a smile of greeting. Zola took the chair on the opposite side of the desk, taking off his jacket as he did so, looking around the room for somewhere to put it, and – finding nowhere suitable – handing it to the Scot, who hung it on a coat hook in the far corner.

He looked straight at Stubbs:

"Apologies about the surroundings, this place belongs to a dear friend of mine, it's useful for the city... I do hope my boys have made you feel welcome Mr Stubbs?"

Stubbs said nothing, confused, yet somehow almost a little relieved, as if the presence of the Italian might help.

"Oh I see..." Zola took the silence to mean something at least, "I'm sorry about them, they still like to work the old ways... But I have told them." He shot an accusative glance at the Scot, who just shrugged, as if to say – 'didn't touch him, honest...'

"But they are good boys really, they just get bored. Bryce, have you offered Mr Stubbs some coffee?" The Scot left the office, Stubbs noticed that he was still smiling, the other was still smiling too. They had enjoyed the game they played with him.

Stubbs suddenly felt a surge of anger, which at least helped him to find his voice:

"What's happening here, why have I been brought here against my will?"

"Against your will?" Now Zola was smiling again, "were you not invited?"

Stubbs said nothing, yet there was so much going through his head now, so much confusion, all those questions that he should have asked, all those questions dammed in by the solid wall of fear.

"You see, an invitation is all you need. My boys asked you along, for the ride, no? And you accepted their invitation, it is a question of manners, a great English thing yes? Manners.

"But to come uninvited, that is bad manners. When you visit my factory, that is bad manners, stealing from us, that is bad manners..."

Stubbs moved to protest, but Zola raised a hand, cutting him short:

"That is no use: we saw you, I myself saw you – we have you on film, a thief in the night."

"Okay. Call the police then." Jesus, sweet Jesus he wished he would, call the pigs, get him from here, any way to get away...

Zola smiled again: "It is not our way, the police – and besides, what you have stolen... it is ermm, delicate yes? But of course you know this, which is why you have passed it on already – to DBM yes, to Kessler, or to that Fraser?"

Stubbs said nothing. Better to let him talk first, see what he knew.

"The boys visited yesterday you know, could find nothing, no trace of the disk..."

Stubbs thought of Sarah tidying the office and wanted nothing more than to be with her, away from here, away from the spike.

"But then you have had much time," Zola continued, "it took me longer to find you than I expected."

He seemed to think on what he had said for a moment, then added: "My fault then, but what are we to do with you Mr Stubbs?"

Zola stared at him for a whole minute, saying nothing, just staring. So that Stubbs had nowhere to look, either the spike, or those cold, cold eyes. Then, suddenly, he stopped staring.

"You arc afraid Mr Stubbs. That is okay, it is natural. The boys they play with you, and they are good. You have learnt... Now business."

It was as if Zola had flipped a switch, or even swapped heads, even the accent was flattened, into something more pan-European, something for the boardroom, something for getting down to business.

"If I was quicker I might have stopped you, but it is too late for that now. We must assume that you have given DBM the disk, so they will know how we do it. They have two options, lodge a protest, which might take time – and who's to say we are cheating eh? It's such a grey area, that software could have many applications... So they will have to develop their own system, time again, and lots of money... But money they have I suppose...."

Zola paused, and bit at a thumbnail for a moment, staring at the lighting tube above him in what Stubbs was sure was mock contemplation, the re-enactment of a thought process, the build up to a decided decision. Then in a eureka snap of the finger against the thumb, it came:

"I think they will come to me. We will agree not to run it or they will go to the top, that way is the safest, for all – but at least we will have one more race, we have stalled well I think, argued well, there is not the time before Belgium..."

He seemed to be talking to himself as much as Stubbs, but he'd read it well. Exactly what Fraser had told him: they would threaten to go to the top, to the writers of the rulebook, if Sultan didn't stop using the system. Less risk that way. Okay, they might get them banned immediately if they went to the top, even get some points deducted, but there was no guarantee. Best to level the playing field again, Chico was still far in front after all.

"And you my friend?"

Stubbs gulped. Zola smiled again.

"You did well, very well. It is to be expected I suppose, you are a professional I see." From nowhere he had magicked one of the Justin Stubbs promotional leaflets, and was scanning it with interest. Stubbs guessed that one of the boys would have taken it on their visit last night.

"Yes, you have done well. Very efficient, very English." He looked up from the leaflet, again staring into Stubbs's eyes. Then he was off again:

"I am a great admirer of you English you know, so passionate, yet so pragmatic, like Kinsella... Yes, I know, they say he is other things, a fool, a playboy, an acrobat, a lover... but he uses well – so pragmatic, he will be good for Sultan, no?"

Stubbs nodded, and Zola seemed satisfied.

"I will tell you a story, about you English. During the war, my father was here, in Wiltshire, you know this place?"

Stubbs nodded again.

"Yes, the English capture him, in North Africa. But they do not lock him away, not like the Germans lock away the English. No, they use him, use him on their farms, treat him well too, so he loves them in his way – he wanted to stay you know...

"They know the value of a man see. Like the spies, the German spies the English find. You know what they did?"

Stubbs shook his head.

"They leave them free, feed them with the wrong information, so that the Nazis get all the wrong intelligence, make the wrong moves. That's the way no? That's the way it should be done..."

He stared at Stubbs for some long moments again, and then:

"That is what we will do with you my friend..." then with a smile, "we are friends now of course?"

He matched the DBM offer, then piled another £3,000 on top, unbelievable. £10,000 up front. Yet Stubbs would have accepted anything to get out of that place, get out of that place before the bloody Scotsman came back.

They shook on the deal and Stubbs pocketed the cheque just as the Scotsman came in, pushing the door with his back and pirouetting through with a tray balanced on the palms of his hands.

The Scotsman put the tray on the table, before pouring a coffee for Zola and another for Stubbs. He was about to ask for milk, but still the words wouldn't come. The cup, on its saucer, hovered in front of him, just out of reach, as if the Scot still teased him. Zola spoke again:

"Just one thing Mr Stubbs... don't you ever play with me."

He didn't catch the look on Zola's face, just the tone, then there was the pain of the hot liquid in his lap.

Stubbs stood by the Sierra, they had given him his car keys and he was free to go. He had been sick again, and his crotch sang with the pain of the scalding liquid. He had apologised, the Scot, but it was sarcastic, this was no accident. Their faces said that, and Zola's warning still echoed in his skull.

Chapter Fifteen

"Is it true?"

"*Yes... But please...*"

Chico put the phone down. He hadn't needed her to say it, the British newspaper was in front of him, on the hotel bed. He hardly trusted it, of course he didn't, but a picture doesn't lie. A picture of her and Kinsella, on the balcony, next to nothing on, on the balcony of *his* apartment...

"Are you okay?"

Fraser had come in from the adjoining room. It had been Fraser that had shown him the paper, shown him the picture.

"Yes... I'm fine."

"You sure?" The Englishman rested a hand on Chico's shoulder.

"Let's go." It was the only thing he could say. He had to go, on to the race. He had to face the pit lane sooner or later, face the sniggers, face the gossips – all summer close together, it's just another village really, problem is that all the world wants a piece of it.

Yes, the sense of betrayal was palpable. He knew it had been hard for her, but hadn't he given her everything and more? That hurt. But – and this surprised him a little – it was of the smallest consequence when held against the hatred he felt for Kinsella. Always him. The man was a demon, always there to haunt him. God, if it had been any other but Kinsella he might have understood, she's a lonely girl after all and... But Kinsella, the damage that fool had done, had she no idea what was at stake?

They stood in the lift now. There was another too, a middle aged gentleman in golfing attire. The man asked for his autograph, but Chico blanked him. They had had enough Chico for now he decided, enough to fill their papers. He watched the lights flash their count-down as the lift descended to the ground floor, his mind on one thing and one thing only.

...What more could they do about Kinsella? Yes, he had not wanted to lose at Silverstone. But it had been a cheap price to pay to be rid of the fool, and Fraser had made sure that Kessler had kept his word...

The doors opened out into a cavernous lobby of palms and marble, dotted with an archipelago of luggage. There was a strong smell of good coffee and freshly baked bread wafting in from the restaurant. Someone shouted over to him, but he ignored them, concentrating instead on the prints that hung from the walls: scenes of the Ardennes forest, and of Brussels.

...And yes, it had always looked likely that he would go to Sultan, have them discard poor Thierry like so much useless baggage...

The main doors of the hotel opened with a whisper as they marched at them and Chico found that his eyes were automatically drawn to the sky – something about Belgium: rain always had some part to play over the Grand Prix weekend.

...No real surprise when Kinsella won the Austrian Grand Prix at the fiddly little A1 Ring. No, everyone knew the Sultan was bent, suited to the tight turns of the once majestic Osterreichring. And that second stint Kinsella put in when the track was wet? Even the British press were asking the questions now...

There was a little silver A Class Mercedes ready to whisk them away to the circuit. Fraser let Chico slide in first, then joined him on the back seat.

"Are you sure you're okay?"

Chico nodded.

...Rain... Likely, and it wouldn't look good, Kinsella beating him here, not now, when Chico should be putting the fool in his place... Fraser had promised that they had the proof, something would be done and after Spa they would force Sultan to drop the system. The promise of a level playing field, and Chico still 21 points ahead of Solé and 30 ahead of Kinsella: comfortable – and with just four races to run it should be enough.

...But the level field was never enough for Kinsella was it? He had to play dirty, make a fool of Chico, a fool to the world. He would teach him...

It was an hour's drive to the circuit at Spa-Francorchamps – perhaps the most demanding and certainly the most evocative track on the tour. Outside the circuit the car dodged through the queues of spectators with their badges of allegiance: silver and blue caps for DBM, orange flags for Sultan, red for Ferrari. There were more still at the gate to the paddock car park, always plenty there, the fanatics, hoping for a glimpse of a driver, a glimpse of celebrity, something to say – 'seen him'... Makes them feel part of it, Chico supposed, but it always somehow disturbed him, the way they would wait and wait – just for a glimpse of him. After the little A Class passed through the gate into the paddock car park a host of photographers – tipped off as to the identity of the passenger – pressed their lenses against the smoked glass of the car, lighting up the grey of the morning in a penetrating strobe. The driver of the little Merc jabbed at the throttle and they accelerated through the press of press, sending one spinning to the floor as they did so. But Chico still had to run the gauntlet to the paddock and the safety of the motor-homes. Run the gauntlet as he held his paddock pass to the sensor to operate the turnstiles, run the gauntlet down the avenue of motor-homes, run the gauntlet up the small flight of steps and into the sanctuary of the DBM base.

"It looks like rain," Fraser said, as they stepped through the doorway.

Yes, the punishment, it never stops....

The rain held off through the morning warm up and Chico was quickest. So he could be content in the knowledge that his race set-up matched his pole winning qualifying set-up from the day before – you can never be sure how they will change, these nervous, sensitive little beasts, when they are loaded with fuel. Kinsella was second quickest again, 0.2 seconds down.

After the warm up Chico had spent most of the morning holed up in DBM's travelling base, the aluminium and smoked glass structure that folded out of the two motor-homes. But the photographers had camped outside, ready for when he emerged for the race. He knew that the pit lane was abuzz with the talk of the day – Teresa and Kinsella – not because he had heard it, no, but because he knew the pit lane. Some of the journalists had tried to draw him into conversation earlier as he walked across the paddock, starting with the usual questions: 'what's your strategy for the race', 'what of Sultan and the rain they have forecast?' But he knew them, knew their game, knew what they really wanted – another piece of Chico for the world to laugh at, and so he had cut the interviews short.

Now, as he waited, he tried to think himself through the race, closing his eyes tight and picturing himself leading away, into the *La Source* hairpin in front of Kinsella, down the hill in front of Kinsella, through *Eau Rouge* in front of Kinsella... Always Kinsella. And the more the race progressed in his mind's eye, the more he would see the orange car – always in front of Kinsella, always him, no-one else to race, as it had never been before...

There was one interruption. A phone-call. He had told them not to call him on race days. But it was important, they said, more problems with the Ministry of Works, they would have to pay off the Minister again. Chico agreed, but then there were other problems with the Chicodrome too: drainage for one, and the papers were beginning to ask awkward questions – some were saying the circuit would not be finished in time for the championship finale. In the end he had to cut them off, had to get back to his mental preparation, to picturing the race, to picturing the race against Kinsella.

Come 1pm it was time to go. Fraser helped him press his way past the photographers as they walked across the paddock and into the back of the DBM garage through the alley formed by two massive DBM transporters, both bristling with telecommunications equipment. Once in the garage he climbed inside his gleaming silver and blue car as soon as it was ready for him, hiding in his helmet, having the mechanic strap him in safely – safe from the world.

Before taking his place on the grid he did two laps of the mighty circuit, each time feeling his heart sink as he noticed the long stretched bruise of cloud that seemed to edge the horizon, each time coming into the pits to make slight changes. But none that could match the advantage that Sultan would carry after the first pit stops should it rain. And then he took it round once more, took it round the full 7km until he was back to the grid, threading the DBM carefully through the cars that were already lined up for the start and the grid people who milled about them: mechanics, engineers, TV. He brought the car up to its grid slot, so that the backs of the grid girl's knees were directly in his line of sight. A gust of wind lifted her skirt a little, and he found himself watching the little piece of cloth, the little piece of Sultan coloured cloth, hypnotic orange cloth.

Some minutes later he caught sight of Kinsella, the Sultan pulling up behind and to the right of him. Chico wanted to put the man from his mind, concentrate on the race, on the first corner, but still he watched him as he unstrapped his belts and climbed out of the Sultan. Kinsella was talking to Thierry Michel, the older man now in the shirtsleeve uniform of a French TV channel, interviewing the one who had taken his drive. He looked to the front of the DBM where Fraser and Burgess, now Bobby Drake's engineer, were discussing the race plan – two stop, Chico knew it.

Then there was a tap on his helmet. Strapped tight into his seat it was an effort to turn and look over the high cockpit sides. He had guessed it would be someone wanting to wish him good luck, or perhaps even Thierry wanting a few words for Chico's French fans. The one face he had not expected to see was that of Kinsella's. Some photographers and a TV crew had noticed, and were beginning to rush towards the DBM, no doubt hoping for some kind of confrontation, but Kinsella's head was level with Chico's before they were near enough to catch a word of it. A word of:

"She was bloody good Chico mate..."

Chico forgot himself, forgot that he was strapped into the car, lashing out at the Englishman. But he was gone, back to the Sultan, leaving just a scrum of pressmen to witness Chico trying to struggle free. Fraser burst through, scattering the photographers, and pushing Chico – who had finally managed to loosen his harness – squarely back into his seat. A siren sounded and the red lights on the start gantry flashed on and off. The mechanics began to wheel the equipment to the side of the track, unravelling the electric tyre blankets from around the wheels. Further down the grid a few of the engines caught and roared into life and Fraser, still pressing Chico into his seat, had to shout to be heard:

"Leave it Chico – leave it, can't you see it's what the twat is after, he wants to rile you man."

There was no way he was moving anyway, the cockpit of a modern Formula One car is a confined enough place at the best of times, and with Fraser pushing down on him, now re-tightening the straps, revenge would have to wait. But not long.

"Just beat him Chico – just beat him..."

Burgess pulled Fraser clear and one of the mechanics made the signal to Chico, the signal that asked him if he was ready. Fraser was right... just beat him. Thumbs up, then left arm skywards and gloved finger spinning in the air, the engine turned by the remote starter at the rear, and a moment or so later Chico squirted the gas to keep it alive. Just beat him.

Chico had always believed that this was part of the race, the warm up lap, had to treat it as part of the race. Had to keep the speed up to make sure the equipment was at working temperature, but also had to make sure you weren't too quick – couldn't afford to sit on the grid waiting for the others to form up, couldn't afford to burn out the clutch. So his mind ought to have been focussed – just on the race, just on the warm up lap. Yet today his whole being consisted of just one sensation and one emotion: the sight of the orange Sultan weaving about to warm up its tyres in his mirrors – and hate. The sort of hate that lives solid in a man. And at another time he would perhaps admit – not the sort of hate you take into a 200 mph racing car around the world's most challenging – and some would say frightening – circuit.

Lined up. Two by two, staggered; the reds flick on – then off. Plenty of boot, almost kicking it, the orange car is almost alongside on the right for the short drag down to La Source, the tight right-hander. Chico chops him, it's brutal, and the smoke's pouring off the tyres of Kinsella's car. Someone hits someone else behind, in the mirror Chico catches a glance of the other DBM – Drake's car – broadside across the track, but the rest of the field splits and funnels through on both sides of the stalled car. Time to put in the lap Chico, time to put in the lap to break them...

Down the hill to *Eau Rouge* the corner they always talk about, an echo of a distant age, an age of heroism in cigar shaped death-mobiles. Left, right, through the compression where Chico felt himself pushed into the well of the seat as the car bottomed at its base, then up the steep hill the other side. He keeps his boot in: almost flat in sixth, perfect. The rest would lift off a bit more, they always did first time through. Not Chico though, break them first lap – and never look back...And where's Kinsella?

Never look back... Shooting out of *Radillon* at the top of the hill, feathering the track fringe, winding it up along the long, long straight, nudging 192 mph, concentrate on the braking area for *Les Combes*... and never look back: break them Chico, break them. And where's Kinsella? Clean through *Malmedy* and into the long right handed loop at *Rivage* a little understeer there, but nothing to worry about. On the exit, picking up the blur of colour that's the field pouring into the turn... Was that a flash of orange in the middle there... way down?

Pouhon, another *man's* corner, this track was everything a track should be, clip – let it drift wide – clip again for the next part, a little slide midway through, but clean on the exit, down towards *Fagnes*. But don't look back...

Through the esses, then two vital fourth gear right handers that turn the track, point it in the direction of home, out of *Stavelot* and then the long blast, precise through the double kink at *Blanchimont* at over 185 mph, inch perfect – has to be. A clean dissection of the turn in a slicing arc that takes the DBM from track fringe to track fringe. And then he's nearly there, the damage should be done by now, approaching the mortise shaped *Bus Stop* chicane, worth another glance now – firing it down through the gears with the bypass button, sixth to second quicker than you can say it, much, much quicker. Yes, worth a glance... There, the flash of orange behind, closing quick as the field compresses under braking for the chicane. The flash of orange growing so big, locked to Chico's retina for an all too long shaving of a second, and then he's collecting the moment, sliding wide, two wheels on the grass, the underside of the DBM clouting the chicane kerbing, briefly airborne, and down with a thump. Still in front. But the mirrors are orange. Should never look back...

Lap one past the pits. 0.5 second gap. Nothing, and what's Kinsella's strategy? Chico pulls another quick one out of the bag, flat through *Eau Rouge*, on the edge at *Blanchimont*, past the pits again: 0.7. Another lap: 0.9.

"We think he's two stopping... he must be...they'll be hoping for rain in the second stint..."

The first from Fraser over the comms. Pump them in, as Fraser would say, make the gap in case the rain comes.

One-point-one second gap; 1.3; 1.6 – Kinsella must have made a mistake – 2 seconds; 2.2, 2.5, 2.6 – lapping traffic already and Chico has a clear view of Kinsella as he exits *Rivage* – the Sultan braking for the same turn as the DBM accelerates out. 2.8, 3.0, 3.8 – perhaps his tyres are going off, 4.1, 5.0, 5.5... for much of the lap he's out of sight now, just an orange dot on the longer straights... Then:

"Kinsella's in... do the damage Chico..."

The next two laps were like qualifiers, a clear track, the fuel load light, time to stretch the lead in the pit lane sort out, time for the hottest of hot laps. And then it was straight on at the *Bus Stop*, straight into the pit lane, using all the speed before the line, and in. New rubber. More fuel. First gear. And out, re-joining the track on the run down to *Eau Rouge*, waiting for the voice of Fraser to give him Kinsella's position, the orange car still not in sight in the mirrors... Working heat into the new rubber through *Eau Rouge* and *Radillon*. Then up the long straight at *Kemmel*, looking to the rapidly approaching horizon – stained black with the clouds rolling off the forest...

"It's about ten seconds... Excellent work Chico..."

It's a long circuit by today's standards, Spa. Five miles long, just about. Which means that the race distance, in terms of laps if not distance driven, is shorter than usual – just 44 laps. So with a two-stop strategy – Fraser had told him it should be *tactics*, over a race, but strategy was the word they always used – your optimum pit laps would be 15 and 30. Although this depended on the traffic to be lapped, and depended on the race plan of your nearest competitor. As the race stood Chico looked set to come in again on lap 29. But then, if it rained everything would be turned on its head. And if it rained now DBM would be in serious trouble. How Sultan did it was still a mystery, loading the traction control into the electronic brain of the Sultan in the first stop. At first one of the wheel-men had done the dirty deed, but that was all too obvious. Now the suspicious in the pit-lane pointed to a small device clamped to the gantry, something that might, conceivably, be a transmitter. Whatever, if it rained in this second stint Chico knew he could kiss goodbye to victory. But if it held off until the next stops, well then he'd have him...

Lap 24. The bank of dark clouds still hung over *Les Combes* and the gap was now constant at about twenty-five seconds to Kinsella, with another ten seconds back to Solé, who was dicing with the first of the Ferraris. Almost comfortable. Indeed, the only cloud on Chico's horizon was the cloud on Chico's horizon.

Lap 25, out of *Radillon*, the DBM floating across the road at the crest of the hill. A Bianchi in front, jink right out of its slipstream, put it two laps down. Easy... But watch those clouds.

Lap 27, out of *Radillon*, powering down the long straight, the black mass of cloud over *Les Combes* seems darker, denser, billowing tautly, as if pregnant with rain...

Lap 28. The heavy cloud has sagged, almost touching the track it seems, rolling down the straight towards him. In the mirrors Chico sees the little vortices as the damp air works the rear wing...

Lap 29. A few spots on the visor, little pearls of water, mixing with the oil thrown out from the lapped cars. Chico reaches up, rips off a tear-off visor film, letting it fly free in the slip-stream.

And then the cloud could hold on no more, dumping itself on the people and the trees, and the circuit. At the trackside Chico noticed the little explosions of colour as umbrellas mushroomed to the downpour.

He pressed the comms switch on the steering wheel:

"It's raining, in next time."

"Careful Chico, Kinsella's in, he's putting wets on..."

Good. Sultan had timed it wrong, the wrong fuel load, and their box of magic would not be available to Kinsella for the wet. Good. There were a few more spots at *Pouhon*, just a film of moisture, then to *Fagnes*, here the road is darkening, the trees are alive with the rain, clouds of moisture boiling off the forest... *Stavelot*, long lances of it now, bouncing off the surface of the road, washing out the front of the car, so that he runs wide midway through the turn, lifting off, only for the back to step out on him. He collects the slide, tip toes on.

"Wets... wets..."

They should know anyway, but who could be sure – it was not

unknown for it to be wet at one point of the Spa circuit and dry at another.

He had been lucky, timed it right. But could not afford to ease up yet, had to hang on grimly through *Blanchimont* risk it a little, Kinsella might not have his traction control activated now – unless he aimed to stop again before the end of the race – but he was on wet weather tyres.

Into the pit lane, the speed limit kicks in. The water has already settled, and great spurts of it fly from the front wheels, landing in the cockpit as he turns the car, filling Chico's lap with water. Hit the limiter, find the pit in the gloom... there's the man to guide him in, there's the man with the lollipop. In. Off the throttle, on the brake, keep the car still for the boys to work on, firmly grasp the steering wheel, a look to the sky – as black as the intricately patterned rubber being bolted to his DBM. A glance in the mirror, an orange car, trundling down the pit lane, throwing up the water even at this speed, must be Solé. In front the Sultan crew are ready for the young Italian, the mechanics ready with their air guns, beads of water dropping off their noses, their Sultan overalls orange-shiny, like paramedics at an accident scene. Then the signal, select first, off the jacks, go... But no...

The lollipop man, a look of undiluted panic etched on his face, stays put, reversing the signal in a flick of fear as the orange Sultan cuts in front of him, aiming for its pit slot. But it's too late for Chico, already on the gas, the DBM slewing sideways as it's rear wheels spin on the slick surface. The lollipop man dives clear, but then there is just the gleaming flank of the Sultan filling Chico's eyeline. Solé's wheels are all locked up as the Italian spots the problem and kicks at the brake. The Sultan crew scatters but Solé manages to stop the car. But in doing so he slides broadside across the pit road and stalls, blocking Chico's path out of the pits. The two cars form a capital T in the pit road, T for *temper*...

Chico had managed to snatch at the hand clutch at the same time as he had kicked out at the brake pedal, but now he was impotent as the mechanics tried to pull the DBM away from the Sultan. Through the corner of his eye he could see Fraser shouting at the mechanics, while Zola had come off the pit wall, away from the protection of the canopy, and was shouting at Fraser. Directly in front of him, in all-too-close a profile, Solé, sunken low in the Sultan cockpit, was gesticulating, livid, the orange driving gloves enacting some deranged puppet theatre that seemed to mimic the complete panic in the Sultan pit. They dragged the Sultan back, then pushed it forward, then dragged it back again. The flashes from cameras made starfish patterns on the beads of water on Chico's visor as his own mechanics tried to pull the DBM clear of the Sultan. Car after car flashed by, making their way out of the pits, and the seconds ticked down, while one of the Sultan crew in the garage, in the dry, gave out a whoop of delight.

Chico thought he caught a glimpse of orange on a giant TV screen across the track to his left as it flashed past the pit lane exit, coming out of *La Source*. He swore to himself and punched at the boss of the steering wheel with the back of his hand. At last the DBM was in the clear, angled to drive away, and now Solé's crew had pulled the orange car clear too – just as eager to get their man back into the race. Chico jabbed at the throttle then planted his right boot in frustration, leaving his pit slot in a succession of lock-to-lock power slides. By the time he had rejoined the track there was no sign of the other Sultan, just a couple of huge rooster tails of spray heading up the steep hill out of *Eau Rouge*.

He punished himself over that next lap. He had known Solé's Sultan was there at the end of the stop, should have been more careful, had it in the bag. And now Kinsella was in front... always him. The lap was as quick as it could have been in those conditions, a no prisoners lap. Twice he almost lost it: once through Pouhon when a long ploughing front-wheel slide switched to an arse-kick of a tailslide as he lifted. Then next at the *Bus Stop*, where fastly tapped cadence braking couldn't stop the fronts from locking long enough to turn the thing in – a quick trip across the grass, but he held it.

And finally, that lap done, Fraser was back on comms, the panic in the pits sorted.

"*You're twenty-five down on Kinsella Chico, he's just hud an off at Les Combes, but it hasn't lost him much time... Sorry about the stop, our fault... heads will roll...*"

Into the *la Source* hairpin he had to do the cadence dance again, on and off the brake pedal, gentle little movements of the wheel in-between, when the wheels rolled, slow it enough for the corner too – and still Fraser talked...

"*Look, best to leave it, six points... it's okay, we are still way ahead remember, it's not worth throwing it away Chico... Not worth the risk...*"

Let it dawdle through the turn a little, the water thrown off the right front coming into the cockpit, then a little throttle, just a tickle, bring the rear around a little, pushing the front out, more gas, round she comes, kicking round, correct the slide, a flick of the wrists, she's pointing down the hill... Feed in the power slowly, wind it up for *Eau Rouge*.

And press the comms:

"I will race him."

No reply, a pause for thought, but then there's Eau Rouge too, the need for concentration, Fraser would know that. It's much slower now, two gears down, a series of little steering corrections as the car slithers through. Peripherally, Chico notices a blue car, beached in the gravel trap. Then the crackle coated voice of Fraser as the DBM crests the hill.

"Okay – it's your shout Chico... But please... be careful..."

Chico had tried to explain it to Teresa once. Formula One in the wet. They had been driving down an Autostrada in one of the Ferraris during an autumnal storm, he remembered. And how the trucks had kicked up the spray, big blankets of the stuff, hanging in front of them. But nothing on this, as he told her. That's the thing with an open-wheeler, nothing to keep the spray down, no arches, no mud-guards, just the fat tyres with their deep wet-weather treads. Treads that cut through the surface of the water, sending it back to the sky, where it hangs behind the car like a smoke screen behind a destroy-er. So the man behind, the quicker man, the one lapping or overtak-ing, what does he see? Nothing, zero – except for his own front tyres. Nothing but the spray, and who's to say what's in front of it and how fast it goes? Driving in these conditions behind other cars was like driving in a box. Even the greats can be caught out by that, misjudge the speed of the car in front – Senna had in Australia one year, Schumacher had here one year – an easy mistake when you're pushing in the wet. And, of course, that's the thing about the greats – they always push in the wet.

It's really like walking on the water you see, nothing natural about it. You can't see a thing because of the spray, and half the time the car is floating, tyres not in contact with the asphalt – aquaplaning they call it, scary he called it: even Chico called it scary... How it was down towards *Fagnes*, up through the gears to sixth again, and then the buzz of the engine, the wedge of rapidly growing orange then red on the dash read out, wheelspin in top gear, wheelspin at 160 mph – yes, scary that. And half a lap later he had every right to be scared again, on the way into the double kink at *Blanchimont*, a needle threading –take a deep breath – flat in top in the dry. But much slower now, even down a cog... But surely not as slow as the cloud of spray in front of him.

Judging the speed of the car in front was the problem, as the slow-er car's completely masked by its wake. In the end it's just a matter of slotting to the left of the huge ball of spray and getting through before the turn in for *Blanchimont*, praying all the time that the other car doesn't reach the turn in point first. Chico made it, the other car blurred red and white just half a metre from his head as he passed at something like twice the speed. Then Chico put the DBM into the kink, sliding through, balancing it on the throttle, then out with a twitch of a powerslide.

The steering was on the bump stops as he drove it through lock-to-lock-to-lock through the *Bus Stop*, the intended over-correction for the first slide becoming the first input for the second part of the chicane – but watch those kerbs, there's nothing as treacherous as wet concrete. Perfect – and the flash bulbs flickered in appreciation at the edge of the circuit. And past the pits, the board is out: Kin + 16. + 10 lap. Lap old data. He eased it into *La Source*, and powered it out in a series of delicate little jabs of the throttle, so that the tail wagged close to the outer wall in a dance of delightful little twitches.

"*Just 15 seconds Chico, I think you've got him on the run...*" said Fraser over the comms, speaking in real time.

Good, two seconds a lap, at least. No problem. Out of *Radillon* that same lap he glanced at the sky, a peep of blue there, or at least a lighter grey? End of the lap and Fraser was there with the gap: 12. Next lap: 9 seconds and the rain is easing. Next lap: 6. Next lap: 8 – traffic, an Arrows spinning in front of him, but the rain has stopped. Next lap: 5, he can see the ball of spray at the end of the straight. Four laps to go, then three, always closing. Then Chico's with him, right with him, tucked up tight behind the Sultan, judging his braking and turning points by the landmarks at the edge of the track. Driving on instinct, driving on faith, driving on the parallel bands of drying tarmac that the car in front seemed to lay before him.

This was how it was into the penultimate lap. The rain had caused havoc down the field, catching many out – including the other Sultan of Guido Solé, which was now parked in the gravel trap at *Pouhon*, Chico noticed. Yet there were still ten of the twenty-six starters circulating, ten fat-tyred machines circulating almost precisely on the same line. Ten machines drying up the line, pushing the water from the surface, etching out the little parallel tramlines that mark the safe parts of the track – just where the wheels go, that's all. But stray off the line then there's trouble.

So, penultimate lap. Into *Eau Rouge* again. The drying line is clear now, still damp but getting there. Chico follows Kinsella through, as close as possible without upsetting the air over the wings – and the spray is down now, with most of the water off the line. Kinsella's slow through *Eau Rouge*, cautious, and Chico closes in on the run down to

Les Combes. Not close enough this time, but there could be a way – the question is, are those tram lines dry enough – dry enough for *Eau Rouge* flat?

The calculation takes a heartbeat. The decision's made and Chico hangs back a couple of lengths for the rest of the lap. Every so often he catches a glimpse of Kinsella looking back at him in the mirrors, wondering no doubt where Chico would make the move, wondering, no doubt, whether Chico had the balls to take *Eau Rouge* flat on a line that was perhaps not quite dry...

Kinsella had a little sideways moment out of *La Source* as they began their last lap, but he collected it well enough. Chico had dropped back a couple of lengths now, looking for the clean run through the corner – with just the one line it would be all too easy for Kinsella to hold back, spoiling tactics. So it was that the Sultan entered the downhill flick left and uphill flick right some four lengths ahead. But he lifted, no doubt about it, those at the trackside would have heard it, the caution of a man with a lead, not a comfortable lead but a lead in a Grand Prix all the same. Then Chico came through.

How clear can the limit of adhesion be marked? The sun-sparkled wet asphalt, the two dry lines, just wide enough for the wheels of the DBM, not a centimetre's room for error either side. It was – and he had the thought there and then – like riding a bike on a tightrope. In at 180 mph, out at 175 mph – the car squirming beneath him as it compresses in the bottom of the dip, the tail kicking out just that little bit, in line with the turn, in line with the tiny envelope that Chico had to work with. From the front left a pencil's-width arc of water is kicked up as the DBM trims the edge of the drenched part of the surface. And then it's up the hill, closing all too rapidly on the Sultan as they go through *Radillon*.

Momentum's the thing now, and Chico has the momentum, carrying the speed from *Eau Rouge* through *Radillon*. By the time the long straight kinks at *Kemmel* the DBM and the Sultan are running side by side, running into *Les Combes* side by side.

Because the cars had been moving about onto the wet parts of the straight to cool their tyres as the track dried most of the surface had been cleared of standing water. But Chico would still have the damper line into the right-hander at *Les Combes*, unless he could pass on the straight before the braking area, which, with the momentum, looked possible. But then Kinsella moved across on him, just as the DBM was inching ahead. There was nothing subtle about the manoeuvre, just a flick of the steering wheel on Kinsella's part, a flick of the wheel that brought them both close to disaster. And for the split second that the Sultan's nose came for the front-left of the DBM, Chico lifted – just the lightest feather of the throttle, a reflex thing, a spasm in his foot – but enough to spend the momentum, so that both cars were as one going into the braking area, speed matched. Chico glanced over at his left front tyre. The Sultan's right front ran alongside it just an inch apart, as if they were joined by some tiny axle, running just an inch apart at 200 mph...

Chico could only hope that the inside line into the corner had dried, for now the race rested on one thing and one thing only – who had the balls to be on the brakes last, for the latest of the late-brakers would take this corner. Chico found his mark, where he would normally brake, and as they shot past he had to force himself to stay off the pedal. Then longer, then longer, the sole of his racing boot kissing the pedal, aching for pressure – but still he held off the brakes as the second was split and split and split in some Zenoan nightmare. And still the Sultan stayed alongside, and still Chico stayed off the brake...

For a second, nothing more, the two drivers were locked into the greatest battle of wills, the greatest game of chicken, of their lives. And neither would admit defeat. So that by the time Chico's reflexes – Chico's will to live – took control, both cars were sailing off the track. Through the corner of his eye he could see the Sultan kicking up some mud, then taking to the escape road. Then Chico was on the slippery grass, trying to turn it but finding no response before the nose of the car bottomed on a rut which sent it upwards, then sideways, and then into a graceful spin, the back coming out slowly, slowly... He tugged at the clutch paddle and blipped at the throttle to keep the engine alive, and then the DBM snapped around viciously as the car bounced against a tyre barrier. His head was jolted to one side as if it had been struck by a passing train, and then the steering wheel was ripped from his grasp as the front of the car made contact too. One of the wheels collapsed in onto the suspension components, then bounced up in front of him while in his mirror Chico could see the right rear wheel, flapping against its tether. And then the car spun once more, through a huge sodden patch of grass that splashed great waves of mud over Chico, obliterating the view through his visor. Then, finally, it came to rest, on the track once more, at the exit of the corner. Engine dead. Race over.

On the run down to *Pouhon* Kinsella checked his steering, all seemed well. The escape road had done its job, as it had earlier in the race – always well to remember these things, remember where it's safe to go off. In the gravel trap he could see the other Sultan, Solé's car, which had gone off earlier – the Italian, he had noticed, was shit in the wet when they couldn't use the traction control. Then behind the tyre wall he caught a glimpse of one of the giant TV screens that were dotted around the circuit. Just a glimpse: a glimpse of Chico, covered in mud so that the Republic's colours on his helmet were lost in brown. He had already clambered from the wrecked DBM, marshals frantically wind-milling the yellow hazard flags in the background. The South American grabbed at the strap of his helmet, tore it clear then wrenched the mud spattered dome from his head and slammed it against the car before flinging it to the floor... But then the image was lost as Kinsella guided the car through the turn, and out to complete his final, victorious, lap. Better get it back Kinsella, time to laugh at that later. Laugh at Chico, laugh at how you had sucked him in: into the corner – there was no way he would brake was there? And you knew the room was there – for one. Sucked him in from the beginning. Sweet.

Chapter Sixteen

Helicopters at dawn. Zola had told him how it had gone, the two bosses flying in to the abandoned aerodrome, shaking hands on the matter. Not that he cared too much now, after Spa he felt he could beat Chico on his own terms, felt sure of it. Besides, just for today there were other things to occupy Kinsella's mind.

He had met her off the plane. Or rather, he had waited at the pick-up point – too many prying lenses at Heathrow, more lenses to upset her. Teresa had moved onto the boat when he was in Belgium, pushing Pablo – who had just brought *Akrasia* back to Monte Carlo – aside. There had been a few more pictures then, just a few. Some of the papers had used them in comment pieces, linking them with the shot of Chico abandoning his wrecked DBM at Spa. Her on *Akrasia*, soaking up the sun, him with his head in his hands, soaked in mud. In the Republic there had been a feeding frenzy – they couldn't blame Chico could they, couldn't see the god had made a mistake – so blame the girl. Distracting him, abandoning him, emasculating him... What was it with the place, that last was always the worst? Teresa's mother had been distraught on the phone, she had told him, while her father would not talk to her. She needed someone, her only friend: Kinsella.

Yes, and they had fucked, and fucked. Then to England for him, camping it up in a petrol station, all togged up and sitting in the Sultan, filming for an advert for one of the secondary sponsors: *'can I get you anything else sir?'* the girl had said. He had grinned, a wicked grin as per script, and she was something – normally it might have been worth a go. Not now though. Not with Teresa on the scene, not with him wanting Teresa on the scene...

It had worried him at first. When you spend the greater part of your adult life trying not to get involved it's a shock to find there's someone – a greater shock to find that you are the only one on the planet for this someone, the only one she has to rely on... Especially when you are aware that her loneliness is all your doing. And there was no hiding from it, there was the guilt again, something new to him, like so much sick inside... Christ, he'd screwed her well and proper.

The long red roadster nosed off the slip road and onto the main carriageway of the motorway. West, always west. They hadn't discussed it, just said hello, a peck on the cheek. It was warm for September, but she wore a long leather coat, which she had taken off and stowed behind the passenger seat before crouching and folding her long frame into the cramped cab of the E-Type. She wore jeans and a sweater, something for the country, as he had advised. So, 'M4 West', he had taken it. Forget Mossup, forget his arrangements, the table, somewhere classy, he'd said – what does he know about class? The slime. He had had his pound of flesh and more. Fuck him. Besides, when Kinsella needed to get away it was always west.

Despite the warm weather he kept the roof up. The slipstream thrumming in the canvas made conversation difficult, but it didn't seem to matter, and every so often he would glance at her and she would smile a distant smile back at him. He hardly stretched the big V12 on the motorway, just kept it to 80, letting it come awake gently as he had neglected it for most of the year, a busy season. But now, with a little time before the next test, he could exercise it in the hills. Stretch it a bit, let it take him back to reality again, and give her a chance to see the real him, before she found out for herself in some other way beyond his control.

The Severn Bridge was always the mark, the older of the two. When the E-Type was at the crest of that beautiful, long white arc then he was there, then he relaxed. Games forgotten. He had never been able to say why. He supposed it represented something so different, so removed from Formula One. Memories first, summer holidays at Grandad's farm in Gwent, then the recent escapes, to walk in the mountains, hide in a cottage. Christ, he had sometimes thought that he might bump into the real Kinsella here one day: but then the next test called, the next race called.

Of course, he had played the game here too. In the early days. Mother's Welsh, had to give it a go. On some advice he had played the papers to his advantage – no one seemed to care that his accent was more Swanley than Swansea. What mattered was that the little taffy boy was winning, winning in this Formula Ford, winning in this Formula Three. And they had loved it when he painted his helmet red, white and green. With the column inches came the sponsors, one or two from the Principality, and for his part he had kept in touch, kept them up to date, fed them the choice stories – TV and newspapers. Why, he had even cheered when Wales had beaten England at rugby.

But with Formula One the backdrop shifts. Playing on a world stage now, and they all wanted a part of Kinsella, not the little fishes but the sharks – and he had given them far too much... But Mossup would have to do without him this time.

They stopped at a service station to see to the Jag's thirst and Kinsella pulled back the roof with some difficulty, out of practice. Then he drove. It's a funny thing, and if he was put on a couch for a day he was sure the best shrink in the land could not get to the bottom of it, but when all was said and done this was how he relaxed... Well, there was this and girls. Driving and girls. Not driving the Sultan, or the DBM before it, no – that had long since become part of the game, part of work. But this, driving this roaring creature through the Welsh hills, feeling it breathe to each tickle of the throttle, feeling it squirm under acceleration, its long nose pointing skywards. Feeling it bow to the turns under braking. Feeling it float, slowly arcing from the rear in long time-consuming tail slides – a reflex of the moment in an F1 car stretched to a full two seconds of undiluted pleasure in the E-Type. This was what it was all about, or at least should have been. Doing what he did well in this car, with one of the world's most beautiful women beside him.

Sometimes he would glance over at her, looking for something, something other than the enigmatic smile she would offer in return, or that look of elsewhere-calling that worried him in some way that was beyond the grasp of his emotions and his imagination. One such time they had taken a bend in a long arcing tail slide, drifting close to the edge of a drop into the valley on the exit. He looked at her, she looked back, just that smile. It occurred to him then that he wanted more from her, much more. And, in truth, it was a shock to him – a shock that he wanted her to enjoy this so –this thing of him – a shock that it mattered that she should recognise his skill – even fear would be something, he conceded. But there was just the smile, or the look of elsewhere. Perhaps it was something she was used to? How often had she ridden with Chico after all?

This thought stirred the competitor in him and at the next turn in the road he pitched the Jag in a little more violently, the tyres screaming the cat's protest, the lip of the windscreen masking the horizon at 40 degrees. The car leaned over, tail out, then popped out of the corner under power, Kinsella applying armfuls of opposite lock. As for her, she stared straight ahead. And so he pushed some more, pushed beyond the sensible, pushed beyond the limit he judged Chico would have pushed in one of those modern Ferraris of his.

Only once did he come close to losing it, and this is where she seemed to snap out of her spell. In truth it wasn't his fault, but rather the driver of an under-powered and over-loaded brown Vauxhall Nova travelling in the opposite direction, who was using all the road and more in an effort to maintain momentum for a steep hill. Kinsella had to use a little of the grass verge to get by, but at least it seemed to shake her a little, as this time the smile was laced with a *phew*, of admiration or relief he could not be sure.

Another time, soon after, as the car came out of a long tyre-burning skid she reached across, touched him there. Massaged it for a little while. He grinned, planted the throttle and lit up the rear tyres, sawing at the wheel so that the long red car fishtailed down the narrow Welsh road. And then she laughed with the pleasure of it, before taking her hand away.

He took the Jag up past Brecon, letting the needle lick at a ton-ten along the dual carriageway. And after that it was corners all the way, while the ever-twisting ribbon of tarmac was forever jumping from the light of the midday sun to the lace like dapple of the shade thrown from the trees. Then, almost suddenly it seemed – so engrossed he had been in his efforts to impress Teresa – they were crossing the old stone bridge into Lampeter. By this time the brakes were cooked, as always, and the driver was famished.

It's a little town, tiny town. A what-might-have-been town for Kinsella, with its university – the oldest in Wales – filling out the shallow valley. The plan had been for him to come here, in the early '80s – English and History joint honours, some vague idea of a media career on his part – another Mossup in the making maybe? It had been the only place willing to take him, with those grades – too many girls, too much booze, even then. He hadn't liked the idea, three years in the wilderness. But Dad was keen, keen that he should get a degree before coming onboard, becoming part of the firm, or finding himself a job. At least Dad had tried to ease the pain, money for a summer's trip around Europe. A ball, yes, the trip was great – but he hadn't got out of France. Then, a week or two into September, when he should have been thinking about getting back, he bumped into another traveller. A young lad, eighteen like himself, on his way to Paul Ricard in the South, a racetrack, he had said. Someone had dropped out of the course at the racing driver school – it seemed like a good way to drain the emergency credit card Dad had given him. Some days later, after just one hour in one of the school's Formula Renault cars, Eoghan 'Egg' Kinsella had decided what he was going to do with his life.

With the Jordan money three years ago he had bought a new Mercedes and the Jag, then it was to Wales to give the cat its head – a good way to forget about a disastrous Monaco that year. Lampeter, a name in his skull, a name he had then aimed for, but now the place he saw himself when the game got too much, too much even for Kinsella.

He pulled the car up in a gravel car park near the market place, switching off the engine and letting it roll to a well earned rest. They sat there for some long moments, saying nothing, while the hot steel of the Jag pinged as it cooled.

"Where are we?" she said, finally.

"A little place I know – I've never brought anyone here before." And he hadn't. He hadn't thought it through either, bringing her, but here she was in the place he went away from the game. The first ever. If he could just explain it to her, it could make her happy – couldn't it? But how could he explain it all? Explain how he had pulled her into the game, and how he now wanted her to forget it, meet the real Kinsella – somewhere here. As it was he could only look for some kind of recognition, she was the first he had brought here, he'd said. Her? She said nothing, her smile said nothing.

"Shall we eat?"

"Yes... Please."

In the three years since he had first been there it hadn't changed a bit. No big deal in that, no, but then it looked like it hadn't changed a bit in a hundred years – for someone from the perpetual state of flux that is Formula One that really meant something. They walked down a short row of stone houses and on to the wide main street. He reached for her hand, she gave it, her fingers closing around his rather loosely, as if more reflex than intentional.

Wide street. Market town. Where the farmers come for treats: pubs with pockmarked white facades, gents outfitters with suits and blazers, boutiques for the wife – weddings and so on – loads of churches, loads. The main street is part of the main road through the town, although a portion of it shoots off, off somewhere else, some-where Kinsella has never been. Some people seemed to recognise him, he could tell by their expressions, expressions followed swiftly by equally transparent looks of: *'no, not here, not Formula One.'* There was a café on the high street: place mats, homely smells and pictures of prize-winning cattle. He had found it before, the *Newbridge Cafe* – all the stuff he shouldn't eat, all the more reason to eat it when he was here – besides, the Sultan trainer was a great one for allowing a treat, once a month. The service was wonderfully slow, reassuringly polite. On a table next door some youngsters in green-dyed dreadlocks gave them a wide berth – even in their scruffiest country gear Teresa and Kinsella just shouted wealth, glamour – enemies then, so be it. He hardly cared, this was his place he thought, as much as anyone's. The kids talked about Wittgenstein with the sort of seriousness Kinsella would have reserved for gear ratios. On another table a farmer – had to be – in a worn-out cardigan and a faded red-checked shirt that matched his wind-etched complexion, treated a young child to pop and cakes. They didn't say much, just the odd phrase in Welsh, accompanied with a smile. A bit like Kinsella and Teresa really, he thought. He had ordered for her, a delicacy, he'd lied – no way out for her then, these girls and their fancy diets. His mother would have loved it, feeding her up, put some fat on those bones. Sausage, egg and chips – Christ, you couldn't match this in Monte Carlo, and certainly not in whatever fancy place Mossup had had in store for them. Bloody Mossup…

After lunch – which Teresa had made a fair stab at – they tried to walk off the excess, hand in hand again. They walked through wide open wrought iron gates and into the college grounds. Kinsella would always stroll here, through the peaceful green grounds where even the birds seemed to walk, and then into the old stone quadrangle to dawdle and think of things he couldn't – shouldn't – think elsewhere. It was a thing of his, the only time he let himself play 'what if.' No place for it at the track see, no place for it in Melbourne, after the spinning wheel of the Bianchi had almost rubbed him off the backdrop of existence. But here, away from it, he could wander slowly, picture himself in another life for a few precious moments. And if he didn't like this other life, so – he could feel good about himself, feel good about Eoghan 'Egg' Kinsella, Formula One driver.

In the centre of the quad stood a circular fountain, and four paths lead off to doorways. It would, he realised then, mimic a Celtic cross in plan elevation, with a background of green, fringed brown by the shortcuts of lazy students. The paths ended after some five metres at the rooms for students, or at departmental offices. The sun was high now, high and warm, angling into the quadrangle, splashing the pathways white, slapping a shimmer on the still water around the dormant fountain. There was a low concrete wall surrounding the fountain. Teresa sat on it, her knees angled up and inwards.

"It is beautiful here… so quiet."

He sat beside her:

"You should come here during term time... then it's not so quiet."

They sat silent for a while longer, so silent that a small bird landed close by, very close, pecking at a crumb of something on the pavement, oblivious to them.

"Was this your school?" she finally asked.

"Nearly."

"Why nearly?"

"Oh, you know...racing sort of took over."

"Like Chico then..."

There was some sadness there, he thought, and again the guilt was something solid within him, as solid as the lump of sausage, egg and chips that sat in his stomach.

There was another long pause as he elected to say nothing and she dipped her head in thought, twisting a strand of hair around her finger. He loved it when she did that. And then she looked up at him again and said:

"Earlier, in the car?"

"Yes?"

"Were you," she coughed, then smiled, "when I touched you, were you... you know... aroused?"

He laughed: "Well, of course my dear – you have that way with me as well you know"

"No, I mean before – when you drove?"

He feigned shock and laughed again: "Well I love the old Jag as you know – but not that much."

"No, it's silly I know – but I wondered, that's all. You don't mind do you, it's something someone told me... once."

"Let me guess – something about racing drivers getting a stiffy when they drove quickly was it?"

"Stiffy?"

"You know what I mean," he smiled at her, a smile that said, alright, how about here – here and now?

She smiled back, perhaps reading his mind, then said:

"It is silly isn't it?

He nodded. Yes, it was all pretty silly, but there were always the stories, something about racing cars and sex, difficult to separate them – if he had lived that other life perhaps he might have written a paper on it. He pictured himself in a tatty tank-top, bent over a book in a musty library, then shuddered at the thought. Teresa was still speaking.

"With Chico I sometimes believed it, the racing, the car – it was everything to him..."

There had been one story, he remembered, a story that did the rounds in the 80s, when he was in Formula Ford. A Grand Prix ace of the time shooting his load every time he did a hot lap – but he had never believed it, it was a different thrill to that, surely?

"... And because he had no time for me..."

She let the thought hang there, obvious that he should finish it, clear up the girl's confusion.

"I'm not sure about that – but you can never be sure with Chico can you?" He had meant it as a joke but she didn't smile.

"The thing is," he continued, "people have been trying to figure out why people do this racing thing since the invention of the wheel. I mean, it's quite a mystery isn't it: why a man will risk his life and spend every penny he has – and every penny he doesn't have – driving around in circles, it's no wonder they bring sex into it.

"The trick cyclists used to love it, they'd say we were all screwed up little boys who confused the tracks with our mother's bits and the car with our father's bit – they even said the spraying of the bubbly on the rostrum represented ejaculation... Ridiculous." He snorted.

"Other people say it's some kind of war substitute, you know, the danger, the competition... And perhaps there's something in that I suppose..."

"Is the danger important," she interrupted, "surely you all try to make it safer?"

"Yes, I suppose we do... every time someone lands in God's great gravel trap these days there's a hell of a stink. Which I suppose is natural enough, I mean there's no way we would be able to carry on like we did in the sixties, killing two a season – no, we'd all be out of a job then...

"But there has to be something there, some element of danger, otherwise the limit means nothing – and Christ, what's the limit if everybody could go there? Free trips to the moon? No thanks..."

"So you like the danger then?"

"Just a little... maybe."

"You are crazy... you are all crazy."

"Yeah, maybe... But then we only do what everybody else does – life and death and glory, only it's distilled into two hours on a Sunday afternoon. It's a theatre in a way, the plot is simple, beat the other guy – and don't get yourself killed."

"And you and Chico are the stars?"

"No, just me." He smiled at that, then continued:

"That's the beauty of it all you see, for your man on the sofa. He gets life at its barest, its simplest, at a touch of a button – forget about the council tax demand for an hour or two and just sit back and watch some idiot trying to dash himself against a steel barrier."

"And they like the crashes – everyone likes the crashes..." she put in, as if she was suddenly with him.

"Yes, everyone likes the crashes, and it's easier to like the crashes now. At one time to crash might mean death. Now there's every chance you will live, death has been pushed along a bit, further down the chain if you like, so we get more crashes, comfortable crashes, and the real limit is hidden somewhere in the biggest of shunts, the freakiest of shunts."

She thought for a moment, then asked:

"And this is why you do it, this drama, for others?"

"No – of course not, I do it for me."

"Why?"

"Christ, Teresa, you're like a little kid with your questions you know..."

He had said it as a joke, and she smiled with him, then:

"Why?"

A dog, a young Border collie, was sniffing about in the far corner of the quadrangle, Kinsella watched it for a while, thinking about the question, thinking about the words. That was the problem with the place, made you want to think about things you shouldn't think about, things that can't help.

"Why?"

"Why? Many things I suppose. First, perhaps it is something in me, a need to be in control of myself and in control of something more – the car. I suppose it gives me a feeling of power... Yes, there is that, definitely – but then it's no secret that the F1 paddock is stuffed to the wire with egotists is it?" He laughed, but it was an awkward laugh, almost a shy laugh, something he recognised – with some surprise – himself.

"And?" she said, eyes on the dog, which had now lifted its leg in a steaming, wet salute to the old stone.

"Why should there be an and?"

She shrugged, and he laughed again, shaking his head:

"Okay – and it's because this is what I am good at – is that enough?"

"But you are good at other things..." Now they were both smiling.

"Yes... But I need to be the best at something."

"Driving a racing car?"

He nodded.

"But Chico's the best at driving a racing car... they all say that."

146

She had said it so matter-of-factly, without a hint of malice, no doubt about that – it wasn't in her he was sure. That's what made it worse, that's what hurt. Okay, it was what they all said, everyone: journalists, team bosses, other drivers even. It had never worried him, in his heart he always believed he was the more complete driver, the stronger driver, he was the one who would win the game. And as far as he was concerned that meant he was the best.

But this, coming from her, coming from the girl he had taken into his life for all the wrong reasons but who he wanted in his life for all the right reasons – coming from her, it hurt. It wasn't her fault of course. It had been stated as fact, and to most it was fact. But now, for an instant at least, Kinsella felt that he knew what it was to be betrayed – and with that he was ghosted by guilt once more.

He smiled at her, then took her hand, standing up and pulling her up off the low wall. They walked out of the quad. They stopped for a while to look at a hill, an impossibly green hill topped with a wood, so green and distant that the cap of trees looked like a clump of broccoli. He squeezed her hand tight. It felt so right, her being there. No doubt about it, and he wanted it to last forever. But next week it was Monza.

Chapter Seventeen

The cow. After all he had done for her, all he had bought for her –and now this. The bloody cow. Out for a Sunday lunch in the country with her sister Helen and boyfriend, and his friend Steve – the one with the job in the city and the Gti. The twat. Yes, alright, she'd been right. He didn't own her. But after all he had done for her, all he had bought for her...

What was wrong with her. He had even taken her to Barbados for a fortnight, eating into the Sultan money. But that was the thing with Sarah, always wanted more – and he had heard her talk with Helen on the phone, wearing the new yellow dress, she had said, the one from Harvey Nicks, the one he had bought. Didn't she know what he had gone through to buy her those things, all that trouble with Zola, with the Scot?

So she wanted more. Okay, even if it meant paying Zola another visit, he would give her more, keep her sweet, show her which side her bread is buttered. It was just a matter of showing Zola it was working, wasn't it? Stubbs had done his bit after all, feeding Fraser with the fictions that the Sultan engineer had invented – problem was that he had no idea if Fraser had taken them onboard. And how could he be sure? He could get nowhere near Fraser now, he had other things on his mind, the whole traction control episode history to everyone now it seemed. He had tried to ring him, but the man would never come to the phone – far too busy, a receptionist would say. So he would pass the 'secrets' on the e-mail, hardly ideal, but at least he could assume that they got there. He had even asked Fraser for more money, on the e-mail again – why not, would he believe he did it for free? But the man had refused point blank, by e-mail again, needed more proof, how about a drawing, another disk? But where could he get a drawing of nothing, of a figment of an engineer's imagination? At least

Zola didn't seem to mind, it would tie up someone at DBM he had said, tie up someone looking at the possibilities, the possibilities of the things they could dream up.

Of course, if he could prove that DBM were interested, that the decoy had distracted them, then he might be able to tap Zola for a couple more grand, or at least it was worth a try, for Sarah's sake. So he had been up to the usual, hanging about in the pubs, the DBM pubs this time. That's why he had been on the scene when it happened, the incident the papers were talking about – something to keep the story alight between races, kindling he supposed.

He had been sat by the bar as usual, just within earshot of a small knot of DBM men, all fresh from the factory, some in the familiar battleship grey polo shirts with the blue piping. He was wired, a little tape recorder weighing down his pocket, the microphone just peeping over the edge of the lapel of his jacket. But that had been a faint hope, too many closer sounds to interfere: the rustle of crisp packets, the clink of pint glasses and the talk of the barman. Besides, as far as he could tell they were not talking about racing anyway, it seemed one of them had girlfriend trouble and the others were offering advice.

But then the Sultan men came in, about four of them, already pissed. It had been nothing really, just a couple of punches. But the landlord had been on the phone to the police straight away. Stubbs had seen it start, the Sultan men shouting over, shouting that Chico had lost it, shouting that Kinsella had him rattled. Then the DBM men shouting back, calling the Sultan men cheats – he felt a part of that – all that fuss with the traction control. And of course there was the thing with Solé's Sultan coming in at Spa just as Chico was going out – losing the race for Chico they said… Coincidence? 'Bollocks,' they said.

They were all carted away and the local papers had a field day. A stringer for *The Brit* picked up on the story and once again F1 was on the wrong page: back to front. All that stuff about Kinsella and Chico's wife, all that stuff about Sultan cheating, all that stuff about Chico losing it…

Chico losing it? Not how they saw it in the Republic. One man, a student – citizen of the Republic studying in Paris – had made his feelings clear. A Sultan promotion, a display car parked up in the Gare du Nord, the girls handing out the freebies, some PR people keeping an eye on things – but they missed the student. Stepping over the rope barrier, pulling the can of green spray paint from the inside pocket of his jacket, spraying 'cheat' all over the car. In English, French and Spanish. He had tried to get out of it by saying it was a political act, but the police were having none of that – yet, remarkably, his embassy backed him all the way. Stubbs could not help but wonder what awaited the Formula One circus when it arrived in the Republic for the last round of the championship in just a month's time.

But by then Chico should have sewn it up. He could even sew it up today. Some honest part of Stubbs hoped so – he had little time for that arrogant shit Kinsella, even if they did work for the same team, even if the championship had to be kept alive if there was to be any chance of him making more money out of it. He glanced at his watch, half hour until the start. Out of the office and down the hall to the living room – the room where he lived. The sofa bed was still unfolded and a foil carton of half-eaten curry was congealing on top of the television. Then the kitchen area: a complete disaster, he could only hope that Sarah would see to it when she came on Tuesday. The fridge was bare – well, not bare: there was some more three-quarter eaten cartons of curry, from last week, there was some milk, also from last week, and an egg broken into a tea-cup. But no beer. Pub then. For the race. *Sam's* had a big screen, he could be there for the off if he put his skates on, maybe even treat himself to a spot of lunch too.

Sunday pubs come in two varieties Stubbs thought: those for your lunchers and those for your hair-of-the-doggers. *Sam's* was firmly in the latter category. Just a couple of knots of friends – youngsters – bent over pints, or Cokes, talking about the night before – probably here, a nocturnal sort of place that turned into a disco after ten. Stubbs sat on a tall stool and ordered a pint. The menu was on a blackboard behind the bar: burgers, pizza, chips. He ordered burger and chips, then asked the barmaid to find the right channel for him.

Kinsella's head was bigger than big on the big screen, which seemed to accentuate the colour of his eyes so that they sparkled electric. A microphone was thrust in front of his face. Stubbs asked the barmaid to turn the volume up but by the time she had the interview was over. There were some graphics now, superimposed on a wide shot of the busy starting grid. It was a representation of the grid itself, a little cartoon DBM, Sultan and Ferrari – in that order. The locals, the Italian Ferrari nuts – the tifosi – would not be happy: their man beaten off the front row by Chico and Kinsella. But then they would be the only ones who cared at this stage of the season. Everyone else ached for battle to commence.

By the time the cars had lined up for the lights Stubbs had demolished his burger and chips in short order and had washed it down with his first pint. The next was in front of him, untouched for now as he concentrated on the start – always a problem at Monza, he had read, the cars funnelling into a tight double chicane at the end of the start-finish straight. Red lights – *off* ... Kinsella had a flyer while Chico was bogged down with too much wheel-spin, the first of the Ferraris slipping by on the run down to the chicane. Bobby Drake was alongside too, in the second DBM, but paid due deference to his team mate into the turn. Further back a Spando and a Sauber tangled, each spinning in formation and coming to rest in the gravel trap, shrouded in a heavy pall of white dust.

At the end of the first lap Kinsella's lead was up to two seconds while Chico was stuck behind the Ferrari, dodging in and out of the red car's slipstream, looking for a way past. He found it on the approach to the chicane at the start of the second lap, a lovely little move, just a slight puff of smoke from the left front as he gave the Ferrari pilot a lesson in the art of out-braking. Stubbs gave a nod of approval, it was a move of clear majesty.

Within two laps Chico's DBM was right on the tail of the Sultan as they headed down the long start-finish straight once more, the silver nose of the DBM probing left and right, like the jinking head of a boxer looking for a way past his opponent's defences. He tried again at the chicane, but it was no good, the Sultan and the DBM evenly matched, and Kinsella alive to all possibilities, and then it was another lap for the orange, silver and blue train.

So it went on, lap after lap of high speed stalemate. Every now and then Chico would drop back a little to let the air get to his car, help cool it, but otherwise they circulated as one. And – the commentator told him – at this stage it seemed likely that they would both be one-stopping, so there was every chance that the race would be decided in the pits. As the pattern of the race had settled Stubbs had found himself reaching for the pint glass more often. And so it was that he was about due for his own pit-stop soon too. He held on for as long as he could, hoping that they would go into the pits and he wouldn't have to miss anything, but it was no use, there was no fighting Mother Nature when she was in this mood, and so he dashed off to the toilets.

The pleasure of the relief almost made the pain of holding it in worthwhile, but it was not a pleasure to savour in his rush to get back to the TV – a premature zip-up that resulted in a damp, warm patch the wrong side of his jeans. Then, on hurrying through to the lounge bar once more, what was this on the TV screen? Men in red shirts, men in blue shirts, a white ball – someone sitting on his stool....

He couldn't really argue, there were more of them, Arsenal fans – he hoped that they lost. And luckily there was another screen, an ordinary tele' tucked away in the far corner of the bar, over the pool tables where the dartboard used to live. He took his fresh pint there, making a point of cheering an Everton goal as he left.

He had lost eight laps: eight laps pissing about with pissing and being pissed off. But Kinsella was still in the lead, Chico still right behind him. It was a lap or so before the commentator confirmed that they had both stopped, the Sultan crew quicker on Kinsella's car by a fraction of a second – but both with fuel to last until the end, the pundit added, judging by the lengths of their stops. So it was a race to the flag: a race to the flag between the only two drivers in with a shout of the championship. The question was, would Chico risk it, after what had happened at Spa? Surely he would be better off with the six points, as the pundit – a former F1 driver himself – pointed out, deflating the excitement of the commentator for a moment. But it's a grudge match, Stubbs knew that, everyone knew that – for Christ's sake doesn't he read the papers? And so it was.

Into that same chicane, always there, that's where the DBM seems to have something, something on the brakes into the left-right flick. And this time it's on – the deepest of swigs from his pint – Chico has the momentum from the long 180 degree curve before the pits, he's alongside on the run down to the chicane... Kinsella, moving right, moving into him at close to 200 mph, do they touch? Chico, two wheels almost on the grass, but he holds it steady, and in the blink of a camera change Kinsella is smoking his front tyres, far too fast into the first part of the chicane... wide. Chico slips behind the Sultan then up the inside.

It's a brilliant move, even the tifosi are cheering, and Kinsella has lost time sorting out his moment and is now some three seconds behind. Chico has it in the bag, has the championship in the bag to all intents and purposes, and Stubbs could not help but marvel as the man from the Republic began to stamp his authority on the race. And now Stubbs really watched.

When he had first watched Formula One, those long gone sleepy Sunday afternoons, it had meant little to him, the driving side of it. Like many, he supposed, he secretly believed that – given a little practice, given the breaks – he could do it himself. After all, it was just a matter of pointing the thing in the right direction and hanging on wasn't it? And he'd been as hot as hell on the arcade games, and that time when they went indoor karting. But now, with the education of being involved, of really seeing, he understood what it was all about, he understood the sheer genius of what he saw before him. It was more than getting the lines right, they all did that, give or take an inch or two there seemed little difference in any car's route around the circuit. Okay, some turned in a little earlier, he now noticed, some turned in a little later, but mostly on or around that same optimum line of least resistance. All tiptoed the line, flirted with it, some dramatically, kicking out the tail on the entry, some smoothly – almost effortlessly to the TV viewer.

Then there was Chico, right on the edge, all the time. Yet to watch the car from the outside it all looked so smooth, so precise, robotic almost... But it was with the onboard camera shots that Stubbs tasted awe. It had taken him a while to figure it, playing a video tape of the French race, stopping, rewinding, playing... Chico's arms were everywhere in the cockpit, violent stabs of opposite lock, swift flicks of the wrists to pitch the DBM into a corner, par for the course with every driver – yes, of course – but somehow different with Chico. Different in that he seemed to be applying the steering correction before the slide, driving purely on anticipation, driving as if one with the car... never correction, always anticipation. Until, that is, something seemed to get in the way, like at Monaco, like at Spa – but then nobody's quite perfect...

Stubbs dug deep into the front pocket of his jeans, marshalling together some change, enough for another pint. The implications of a Chico win were beginning to sink in. Yes, the guy deserved it, the best of course. But where did it leave Stubbs – after all, would Zola be so keen on using him now, just when the season was dead and buried? He would have to hope so – he had promised the bitch so much more...

The guys at the bar were on good form. Arsenal had stolen two back and were camped in the Everton half – how moods can switch across an hour watching sport. He had to wait a little longer for his pint as the Arsenal fans had already began to celebrate in some style and by the time he was back at the little tele' in the corner of the pool room moods had switched at Monza too. They were showing the replay. A shame for poor Chico, the DBM converted into a high speed cloud factory on the run down to the final corner, with just two laps to go. Blown engine. Still, at least there was everything to play for. Everything for Kinsella to play for, everything for Sultan to play for, and yes, everything for Stubbs to play for.

Kinsella took the flag, and a long shot from a helicopter showed the tifosi aficionados pouring out of the parkland circuit: a bad day for Ferrari, neither finishing, and a bad day for racing in a way, he supposed – the rightful victor robbed by the worst of bad luck. Stubbs tried to think of a way he could use it to his advantage. After all, who is to say that the DBM engine technicians had not been distracted, angling for one of his red herrings? But no, Zola wouldn't buy that. He needed something solid, he needed to make sure that Fraser got the message, saw the urgency of what he was saying, sell him the herring – hook, line and sinker – and then get off to Zola with cap in hand. And who could tell, he might even be able to pick up some DBM secrets too, something to sell to Zola, that would keep him sweet... Keep the Scot friendly, keep Sarah happy.

He took a deep draught of the lager. It would take a heap of cash to get to Japan – but speculation, accumulation and all that crap eh Stubbs? The only way.

Chapter Eighteen

The bag with the laptop computer missed the chair and clattered into the bedside table. The tiny Japanese hotel cleaner was frozen like a rabbit caught in the headlamps, transfixed by Fraser's rage, complete shock and fear, big-eyed, a stack of white towels hugged tight to the flat plane of her chest.

"Out – get out!"

She ran to the door, turning sideways on to brush past Chico as she did so, slamming the door behind her.

Now Fraser turned to Chico, and Chico felt it there. Not fear, no – when you've spent the weekend braving *130R* flat... well, then rage is a small thing – even Fraser's rage. No, it was shame, shame because he had let him down.

Only Fraser could speak to him like this, shout at him like this, make him feel quite like this. Chico started to peel off his race suit, opening the adjoining door to his room and walking through.

"For Christ's sake Chico, you threw it away – what's wrong with you man, it was a kid's mistake?"

Yes, he was right of course. First lap, trying to break them as usual, just a little too fast at the hairpin –straight-on, into the barriers, just a tap really, but the steering arm was bent...

"When are you going to get that tosser out of your head man?"

Yes, he had looked back, taken a glance in his mirrors, just to see if he had broken him in the first part of the lap, just to see if he had broken away from Kinsella.

"You know what you've done – do you?"

He had sat there, on the wall for a while, watching the race unfold. Then he had walked back to the pits. Fraser hadn't spoken to him then, and Kinsella was back in third, Bobby leading.

"You've thrown it away, thrown away the lead in the championship..."

Yes, both of them on the way back to the hotel, crammed into the back of a people-carrier, saying nothing while the driver translated, gave them the news that came over the radio. Embarrassed as he told them: Bobby Drake out, engine blown, Solé letting Kinsella through to win, team orders.

"Bloody hell Chico, what's wrong with you man?"

Fraser had followed him into his room, where he now stood naked, rubbing the sweat from his body with a little white towel he had taken off the bed.

"Talk to me..." Fraser kicked at one of Chico's discarded driving boots, sending it flying across the room. "Talk to me..."

Chico pulled the towel around his waist and sat on the edge of the bed. He could hardly look Fraser in the face, but when he did he saw the tears that were there, and he felt the shame again. Yes, he had let him down.

"I'm sorry," he said.

"Sorry!"

"Yes... sorry." He looked into Fraser's eyes once more, which met his own. He watched as the Englishman's anger seemed to melt away, watched as the fight slipped from his shoulders, as he let out a big, big sigh, slouched, and sat down on the edge of the bed beside him.

"What now?" Fraser asked, suddenly sounding so very tired.

"We will win next time, we will win at the Chicodrome."

"Do you believe that Chico, I mean... do you really believe it?"

He shrugged, but didn't answer. Yes, he did believe it, somehow the whole season was beginning to make sense. It had all led up to this, the finale in the Chicodrome – it all made sense that way... Then finally he answered:

"Yes," he said, "I am positive." And, strangely enough he was.

"What, the perfect lap, the perfect track, the perfect race?" Fraser seemed to snort a little laugh.

"Why not?"

Fraser looked pained for a moment, as if he weighed up the import of what he was about to say.

"Look Chico, you're not on form, surely even you can see that, we have to do something about it..."

"You are not helping my confidence, friend." He smiled as he said it.

Fraser smiled back, apologised: "Perhaps not, I'm sorry – there's still time I guess..."

"I promise you Gordi', all will be well at home. I am convinced."

Fraser stood up and went to the mini-bar. He took out a miniature bottle of whisky and dropped its contents into the bottom of a tumbler. He grimaced as he sipped at it, it was the first time that Chico had seen him drink since that time here in Japan two years ago, when he had wrapped up the championship.

"I hope you are right."

"I am." He stared at Fraser for a while, he had been meaning to tell him for some time now, but always the focus had been on the now, on the race at hand. But here it was, here was the time – there was little doubt of that.

"I have to win it you see... It's my last chance to get what I want from racing."

"There's always next year..."

Chico said nothing, just sat there, looking at his engineer, looking for that moment when the penny dropped, looking for the change in his face, the change that signalled the recognition that – from the Republic on – all would be different.

"You mean it's over?" Fraser looked bewildered.

"Yes."

"But why?" He half sat, half collapsed, down beside Chico again.

Chico took a deep breath and started to explain, started to explain why he had finally decided to retire.

"My heart isn't in it these days. To win you have to be like Kinsella, I see that now, and it is not for me. Then there are other things, always they want a part of me, always we must hide – I'm tired of it Gordi."

"What will you do?" He sounded shell-shocked.

"I'm not sure. Now that I am tied on points with Kinsella and the title is going down to the wire we should have many people at the Chicodrome, it will help replace the money I have lost building the track. And there are other business interests in the Republic, as you know... I will be busy enough, it's not a problem – and there is still the chance that I will finish as champion, finish with that perfect lap at the perfect track. Now that would be something would it not Gordi?"

"Yes – of course." The Englishman drained the dregs of the scotch, swallowing hard and looking up at Chico. There were still pools of dampness in his eyes, tiredness etched deep into his face: again Chico could only wonder at how hard he worked for him, so that he could win. Then Fraser asked the question, the question that Chico had waited for, hoped for:

"And what about me?"

Chico stood up, the towel falling from about his waist. He stared down at Fraser, then asked him the question, the question he had wanted to ask for so long:

"Will you come with me, leave DBM, help me with the Chicodrome, with everything – be there for me?"

Fraser seemed to think on it for a moment or two, then he stood, his face but an inch or two from Chico's.

"Of course."

The Englishman leaned forward and kissed him, a little kiss at first, then his tongue found Chico's, and his hand reached down to where Chico was awakening to the feel of the engineer, awakening to the familiar...

The door through to Fraser's room was still open, so that the light that shone through lay in a rhombus across the darkened floor. Chico had meant to switch off the light, Fraser's light – it might have helped him sleep. But the bed was comfortable, and the room a little cold. So he just lay there, beside Fraser, listening to the Englishman's easy breathing as he slept the sleep of the wholly exhausted.

He could not sleep himself, and not only because of the light. No, too many other things at play in his head – how he wished for the days when there was just him, him and the lap to drive, that's all. Simple when you're young. But not now... and he was so very tired. Yet now, every time he closed his eyes, there was Kinsella, or the back of the Sultan, or Teresa – poor Teresa, who could blame the girl?

She had been given a hard time at home, by the press. It was as if they wanted to blame her for it all, for his mistakes. He had never understood that, never understood how the papers had treated him: as if he was above the faults of other men, like a god. At one time he had almost believed it himself, when he was younger. And then he had feared it too, feared that they might find out who he really was – was this the way they saw their heroes in the Republic – as one with another man? They could not live with it there, he knew that – progress, if that's the word, is for Europe. And so he had used her, there was no hiding from it. In the same way that the PR man had used her. He had used her to show them that all was well, all was correct – a thing of panic it had been, marrying her, but unforgivable all the same. A rumour, bouncing back, why always the adjoining rooms? And my God they were getting hard to find. So, he took her, and there had been one or two nights when he had managed his duty, when she had wept with pleasure and he had wept in shame... Just an adornment, that's all, the missing piece of the puzzle for those who wanted everything of him... Wanted him to live their dreams. What

158

right have they? But life throws things at you, shows you are mortal – things like Kinsella, the man who had almost beaten him.

Yet they didn't believe that did they? No, the papers in the Republic, the people in the Republic, they didn't believe he was beaten – and he could only hope that he could take strength from them when the time came, when the time came for the race of his life at the Chicodrome.

There had been trouble there, he had been told, almost a riot in the streets of the capital after Kinsella had moved over on him at Monza. The mob had thrown things at the British Embassy. The Government had ordered him to go on TV, calm them – but for this coming race they would take more calming. They expected so much of him; and that's the problem with being a god. You soon run out of excuses.

There was more to keep him awake too. Even now, at this late stage, the race was threatened. The government had bled him dry, nothing had been passed for construction without massive bribes to ease it along. And now there were but two weeks to go and the money was running out – couldn't they see that the country needed the victory, couldn't they see that he was all that the people had?

There was a knock at the door, Fraser's door in the adjoining room. Chico ignored it. Whoever it was knocked again, insistent this time, and he felt Fraser stir beside him.

"What's that... who is it...?" His tongue was thick with sleep, and he waved his hand in the air, probing for the light switch above the headboard.

"It's the door – leave it, they will go away."

"My door?" He found the switch and the room was suddenly flooded with bright light, Chico covered his eyes.

"Yes."

"Good, that'll be my laundry." Fraser looked at his watch for confirmation and then slipped out of the side of the bed, pulling the towel that Chico had discarded about his nakedness.

"The door... please." Chico pleaded as the Englishman left the room. But Fraser hadn't heard him, or had just not pulled the door hard enough in his rush to get to the other door before the caller ran out of patience. Chico reached up to the light switch above the headboard and switched it off, so that the only light in the room came from the adjoining room once more, where Fraser, at the door, was framed precisely. Chico peeped over the edge of the sheet and watched as Fraser tightened the towel about his waist before opening the door. He hadn't locked it, hadn't thought to in the tumble into

bed, and it was just a matter of pulling it towards him. Even in profile the shock, then the anger, was clear. No laundry this, no welcome
visitor this...

"You – what do you want... what are you doing here?"

"I have something for you, it's hot, believe me..."

"Just get lost... I've no time for all this. If you want to speak to me
arrange a meeting through my secretary, I've told you before." He
went to shut the door on the visitor, but was stopped by a foot, and
then a shoulder, and then the man – a rather flabby man – pushing
himself in through the door.

"Look, come on, this is good stuff, give us a chance...You wouldn't
believe what those Sultan boys have got planned for the
Chicodrome..."

Fraser just stared at the man in disbelief, in 'how dare he'. And
then he grabbed him by the shoulders and pushed him back towards
the door.

"Please..." begged the man, now roughly massaging an ugly little
scar under his nose "...just five minutes please..."

"No, fuck off out of here – now!"

He had him half out of the door and the fatter man was already
breathless – people underestimated Fraser's sheer physical power at
their peril.

"Just a minute of your time, that's all I ask..."

"Out."

"Thirty seconds, for Christ's sake, I'm trying to help..."

"Through my secretary I said – I'm busy..."

Fraser had managed to squeeze most of the fat man out of the
door, so that only his head was now in the room, the face squashed
comically scarlet between door and frame. Then the towel slipped
from Fraser's waist and Chico gave out a little giggle, a little giggle at
the sight of that little white bum, pressed sideways against the door,
and that big red face in line with it, squashed up on the other side of
the door.

The flabby man seemed to hear the laugh, or at least his eyes were
drawn towards Chico's room for an instant. Chico ducked beneath the
sheet – although, he thought, there would have been little chance of
him catching sight of him, not in the depths of the room. Then he
heard the door slam and Fraser shouting through it:

"You know the drill, through my secretary, now clear off!"

He locked the door and came back through to Chico's room.

"Who was he?" Chico asked, "an old boyfriend?"

They both laughed, and Fraser slipped in beside him again.

"No... Believe it or not he's a spy, he's the one who got the traction control stuff off Sultan for us – hardly James Bond though is he?"

"No. But shouldn't you listen to him, he may have something?"

"I doubt it, and if he has there's little we can do about it now. Besides, he's been trying to peddle all sorts of rubbish lately, there's no way we can tell what it's all about – I think he's just got a bit greedy, he made good money on the first deal you know..."

"But still..."

"But still nothing... Tonight's for you... No one else. I will see the fat slob as soon as we get back to England."

Chapter Nineteen

Passport control had been bad enough. As soon as they had clapped eyes on that little red book Stubbs could see that he was in for trouble. But that was nothing on this, on the customs men, scattering his belongings with glee, working their way through the suitcase, laughing at his underwear. There would be little laughter when they came to his hand luggage though, all that he could hope for was that they would be as flexible as the passport control cops – or as cheap.

He had been warned, everybody had been warned – a trip to the Republic at this time would be no picnic. All that anger and frustration, all that poverty and hate, focussed on one thing – the race for the championship – and the government just glad to have the pressure taken off them. But pressure there still was... and when there's this much of the stuff something is sure to blow. For a week or so the race was in doubt, and some teams threatened to boycott it – including the team with the most to lose by missing the final round, Sultan. But then there had been guarantees from that same government, guarantees of safe passage, tightened security at hotels and track – plus the guarantee of the most eagerly anticipated TV show of the decade, and not one of the sponsors would want to miss out on that.

How had the Foreign and Commonwealth Office put it in their advice to travellers? 'Essential business only.' But Christ was this essential for Stubbs... One of the customs men, an AK47 slung around him, magazine detached, snatched Stubbs's hold-all from him, slinging it onto the counter and unzipping it. Stubbs found himself rubbing at that little scar again, Sarah hated it when he did that – and he always seemed to do it when he was with her these days. She had said nothing when he had told her, told her that he was coming here, to the place Kinsella had made dangerous for the British, tampering with their god, the fool. She should have said something...

Surely something...

The customs man pulled out the plastic carrier bag, its handles stretched taut and transparent by the weight of the huge bottle of cognac he had picked up at duty free. He grinned at Stubbs, shook his head in mock reproach, then rattled off some excited Spanish in the direction of his colleague, placing the bottle under the counter. The large plate glass windows behind Stubbs shook to the take-off of a jet. He turned to look out, turned to hide the panic that he felt was slowly filling his face. The big jet was lifting its nose into the early morning sky, heading for home – for a moment he wished he was on it. On the tarmac a group of soldiers in olive drab, some wearing red neckerchiefs, others with forage caps, played a spirited game of football. They folded themselves in laughter as the ball was kicked high and far, into the line of camouflaged fighter planes, bouncing off a jungle-coloured wing. Further along the field a freighter was disgorging its cargo from a nose hinged open: big silver boxes with a logo on them: *DBM*, all 22 tonnes of the stuff that he knew they took to the flyaway races, 22 tonnes in 110 lightweight boxes. While half hidden behind the freighter sat one of the silver and blue cars on a pallet: nose-less, tail-less, and shrink-wrapped, but still somehow beautiful. In stark contrast, a squat armoured personnel carrier trundled past, its gun-bristled cupola spinning slowly through 180 degrees, then resting on the DBM for an instant, as if in salute, one vehicle of power to another.

He had spoken in Spanish, the customs man. But there was no doubting the question was there? Yes, Mr Stubbs what is this for: the tiny little video camera, gleaming in the guard's sweaty palm, the listening devices, clustered like robot insects in the old tobacco tin, and the long, long lens that made his camera elephantine. He reached for his wallet – sometimes you have to cut the crap, get to the point: the passport people had cost him $100 – this would be more.

"I am a journalist," he said, "here for the race." He thumbed through the fan of fifty-dollar bills that fringed his open wallet, watching as the customs man did some quick sums in his head. It was as the guidebook had put it: nothing is impossible in the Republic, as long as you have enough dollars to oil the wheels: $500 US. Big bucks, but nothing on what he could make from Zola when he blew this little pile of porn. And if Zola didn't want it, well – there was always *The Brit*.

When the taxi driver realised that Stubbs was British he increased the fare by 100 per cent, but Stubbs was not about to make a fuss, not in the middle of Avenue Colonel Watson, Watsonville. Not in the festering heart of the sunny old – make that sweaty old – Republic. It was about now that Stubbs realised why Chico did not keep a home in the capital – Lord knows he had one just about everywhere else. The thing is, and not to put too fine a point on it, the place sucks. Picture it, no, not yet – smells first... Shit, that was the main one, all pervading, the smell that every other odour had to compete with to get itself noticed in the olfactory jungle. Those smaller smells of meat – pork, chicken, could be anything – roasting in the streets, and the pungent bursts of liberally applied perfume as women rushed past. And, of course, the fumes from the cars. Then, what can you expect? Cram five million Latins into a city and give a third of them a motor, every day's a Grand Prix, every day sees the sky grow heavy with the lead, every day sees the smog wrap itself around the crumbling high rises, trapping in the heavy, wet heat, trapping in the noise. And that noise: if shit was the canvas that all other smells were painted on, car horns were the same for noise – For God's sake, it was almost a constant blare, a break was something to be marvelled at, and he savoured them – one for as long as three seconds.

Stubbs had just stood there at first, in a daze, trying not to be crushed by the mass of molten humanity rushing off to work, trying to find his bearings by rotating the guide book through 180, trying to match the lie of page street with the real street. The kerbside was crumbling into the thoroughfare, and every now and then an impossibly stacked flat bed truck which had somehow squeezed itself into the river of Fiats would rush by, pulverising the little pieces of stone into a fine dust. Everyone, it seemed, was in a rush. Indeed, this was the first intuition Stubbs entertained in the Republic: rush hour or not, this was not a street to linger on.

Finding the hotel – a concrete block that clashed against the grimed colonial charm of some of the other buildings in the street – was surprisingly easy, dollars again. Then there were more dollars, for the information he needed – the whereabouts of Chico's room. That last had been expensive, and he had had to tread carefully, especially with that accent. But then 500 smoothed the way, and yes, Fraser's room adjoined. It was just a hundred or so for a room two floors up from Chico's – Stubbs tipped the bell-boy – who waited for more – so he tipped him again. The windows opened up onto Avenue Colonel Watson, but the smog was thick, trapping the heat in the street – and, despite the hotel's stars, the air-conditioning did not work. Water off too – trouble up town, they said at reception. Stubbs collapsed onto the big soft bed. Using the remote he switched on the TV. There was a western, Clint Eastwood dubbed Spanish, and he fell asleep to the sound of horses galloping...

Not the nicest music, not the nicest way to wake. He recognised the martial strains, the national anthem – always played when Chico made the top step of the podium. It was over-playing some footage of the President of the Republic inspecting a formation of soldiers. Then there was a montage: jet fighters streaking across the sky, tanks on manoeuvre, a hydro-electric dam, some factory workers, school-children welcoming the President, then Chico, spraying the champagne at Melbourne earlier in the year. It was dark outside now, and Stubbs's tired eyes were struggling to readjust to his surroundings. On the TV the music stopped but the flag of the Republic still fluttered, filling the screen, until it faded to black and then there was more music: urgent, electronic, tapping out the wake up call. Stubbs lifted himself up on to his elbows and focussed on the newsreader. She was pretty enough, but the earnest expression she wore sat uneasily on that young face. He turned up the volume but understood little of it, except the odd name: *Kinsella, Sultan, Chico...* Pictures said so much more though: a large group of men, outside an ornate building ringed with a high fence, burning the Union Flag, burning the orange T-shirts with the Sultan crest...

Chapter Twenty

When sleep becomes an issue you know you are in trouble. That's what Chico had always believed, that's what Chico's trainer had always told him: when sleep became an issue there are other issues which must be sorted. And yes, there were so many other issues to sort...

And here he was, the Wednesday before the race of his life, trying to sort them, helping with the finishing touches – and he had hardly slept. Thank God Fraser had been there, the thinnest of partitions away, some crumb of comfort.

Chief issue? The circuit of course. Yes, he had ironed out the major difficulties – funny how problems evaporate when you throw a million dollars at them. So now all the building was completed, save for the levelling off of some of the gravel traps and a lick of paint here and there. He had even helped himself, hands on, bolting two lengths of Armco barrier together – the papers had loved that, the DBM PR man had said they would.

Then some of the drivers began to voice their concerns: that's the problem with scale models, with maps. They just hadn't got the scale, hadn't got the immensity of the thing – six hold-your-breath-and-hope corners per lap... Yes, of course it was something – what did they expect? One or two of them had whispered, whispered to the little big man, whispered to the circuit inspector. One had spoken to the press, one of the older drivers, always complaining about the loss of all the great circuits him, all the great corners – but now they were back... Well hang on there, isn't this a little dangerous?

But it was too late for all that. Okay, it wasn't ideal from that standpoint: some of the run-off areas were not as large as planned and the surface was still very bumpy in places. And yes, much of the work in the old quarry area at *Spa* was incomplete – even Chico winced at the thought of going off there. But what could they do about it now? Time had run out, and who would be brave enough to call the show off? No, it was too late, and they had all seen the mood in the Republic – here was a pressure cooker in need of release, and the release it had chosen was the race... And Chico winning the race.

Still, for a while it had looked like none of the teams would make it. Even Kessler had his doubts. But money, as always, had the last word. K-Corp had a huge presence in the Republic after all, and it was not about to lose its day of days, the focal point for a nation. So now the show went on, it always does in F1, a little island in this world of affairs, a little island where the budget of a third world nation is used to take a man around some thin ribbon of tarmac as fast as possible... And, in the final analysis, what else really mattered?

Chico shook himself from the daydream. He was sitting on the pit wall, having just finished the seventh interview with the press that day. A German TV crew. The journalist had asked the same questions as the six before him: *will the race still go ahead... Can you beat Kinsella... Had he heard that some members of the Sultan team had been attacked in their hotel?* They were back now, TV and papers, all of them, for the biggest photo opportunity of the week so far.

Up until this point the track had felt strangely empty, just Chico, the press, some hangers-on and the Sports 2000 car below him in the pit road. But now the man had arrived, a forward unit of two jeeps – each mounted with heavy machine guns – and an APC announcing his arrival. Then came the out-riders, big bikes, big guns, big horns – sirens blaring and lights flashing, nothing subtle about this entrance, but then there was nothing subtle about the President, or his car – an impossibly stretched black Lincoln Town Car. Parked at an angle the huge car almost blocked the pit lane, while behind it two more armoured personnel carriers disgorged squads of troops who immediately fanned out to take up defensive positions. He may not have worked for Sultan, but then the president of the republic had never been a safe job and this one was taking no chances. The large man, in the uniform of a full field marshal, seemed to salute the huge empty grandstands opposite the pits, then half-marched and half-waddled along to where Chico waited, his wife walking alongside, seemingly treading some invisible catwalk.

Chico climbed down from the pit wall and pressed his way through the bank of photographers who were welcoming the President – or more specifically his spectacular young wife – with a frantic rustle of shutter action. The President was always pleased to see Chico, for, as he always said, Chico's success was the country's success – and this year it had been the only success, what with the soccer team crashing out of the Coppa America in the first round. For his part Chico hardly trusted the man, too much sweat in his fat-handed handshake. And then there was the little matter of the Chicodrome, the idiot and his ministers had bled him dry there, to the point at which almost every bag of cement had meant a donation to the party coffers.

The original idea had been to open the circuit a day later, on the Thursday – when the Formula One cars had their extra two hours running to learn the track. But someone in the President's office had said no, too many spectators, too much risk. So in the end they had decided on a TV event, a stunt. Chico would drive the first official lap of the circuit in one of the sports racing cars to be used by the resident racing school, which also bore Chico's name and was due to go into operation in the week after the Grand Prix.

The Sports 2000 had been fitted with an extra seat, so that tyro racers could learn the circuit's lines sitting alongside an experienced driver at racing speeds. And the first passenger was to be the President. Yes, it could make good TV. It took a while for the school mechanics to strap the President into the cockpit, he was a big man, and then to find a crash helmet that fitted. Then Chico, in his white DBM race suit, slid in beside him, flicked the ignition switch and jabbed at the starter button. The mechanics had warmed the car up earlier and it fired instantly.

The car was a veteran of an American club championship. It was a sleek machine, with swooping all-enveloping bodywork that hid the wheels, so that it almost looked like a lemon lozenge hovering just an inch above the track surface. Despite its vintage – at least a decade old – it had to be said that it was aesthetically futuristic. Yet to Chico it might have been a traction engine. It had been years since he had sat in anything like it: the instruments were old-fashioned dials rather than the electronic read-outs he had grown used to, with the rev counter big and central through the spokes of the steering wheel. It was rotated so that the point of maximum revs was directly in his line of sight, the clock askew. Then there was the seat, to fit all sizes, a far cry from the seat in his DBM, moulded to every curve and bump in his frame. He had the mechanics tug extra hard at the belts to press him into it, then he felt for the pedals with his feet, all three of them – no hand clutch in this. And that little stubby gear stick... That would take some relearning.

But, strangely, it didn't. Once out of the pit-lane it was if he had never been away, so different from the F1 car that there was never any real danger that he would reach for phantom gear paddles on the steering wheel. It was the first time he had driven the Chicodrome, that out lap with the sweaty President by his side. He took it easy for the first tour, reacquainting himself with the old ways. Reacquainting himself with the heel and toe operation of the brake and throttle on the double-declutch downchanges – clutch once then blip the throttle with the side of you foot as the gear stick moves through neutral, matching the revs, clutch again, into the lower gear… And all the time you're braking for the bend. It wasn't long before he was nearly as quick as always, that little dance on the pedals strangely comforting, bringing back memories of days gone by, laps gone by, when all was hope for the future.

As for the circuit? Yes, they were right, the track was bumpy, but not too bad. And for the rest of it, well he forced himself to reserve judgement until his first hot lap – President or no President he was determined to christen his baby in style.

Past the pits for the first time and the two-litre engine was already screaming, top gear too short for this, the longest straight in Formula One. The straight was something he had fought for, room to pass. The ultimate circuit is not just for the drivers after all, and everyone had always said that there was one sure-fire way of improving the show, bringing the overtaking back – a long straight terminated with a slow corner. The straight was over a mile in length and the first corner was *Zandvoort*, a copy of the Tarzan corner at the Dutch track of that name. The Formula One cars would be topping 210 mph as they entered the braking area, this was screaming at about 150 mph. Chico glanced over at the President, saw the fat leg stretching for a non-existent brake pedal, saw the fat hand gripping at the edge of the seat, but they were no where near the braking area yet… And the F1 cars would be braking a long way past that, even with their increased speed. *Zandvoort* was a second gear hairpin fringed with a generous gravel filled run-off area. Ironically, at this – the one corner designed with spectators in mind – there were no grandstands, just a solid wall of advertising hoardings. It was a concession to the race sponsors, at a point on the circuit where the cars slowed down enough to keep the logos on camera for any length of time. Chico could hardly complain, they had let him have so much more. And after all, without the advertisers, without the TV money, there would be no F1, there would be no Chicodrome.

The Sports 2000 turned into the hairpin surprisingly well, with just a little kick of turn-in oversteer – something that Chico made a mental note of, not novice friendly that, he would have to get the boys to soften the rear anti-roll bar. Out of the corner, having turned through 180 degrees, Chico allowed the car to drift out onto the apron he had designed in, that little bit of extra room to reward an imaginative line through the turn. It was slippery there, a different sort of surface, and the rear of the car stepped out as he applied the throttle. A short straight followed, running parallel to the main straight, and then the circuit plunged down off the plateau through *Brands*. This plunge was why he had chosen the site in the first place, for no circuit is a test without significant changes in gradient. And with the main straight running the length of a natural plateau, and the rest of the circuit twisting and turning down to the base of the valley and then back up again, this was more than a test for both man and machine.

Brands was a facsimile of Paddock Bend at Brands Hatch, only reversed so that it was a left-hander. The entry speed was slower than the original too, but otherwise the character and the challenge was much the same. Chico could only feel sorry for the President as they plunged down the hill, it was very steep, and the man had a lot of stomach to leave behind. Towards the exit the surface of the road fell away to the outside, a vicious little camber switch that was bound to bite the unwary, followed by a twist in the ribbon of asphalt as the track straightened again, leading down to *Suzuka*.

Another mirror-image corner this one. Where the *130R* at the Japanese track that gave it its name turned left, this turned right and dipped into a compression. But it was a similar challenge, a confidence lift in, just to transfer the weight onto the front tyres, then through at close to maximum speed. With the DBM's downforce it might just be flat in top, Chico thought, even with the extra entry speed. The track levelled out after *Suzuka*, levelled out for *Silverstone*, which was similar to the Becketts-Chapel complex at the British Grand Prix venue. Almost exactly like it except for the marshland still to be drained away past the gravel traps – then swap the rolling Northamptonshire fields for the smoky, irregular outline of Watsonville hovering in the distance. It was in fast through the sweeping left, drop down a couple of gears for the right, then out through another left, winding it back up through the gears. It was fourth to second in the Sports 2000, coming into the slowest part of the complex, where the track turned right again. A bit too low, Chico thought, and he was forced to snick into third before the car had finished turning, an act that momentarily took the weight off the rear axle, kicking the tail out viciously. There was time for a quick glance to his left, a quick glance at the President's hands, white knuckles gleaming as he gripped the edge of the bucket seat. They would be lucky to prise him out of the car, Chico thought, revelling in the man's predicament.

Spa was next. The corner that had caused the most problems, carved out of an old quarry with the help of lorry loads of explosives. There hadn't been enough time to finish the job though, not really. So run-off suffered and the circuit inspector had not liked that – a couple of the drivers had blanched when they had caught first sight of it too. Chico had had to call in a lot of favours – for the love of God his stock was low now. It was Eau Rouge really, in all but name. Though, to be fair, not quite as quick – as he had pointed out. Still the plunge though, just a little way after the *Silverstone* exit – where the F1 cars would almost certainly be in sixth – then the left –right snick at the lowest point of the circuit, before the steep climb up the far bank. Probably easier than the original, he thought. But then the proximity of the rough stone walls of the quarry did little for the nerves. All it would take was a quick trip across the gravel – it has been known to launch a car – and then it could easily vault the tyre wall and barrier. But there was little he could do about that now.

The Sports 2000 popped up over the lip of the exit of *Spa*, the laws of physics dictating that it stood on tip-toe, its springs fully extended, almost airborne, before crashing back onto its bump stops with a thump that made the President's fat wobble. The car was just about settled when Chico pitched it into the final turn of the circuit: *Monza*.

It was a crossbreed this: a little of the Parabolica at Monza, a little bit of Gerards at Mallory Park – where Chico had never raced but had once tested before the Monaco Formula Three race, back in the hopeful past. It was what Bobby Drake would call a monster of a corner. A long, long, curve, like the head of an oval, with a stretched apex that the Sports 2000 seemed to kiss for an age, the rubber twitching nervously against the road surface as the car tried to follow the course that Newton had intended. While all the time Chico worked the wheel and the throttle, feeding in morsels of speed when he judged the car was ready for it. Finally, the exit was in sight, that long, long straight stretching down to *Zandvoort* – so long in fact that the high stack of advertising could still not be seen, except for a peak of Sultan orange brightening the horizon. Chico spotted the TV crews, fanned out across the start-finish line to get the best pictures, the best pictures of the people's champion and the best pictures of the President.

He allowed himself a little smile. Despite the problems, despite all those who had stood in his way, he had done it. There could be not the tiniest doubt that this was the most challenging Formula One standard motor racing circuit in the world. No doubt about it. And *Monza* was its crowning glory – a big balls corner that rewarded the brave with a fast run down to the overtaking spot at *Zandvoort*. For an instant or two he imagined himself in the DBM, sling-shotting out of the corner and pulling up alongside Kinsella. Yes, a monster corner... But a scorpion too.

Perhaps it was because he was distracted, perhaps it was because he was tired. More likely the first was a result of the second. But whatever, he had forgotten that sting in the scorpion's tail. It was a drama of a moment really, that's all. But it had started a month before, a shipment of the special surface aggregate held up at the dock, awaiting payment. They had to make do, and the boys had used a different material. It was forgotten, until earlier in the week, then replaced hastily. But he knew the bump was there, that slight wave on the road surface just where *Monza* exited onto the main straight. He had simply forgotten.

The car was travelling at about 100 mph when he hit the bump, and was instantly pitched sideways, so that its yellow flank was broadside on to the TV crews and photographers. In a moment crammed with happening the sports racer teetered on the edge of a high speed spin, while Chico instinctively jabbed at the throttle pedal and wound on armfuls of opposite lock in the direction of the slide...

It might have been embarrassing. Kinsella would have made much of it. But he had saved it. He could tell them he was show-boating, could tell the President that he was fooling around – once the fat fool had slapped his machismo back in place, scraped the fear from his face. But mother-of-God Chico, it was a close one. A wake-up call man, make no mistake about it. You have to get some rest, forget it all except the race. Sleep a little...

Chapter Twenty One

There had been no real sleep. Nothing of that velvet oblivion his body and mind ached for. In the night, despite his promise to himself, he had tapped at the adjoining door, crawled into bed with Fraser. But every time he closed his so-tired eyes a little strobe-like film show played about his skull: the rear wing of the Sultan, the exit to *Monza*, Teresa crying in the flat in Monaco... And then, just as the milky light of dawn filtered through the curtains the images floated aside, there was a dream of sleep itself: something he could touch, something so cold, the colour of champagne. And Fraser woke him.

Then at the track the day had started badly too. It was the new beauty queen, the successor to Teresa's successor. A celebrity race in under-powered little Italian saloons, built under licence in Watsonville, a race to mark the opening of the circuit, something for the spectators as they waited for the Formula One cars. There were already an estimated 80,000 at the Chicodrome and the grandstands opposite the pits seemed carpeted in the colours of the Republic, and many sat there had a good view of the shunt. The beauty queen had stuffed it at *Monza*, a regular novice mistake: the hint of a slide, straight off the power, the back snaps round, she slams on the brakes but by then the car is in the gravel – it digs in and rolls three times. Poor little Maria breaks a slender arm.

The press – and the British press in particular – loved it. They had already made much of the safety issues, what was it the one had written, the one in *The Brit*: 'Is beating Kinsella worth more to Chico than other drivers' lives?' The beauty queen's shunt could not have been timed worse. Chico spent the hour leading up to the first untimed practice – the hour he should have spent with Fraser sorting the set-up – talking to the press, explaining that it was a freak accident. It was really, the girl had panicked, let her arms flail about in the car as

173

she let go of the wheel, fractured one against the roll cage. Some said the race should be stopped, some in the press. But everybody knew that was the last thing they wanted, they had built up the war between him and Kinsella, they were not about to miss it. But their fake protestations were lent some weight when Thierry Michel threw his hat into the ring. He would not race there, he said. Of course you wouldn't Thierry – and who would let you...

It had been a blessed relief to get into the car, to feel the clamour at his ears soften as he pushed in the ear plugs come ear phones, pulled on his Nomex balaclava and eased on his crash helmet. And now he was out there...

There were two reasons for this extra day, with its extra two hours of track time for the Formula One cars. First, the track was green, it hadn't benefited from the passage of traffic, there was hardly any rubber down, and so it was slippery. There was a big support program to help break in the track – Touring Cars, Historics and Formula Three – but there is no substitute for the huge aerodynamic load of an F1 car. The other reason was simpler, track time. It was a new circuit for everybody – and from the very earliest stages it had been very clear that this was not the place for a quiet afternoon drive. The clock was on of course – it's the only measure of how you do. But the times would not count, not these, not tomorrow's. Only Saturday's times would count towards the final grid positions. But only a fool would think that the race had not started, for now's the time for the mind games – put in a quick one now and you would unsettle the other guy – unsettle Kinsella – panic him into switching set-up. But then mind games cut both ways.

It was the end of Chico's first flyer, and it had been a travesty of the art. He should have known that he was not ready, when Fraser had had to tap on his helmet, shake him from his doze in the garage, when the little jabs of cramp started to spike at his right foot. Then, first time quick into *Zandvoort*, he had locked up big time, so that he could count the grooves in the stock-still front left, count them as the smoke poured from the rub of asphalt and tyre, count them as the car slid wide, missing its turn-in. He should have aborted the lap there and then, saved it for the next time – but although there was drive to the back wheels something was not in gear. There were two more mistakes that same lap. First he slid too wide on the entry to *Silverstone*, which meant that he had to get off the throttle in the heart of the complex, so the speed was also down for the entry to *Spa*. But more serious still was his lapse at *Monza*, there was no excuse for it, exactly where he had scared the President the day before. He was almost sideways again and his speed was down onto the start-finish, in effect two laps ruined for the price of one, for he had spilt much of the momentum he needed for the start of the next lap in sorting out his moment.

Chico was past the pits by the time he decided to come in, so he would have to take it round again. With the effort of the hot lap – that wasn't – behind him, with the car stable in its dash down to the first corner, Chico tried to relax. The cramp in his right foot was much worse now, and he tried to flex it a little, tried to get the blood to it. It didn't work, just more pain, shooting through his instep, if only he could lift it clear, stamp it down and bring it back to life... And then, for an instant he lifted off the throttle, just an instant to get the blood flowing, just an instant of respite after the lap from hell...

The DBM pivoted up on its nose slightly for a fraction of a second – and he saw the rest of the accident through his mirrors. And the horror at what he saw was mixed with the horror of realisation: it had been the first time he had glanced in his mirrors for a lap. There was a flash of orange first, then the flat underside of the car as it was launched into the air. It seemed to hang there for a while, before completing the somersault and twisting to the left so that the orange bodywork was clearly visible again. It half somersaulted once more, then landed. But by this time Chico had run out of road... Some instinct had him on the brakes, looking ahead, somehow scrabbling through *Zandvoort*. He parked up in a long skid after the turn, snapping off the belts and jumping from the car as it still rolled to a halt. The track had turned through 180 degrees and Chico had to vault two sets of Armco barriers before he was running up the start-finish straight again.

It was a Sultan, still some 200 metres distant, upside down, astride a barrier, tail trackside and waving in the air, nose digging into the dirt the other side of the barrier. Further up the track the faces of the grandstands had taken on the same bronze-brown complexion as Jose Republic as each and every spectator craned left to view the drama. Chico could see that the driver's helmeted head seemed trapped between the corrugated steel of the Armco barrier and the lip of his windshield, pushed forward by the wedge of the barrier, while his arms hung down loosely on the other side. Chico took on great lung-fulls of air as he ran towards the wreck, air laced with the acrid and unmistakable pong of petrol. Even from this distance he could not fail to notice the spillage of liquid darkening the track surface, yet still he ran on. The Mercedes medical car screamed out of the pitlane while another F1 car, a Spando, had stopped some way past the accident, its driver alighting, running up the track just in front of Chico.

Then there was a muffled *whoof* on the breeze. And the orange of the Sultan was lost in the darker orange of the flames... Chico kept running, but he already knew that there was nothing he could do.

Chapter Twenty Two

There seemed to be an unspoken agreement between them, not a word about it was uttered. And yes, Mamma was pleased to see her, obviously pleased. Papa? Working in the south, helping Uncle Luca with the harvest. It had hit him hard, she realised that. On the way down from Watsonville Juan had filled in the gaps as she sat in the cockpit alongside him in the old mail Dakota.

The reporters had virtually camped outside the farm, he had said, hoping to catch a glimpse of Teresa. She had expected them at the airport too, and she had been lucky that nobody had caught sight of her when she had transferred from the European flight – but then all eyes were on the capital now, either that or the Chicodrome. She had known Juan since childhood and she was always more than pleased when she found him at the controls of the ancient Dakota used to shuttle the post and the people to their little settlement in the north. Juan was embarrassed as he told her what he knew, what the papers said, about her and the Englishman. It wasn't true, was it? he'd asked. And she had said nothing as she looked out of the plexi-glass windshield at the clouds of moisture boiling off the forest canopy below.

Mamma's hug was with compound interest, missing months to make up for, and she had nearly squeezed the life out of Teresa. Then, on feeling the bone, it was straight to the kitchen, to the beef, good beef – if not quite a fatted calf. She fed Teresa until she had to undo her belt and the fastening stud of her jeans. Then there was the coffee, and nowhere in the world could you find the coffee of home, even if the label said it was from home, everybody knew that they never let the best stuff go. All seemed a little better, at last.

After that early lunch they had sat on the veranda, listening to the sounds of the forest and commenting on the riot of colour in Papa's garden. Mamma brought her up to date with family news – no small bulletin – and then they drank more coffee. The overnight flight from Europe had taken its toll, but despite Mamma insisting she take a siesta Teresa did not feel like sleeping. But Mamma was tired too – she seemed to have aged these past few months – so she excused herself, just for half-an-hour. Teresa guessed that she had not slept that preceding night. But she need not worry now, Teresa was home for a little while at least, and things could be as they were. But just how long before she asked her? That was the worry. Just how long before she asked the question everybody asked: Teresa and Eoghan? She knew she would not lie to Mamma. She would tell her everything.

Or at least she would tell her what she knew. Love him? She didn't know that... Not yet. It had been a sex thing, at first, the thing he does she had supposed, with the others, they said. But then the change in him, in the town in Wales, where she had sensed that he wanted to tell her something. If he had it would be easier, less confusing. But then there was still Chico. They had talked on the phone now, no welcome home Teresa, but he had seemed happy, and friendly... And the biggest question? Did she wish it could all be undone, the night in the apartment in Monaco, and everything since – did she wish it? She just did not know...

Teresa walked in off the veranda closing the thin, slatted partition doors behind her. Papa's whisky was kept in a glass cabinet above the writing bureau, perhaps it would help her sleep? Just a little. She found a tumbler in the kitchen then broached the bottle – it was hardly ever touched except for birthdays and weddings. She remembered her wedding with a pang, then poured a golden drop of the liquid into the bowl of the tumbler. Then a little more – good measure.

She switched on the television set, a habit born of lonely, boring days in Europe, and then she settled on the sofa, her legs curled beneath her. It was an old set, and it still took time to warm up. Teresa had given them money to buy a new one, but perhaps Papa had spent it on some new part for the tractor. The reception had never been good in the forest, the picture a fuzzy plaid of colour, but it was good enough. Good enough for her to see that this was the last thing she needed, the very thing she should be running from. And yet, with papa's whisky already warming her throat, softening her head, and with her muscles aching from the hard seat of the Dakota, she could hardly be bothered to turn the thing off – and there was just RTV, no other channels.

She checked the time. Yes, it would be the first laps of the Chicodrome. The camera was trained on Chico, and Teresa found herself watching with an expert eye – she had picked up so much this past year, an eye expert enough to notice at any rate. An eye expert enough to notice the raggedness of that lap, the smoke pouring off the front wheel into the hairpin, the tail of the DBM kicking out through the fast left-right flick, and again at the exit of the very long loop at the end of the lap. But the cameraman was too focussed on Chico – of course, it's his limelight after all – and had failed to pick up the other car, the car that had closed on the DBM during that messy, slow, lap. Then it was there, in the top of the picture for an instant, closing on Chico and...

By the time the orange had registered in her consciousness the nose of the Sultan had hit the rear wheel of Chico's DBM, and then the wheels had clashed, acting like conflicting cogs to catapult the Sultan into the air. It rose gracefully at first, like a jet taking flight as the air rushed beneath it, and then – as the camera panned alongside – with its nose pointing vertical, it flipped and twisted on to its back, still some five metres in the air. Then it fell, down astride the barrier at the edge of the track, like a toy tossed aside.

Mamma rushed in from the back room:

"What is it..."

Teresa's standing, the empty whisky glass at her feet, a dark stain on the carpet.

"What is it... you screamed?" There is still sleep in her face, she looks at Teresa as if it's all part of some nightmare. On the TV the nightmare is played out, the Sultan in flames, upside down on the barrier. An ambulance and a fire truck pull up alongside. Mamma has rushed to her side, holding her, she's shaking, and all of a sudden she feels sick. The commentator is hysterical, Teresa can hear the commotion in the background as his crew searches for information...

Then the flickering graphic, a cartoon Sultan in profile at the bottom of the screen, and the commentator's voice again, on the edge of breaking down, a sob stuck there, somewhere behind the words:

"It's Guido Solé... This is terrible..."

The relief had its own pain, a guilt: poor Guido, she had liked him. No one had confirmed he was dead, but there was little doubt, the car still ablaze as the fire crew struggled with unfamiliar equipment. Then her mother switched off the TV and pulled her away, and Teresa collapsed onto the sofa in tears.

"Oh my dear, that must have been terrible for you." Mamma said. "If you love this Englishman you must go... Please go to him little one, he will need you. They will all need someone now..."

Chapter Twenty Three

She had been lucky to get on the flight to Watsonville that following morning. Many of the places had been booked, people going up for the race, but Juan had let her sit up beside him again. Most in the cabin of the plane recognised her, despite the shades and the headscarf, but nobody had said anything. A man had been killed at the Chicodrome, and the world's eyes were on the Republic for all the wrong reasons yet again, so her part in the Chico drama had been pushed down the pages for the time being. On the national radio station that morning, as she listened with Mamma, someone had rung in. Why had it not been Kinsella they asked. And she had cried again, cried for Eoghan – and cried for Chico.

At the Watsonville International Airport the domestic passengers sped through arrivals with little trouble, those tied up in the red tape of the Republic's passport control and customs shooting them a broadside of jealous looks. It was as Teresa was entering the main concourse – her head dipped a little in fear of recognition – that she caught the tail end of the argument. It was an Englishman, collecting his luggage from one of the customs men, spitting his disgust – been there all night, a day late already he bellowed. He demanded the man's name, saying that he'd get his money back, somehow. The customs man just laughed, while Teresa sped by without a second glance.

"Hey... You there..."

The shout was from behind her, the same Englishman. She carried on walking but then she heard the slap of his shoe leather against the polished tile floor. He was at her shoulders.

"It's you isn't it... Teresa Perez..."

Someone else caught the name and stared at her. She quickened her pace, but the Englishman was alongside now.

"A word please..."

She walked on, heading for the automatic doors that fronted the concourse.

"You don't know me," the man was not about to be put off, "the name's Mossup, Clive Mossup..."

She thought she recognised the name. There was a taxi outside, it's rear door already open, ready for a fare.

"I work for *The Brit*..."

"Leave me alone," she said.

"But I have something to tell you..."

There was a whisper of pneumatics as the glass doors parted for her.

"About your man," he was babbling now, could see the waiting taxi, could see his chance going out of the window. "Tell him not to fuck with me love... that's all, tell him I was waiting in London with the photographers all day for you two – we had a deal, two pictures, two locations..."

She looked at him, slowing a little.

"Tell him if he's going to play the game there's no bloody backing out – and I'm surprised at you lass, he's played you well and that's for sure..."

"I don't understand..." she said, turning to face him now.

The driver had taken her hand luggage from her and had placed it in the boot of the cab.

Mossup smiled, and wiped the sweat off his forehead. The driver brushed past him and slammed shut the door of the cab, climbing into the driving seat while Teresa sat in the back.

"Remember Monte Carlo love? Why do you think he was so keen to get you out on the balcony then – lovely little picture wasn't it?"

The cab lurched forward, quickly slotting into a gap in the stream of traffic passing the terminal.

Kinsella was sunk deep into the studded leather armchair. The discussion had gone on into the night, and now for most of the morning. They should drive in an hour or two, but no one really felt up to it – though they all knew they would. Because of the situation on the streets all the teams had decided to stay in the same hotel in Avenue Colonel Watson. And that night before many of the drivers had found themselves in this bar. Someone had cracked open a bottle, but few had touched it.

Kinsella had been here before, after the Jap' had bought it at Sugo. It was the same there, the situation too, all in the same hotel. And what do you get on the back of the tragedy? Guilt. All of a sudden you have a group of the world's top sportsmen holed up in the same room like a bunch of naughty schoolboys – prank backfired, found out at last. All of a sudden the bravado of it all becomes something dark, all of a sudden you realise it could happen to you...

The night before Thierry Michel had led the drinking, led the talking. He had been the closest to Guido, it had hit him hard. Particularly as they had not seen eye to eye lately, and Thierry had said something on TV, something stupid – nobody likes being beaten, but there's always time to make up after. But not now. Kinsella had asked him whether he would take his old seat, but it was a waste of words, the man was empty.

That morning Kinsella had seen Guido Solé's sister, in the lobby, the light within her extinguished, a suitcase at her feet, one of the driver's wives trying to comfort her. He had wanted to talk to her, comfort her he supposed, it seemed like the decent thing... But he had just turned away, pretended not to see as she wept for her lost brother. Kinsella knew that he was all too much a part of the thing that had taken Solé, all too much a part of it to face her now.

Guilty schoolboys all of them then, in the creaking lounge bar of the hotel. But professionals still. They had picked over the bones of the accident, someone had even brought in a video and they had watched in awkward silence as the Sultan once again performed its back flip, once again landed on its spine on the barrier, once again burst into flames. Yes, it was a freak accident, landing like that. Even the fire – he had been running on full tanks to build on a good race set up, as had Kinsella. There had already been talks of an inquiry, the little big man and the rule-makers had insisted on it, after some in the press demanded that the race be cancelled.

Cancelling it might even have been the decent thing, but with the mood in the Republic it was not a decision anyone would take lightly. In the end the team bosses made the decision, persuading Zola to make the announcement: *'it is what Guido would have wanted after all.'* There had even been talk of a drivers' strike, but too many drivers had too much to prove – and only this one last race this year to do it in.

It was fair enough, Kinsella thought, it wasn't the fault of the circuit after all. But the sponsors didn't like it, their logos over the front pages as a young Italian pays the ultimate price. As for Chico, nobody knew. No one had seen him since the marshals had stopped him plunging into the flames to rescue Solé – it had been a thing of passion, the man was dead by then anyway, no doubt about it.

Far away from all this a newspaper had asked the question that everyone was asking, if only in their heads. Zola had shown him, the newspaper cutting had been faxed through from the Sultan base. Yes, that was the question. How had they collided in the first place? Had Chico lifted without checking his mirrors? Or had Guido simply misjudged the passing move? The question would be asked by everybody sooner or later. And only two men knew the answer: Fraser, who was keeping hold of the DBM's telemetry, and Chico himself.

Kinsella looked about the lounge. It was a dusty room, full of leather, books and hunting trophies. It was how he might have imagined an old London gentleman's club to be. Except for the sullen young racers, slouched in their armchairs – and the two gorillas stood at the doorway. But he couldn't complain about them – they were with him. Zola's personal 'staff' – seen the world, shot at a lot of it by appointment to her majesty, just the type to have in your corner if the population of an entire country wanted to think of you in the past tense.

Thierry Michel was standing now, he was warming to his role as drivers' representative and nobody had thought to question his right, the one man in the room – bodyguards aside – that did not have to drive the Chicodrome that weekend. He was speaking about demands, demands they should make, a couple of tyre barrier chicanes to slow the cars into *Silverstone*, into *Monza*, but as Bobby Drake said, what was the point, the corners hadn't killed Guido?

The quiet Scot and his colleague, Zola's men – used to death perhaps – just checked the comings and goings. Just checked the bell-boy with the message for Kinsella, the embarrassed bell-boy who had broken into the ring of seriousness, playing his part in the drama of the now, handing Kinsella a note. There was someone for him, someone waiting in the coffee lounge. Teresa.

They had insisted on coming with him, but he made them stand outside, each patting the bulges in their jackets as if to say, 'don't worry, a bullet will get there quick enough.' The coffee lounge was the antithesis of its musty counterpart where the guilty racers talked: airy, marbled floor, palms shivering to the air that spilled through an open window, a marble fountain too, and the smell of the Republic's coffee, over-powering yet delicious. Just to let that smell tickle your nasal hair meant an hour's less sleep. She sat alone, head down, listening to the music of the fountain, playing with the spoon in her tiny cup. He left her to her thoughts for a moment and ordered a coffee.

"And for them... *Pour favore.*" Flicking his head in the direction of the bodyguards.

"Can I join you?" he joked. But there was no laughter, there was

183

nothing, her eyes still trained on the little spoon in the little coffee cup.

"What is it... Is it Guido?"

She raised her head so slowly he thought it might be heavy. Then her eyes met his and his stomach folded at a new facet to her beauty, a beauty washed through with complete misery, uncomplicated misery, the misery of a child, pet dead. Love dead. He knew it instantly. And it hurt as sure as a sharp kick to the solar plexus.

"I know," she said. That's all. Yes, of course she would find out sooner or later, it was inevitable. That's what journalists are for after all, spreading the news. Spreading the news that Kinsella had used the one thing he had loved in his entire, miserable existence to gain a fraction of a tenth over Chico. He might have argued, said it was before, before he realised he loved her. But instead he felt a strange sense of relief. Somehow it was right that she should know what he was. But he still played the game:

"Know what?"

"The boat... The lead singer of *Puberty*... You used me."

A waiter brought his coffee and fussed over napkins for a moment or two as they sat there in silence. When the waiter had finished Kinsella watched the curls of steam coming off the surface of the thick black liquid for a moment or two. He had a strange feeling that this was a big, big moment in his story. Here things would change. And although the pain was there, no doubt about that, the relief he felt that she finally knew was something solid too. All he could say was one word.

"Sorry."

Through the corner of his eye he caught a glimpse of the bodyguards, staring at Teresa, sharing a joke. She just sat there, looking right at him, her eyes never wavering. He wished to God that she would scream at him, punch him, kick him – but all that there was in those shining eyes was the transparent misery of someone dead, something dead.

After a space of time that could never have anything to do with a little hand racing round the rim of a Rolex Daytona he asked her the question, just a formality, he thought.

"Is it over?"

"Yes."

"I see." He sipped at the coffee. The steaming brew burnt the tip of his tongue, but it was a welcome pain, something more tangible than the confusion of sensations inside.

"It's over..." he said, more a confirmation to himself than anyone else.

She drew herself up straight, using her elbows as levers. Her eyes were still not quite level with his, and once more he found himself marvelling at just how much of her height was in those long legs. And then she spoke. Speech so measured, so considered, it almost reminded him of Fraser, in some strange way.

"There is one thing left."

"Yes?"

"You owe me – you owe my country..."

"I don't follow."

"This, it hurt Chico – I hurt Chico, I hurt my country. You do not understand how important it is to people here, Chico is the only light in the darkness. Chico winning is the only triumph the people can share in... It is so much more important than you and your cruel games Eoghan. Now I must put things right. How they should have been."

"How will you do that?"

"You will do it Eoghan. You will let Chico win on Sunday."

He just looked at her. There was something of the fanatic in her eyes: a love lost, a cause found. In another time she might have picked up a gun, hi-jacked a plane. But now she just said:

"You owe me."

Chapter Twenty Four

Because Sultan was undoubtedly public enemy number one in the Republic a little corner of the Chicodrome paddock had been put aside especially for it. The area had been fenced off and ringed with the Government's much unloved Special Security Police, in their blue combat gear and berets, each one fondly cradling an evil matt-black Armalite. Inside the little compound – already christened Fort Zola by the Paddock wags – there was a jumble of hired motor-homes and a windowless Portakabin, left over from the building project: the keep, if you like, where Zola, Kinsella and Kinsella's race engineer, spread the traces of the first practice laps. Quickest, just, from Bobby Drake.

That had not been the main talking point that afternoon though. No, the subject that grabbed everybody's attention had been the absence of Chico and when they realised the hero, the god, wouldn't show the crowd had just gone home – they were there for one man only, and the rest of the drivers had performed to an almost empty house. For Kinsella that had hardly registered, through the whole session he had been on auto-pilot. He had the strangest sensation of being badly winded, only in the head. As if his life force had been knocked out of him with one cruel – but wholly just – blow. And Solé? There had been little talk of him today – reporters questions aside. The race was on and for the drivers there was no point in dwelling on the accident, the post-mortem could wait... For most.

One flickering strip light illuminated the interior of the damp little Portakabin, while the noise from the generator outside lent a background clatter to the conversation within. The team had packed in a great deal of equipment – monitors, videos, telephones, laptops – and after going over the traces they watched the video of the session, Kinsella absent-mindedly noticing that his line into *Zandvoort* had been very deep. Finished with the debrief, the engineer had made his notes and returned to the pit garage to tweak the car ready for the morrow's qualifying session. Zola was now on the phone, an animated conversation switching between Italian and English. At other times Kinsella might have found it funny, the rage in the man's face, the sheer violence as he slammed the receiver into place. The sole remaining Sultan driver sat on a moulded plastic chair, one orange Nomex clad leg crossed at a right-angle over the other, his hands in his lap, still and clasped together. Zola looked up from the phone and said:

"It is the Sultan people, they are worried..."

Kinsella shrugged, they had every right to be.

"Guido... it's all hit them very hard..."

Yes, but that's the thing, death comes in many forms: in a burning racing car, or your lungs eaten away by cancer: just a matter of different time scales really, surely they knew?

"... And their sales are down in the Republic, because of this thing with you and Chico. It is stupid, I know, we are here to race, to get the results, but they have to sell their cigarettes if we are to race. No?" He looked at Kinsella, clearly frustrated that the Englishman had failed to enter into the spirit of the conversation.

"They wanted us to pull out. They said it would be a mark of respect. Respect for Guido..."

"And?"

Zola nodded, seemingly pleased that his driver had responded at last.

"It is not possible – they see that. They will lose out elsewhere, everyone will be watching Sunday, it's the biggest prize-fight of the year. You and Chico... If he shows..."

"And I'm sure Guido's accident won't do the viewing figures any harm eh?" Kinsella put in, making no effort to hide his tone.

Zola chose to ignore him, while the shadow of something Kinsella had once read passed through his memory. Imola, '94. Senna hits the wall at Tamburella. It had been a hot day, all of Italy out in the sun. But when the news hit the streets, they all went indoors, turned on the TV to watch the great man die. It had been the biggest surge of electricity demand the Italian grid had ever experienced. That's what they like to see...

Zola carried on talking, he had switched to that other way of speaking, the one for the boardroom, and as he talked he paced up and down the room, his right hand kneading the knuckles of the left behind his back. He was trying to explain everything commercially –

187

the only way it could possibly make sense – with plenty of noughts and plenty of nods to the mighty dollar to get his point across. Kinsella was left in no doubt that a decision had already been taken.

"They have a very great problem you see: they cannot afford to miss this race, it will be the biggest race of the year, the largest viewing figures and no advertising restrictions for the cigarette manufacturers. But they would very much like to hold onto their fast dwindling share of the market here in the Republic.

"So, it does not take a genius to work out that the best possible thing for them –our paymasters you must remember..."

Kinsella said nothing, but he was already one step ahead.

"...that the best possible outcome for Sultan Tobacco International would be for you to lose and Chico to win – then these stupid people would have no time for hate, just for the triumph of their hero, their god."

"You want me to throw the race?" Kinsella said it flatly enough, but Zola feigned shock.

"No, no, of course not... I'm just – how you say it – it's hypothetical, yes? If that were to happen we would be happy no? You will drive for Sultan next year, another chance at the title and perhaps more money, the jet you spoke of. And we remain friends with the sponsors. It is hypothetical, that's all..."

Kinsella shook his head, letting a wry little laugh pass between his lips. Hell, he had been the villain of the piece before and no doubt about it, he had had the odds stacked against him too. But this took the bloody biscuit: a whole country would rather see him dead, his sponsor wanted him to lose, his team boss had asked him to throw the race – even threatened him with the sack, reading between the lines. Christ, even the woman he loved – the only woman he had ever loved – had asked him to do the one thing he once thought impossible of him. Let the other guy win. Could it get any funnier?

"Just think about it seriously Egg." Zola said, "Very seriously."

And then the Italian's mood seemed to soften, as he considered the figure in the racing suit sat before him.

"This accident – Guido – are you okay with it, okay to drive?"

"We've been through this, it's not a problem..."

"You are sure – yes?"

For a moment or two Kinsella wondered what Zola would do if he said no, said that he wouldn't drive the race, wouldn't be there to put on the show, there for the sponsors – to lose for them, to lose for Teresa. But in truth he felt curiously empty about the whole thing, and not just because of the situation with Teresa, of that he was sure.

No, there was more. As stupid as it seemed he felt as if it had happened now, the thing he once feared – landing on his head like the Jap at Sugo. And it had happened to someone else, and that was it. Of course, it was silly, gambler's fallacy and all that, the chance – the odds – remain the same every time. But somehow he felt safe from it... Still, he might have teased Zola, with this other possibility. But there was an interruption.

It was a respectful tap at the door, but Zola barked a come-in. It was not a good time to ask an audience. The Scottish bodyguard, the one called Bryce, showed the man in. Kinsella recognised him – from the Sultan factory before he signed – overweight and sweaty, rubbing at an ugly scar under his nose so that when you first caught sight of him it looked like a finger was working at the nostril. Zola was curt, while the flabby man was scared – the Scot flexed his knuckles. Yet the flabby man – unbelievably – won the day. There was something in the urgency of his voice, something in the panic that persuaded Zola that here was something worth listening to. Kinsella stayed put too – there was nowhere he had to be, nowhere he could be except here or the hotel.

The flabby man pulled up a chair, sitting next to Kinsella. He smelt of stale sweat, a little alcohol too. Dutch courage, Kinsella guessed, Zola could have that effect on people. He reached into the duty-free carrier bag that he had been grasping tightly at the opening – as if there was some wild animal in there, waiting for its chance to escape. He pulled out a video cassette, handing it to Zola. Without a word the team boss pushed the cassette into the slot and it was instantly and electronically sucked into the bowels of the black machine. Zola pressed play.

At first it was difficult to make out what was going on, so the flabby man gave a running commentary. The picture was fuzzy, tinged green. There was a bed, white and glowing in the centre of the screen, the mound of a sleeping figure clear in relief.

"Now watch the door – at the top of the picture..."

The dark shadow of the door swung inwards and a block of furry light was thrown onto the floor. Another figure this time...

"Here... you can clearly see his face."

It was Chico, no doubt about it. Naked too, and clearly aroused. He walked over to the bed and then slid under the sheets.

"They talk for a little while..."

Kinsella tried to make out the other form in the bed, the hair was short and for a moment he thought it was Guido Solé's sister – what they were supposed to do with that at this particular time he could hardly guess. But then the figure turned and the face was big on the screen, while Chico ducked beneath the sheets, his head a lump in the sheets as it travelled towards the foot of the bed, settling at the groin area. As Kinsella's eyes got used to the picture the face grew clearer, and it had registered just before Zola exclaimed:

"Fraser!"

There was more: Chico folded over the edge of the bed, Fraser taking him, the long lens working in and out for long-shot then close-up, and then they were done, collapsed as one on top of the bed.

Zola was obviously uncomfortable with the film but the flabby man didn't seem to notice, shooting long glances in Zola's direction, looking for praise, recognition. As for Kinsella, he thought of Teresa, some things that she had said that now made sense.

After some minutes of watching the two men on the bed Zola seemed to jump, then flush, as if he suddenly felt others watching him watching, and in one fluid movement he stood up and switched off the machine. Then he turned towards the flabby man:

"And what are we supposed to do with this Mr Stubbs?"

"You can break him..." The man looked confused, he had obviously expected more enthusiasm.

"Explain." Zola snapped.

"Well, if the press get hold of this, he will be finished. You know how they are in this country, all that machismo – how do you think they will react to this, the national hero in his true light?"

"Yes, it would be difficult for him. But perhaps he has suffered enough, no?"

Zola looked over at Kinsella, looking for a reaction. But he was a continent away, with Teresa in a small Welsh town, the words in the room meaning little to him.

"But should that matter," Stubbs said, "you want to win don't you? And okay, for this year it may be too late, but you will have this on him, for next year... Think on it. These sponsors, big corporations with an image to project – can you honestly tell me that homosexuality is something an Asian leviathan like K-Corp could put up with...?"

There was an edge to Stubbs's voice now, and absent-mindedly Kinsella wondered whether he had moved on to plan B a little earlier than first intended. Still, Zola nodded and then he pulled the tape from the machine, placing it on his desk, balancing it on its edge like a little black tombstone.

"You have copies?" he asked.

"Not yet, no...I mean..."

"Then wait outside, I will confer with my colleague."

Both Stubbs and Kinsella went to say something – Kinsella to ask what it had to do with him – but Zola waved them quiet, then looked at the Scot, who nodded, opening the door of the Portakabin and showing Stubbs out.

When the Scot closed the door behind them Zola spoke again.

"What do you think?"

"He's scum."

"Yes, but useful scum all the same."

"Perhaps."

"Shall we use it?"

"It's up to you."

"But what do you think?"

"No. What he does in his own room is up to him."

"You surprise me Egg, are you going soft? It is better than Monte Carlo is it not, Monte Carlo and the girl?"

Kinsella was not really surprised that Zola knew, he was just surprised that he had thought he could keep it a secret from anybody – keep it a secret from Teresa. He said:

"The time for games is over."

"Good. I was hoping you would say that. I will destroy it."

Kinsella cocked his head in the direction of the door:

"What will you do with him?"

"Oh, he has worked hard – he will get his due." Zola wore a look of disgust again, the same look as when he had spoken with Stubbs, the look he wore when he watched the tape – even the lawless play by certain rules, Kinsella thought.

For a while in there things had looked grim. Had he really misjudged Zola so badly? He thought the man would jump at it, to have something like that on his closest rival, yet there had been indecision to spare. And Stubbs had sweated as he waited outside the Portakabin. Sweated more when that arrogant twat Kinsella had come out, looking at him as if he was just a piece of shit. But then Zola had called him in, told him it was good work. They would work out the money later, he said, after he had got on to the papers. One more job for Stubbs, he had added, just a little meeting with the sponsors – the Sultan people. Part of his reward, they were very pleased with all that he had done for them.

The Scot, almost friendly now, had kitted him out in Sultan gear: orange knee-length shorts and an orange shirt plastered with the scimitar logo – it was a tad too small and one of the buttons had let go as he tried to squeeze himself into it. They would like it that he wore the colours, the Scot had said, it would make a good impression with the sponsors – team loyalty and all that.

The Scot had driven him from the circuit in a people carrier with smoked glass windows – to be in Watsonville in that uniform without the one-way glass would be suicide indeed. The Scot drove fast, aggressively, hardly speaking for the entire journey. By the time they reached the outskirts of the city the smog had been sucked into the darkness of the night. Stubbs asked the Scot where they were going, but all the man up front would say was 'you'll see'. Out of the windows Stubbs could now see a part of Watsonville new to him, buildings tumbling into each other along the steep slopes of a hillside, walls and roofs of corrugated iron, kids playing in the dirty puddles at the potted roadside. He fished into the depths of his duty-free plastic carrier bag for the guidebook that had served him well, trying to find a street sign that matched a line on the map. After a while he figured he was in the Brigado, Watsonville's Ghetto, but for the life of him he could not understand why the movers and shakers of Sultan Tobacco International would want to meet him here. He might have worried, perhaps he should have, but his head was filled with thoughts of what to buy Sarah when the Zola money came through.

Then, after some time when Stubbs thought the Scot was just driving round in circles, he brought the people carrier to a halt, its head-lamps splashing yellow the corrugated face of a roller shutter door. The engine was still running and the Scot turned to face Stubbs.

"Do us a favour pal – open the door there."

Without thinking Stubbs climbed down from the people carrier and moved to open the corrugated door, he grasped at the handle but it seemed to be locked. Then, behind him, he heard the door of the people carrier slam shut. He turned. Past the glare of the headlights he could just make out the grin of the Scot. And then the vehicle was reversing at speed, turning, into first as it still rolled backwards, and the smoke poured off the front wheels as the Scot dropped the clutch viciously. The people carrier was out of sight before Stubbs really had time to take it all in, jinking around a street corner to a squeal of tortured tyres.

Without the benefit of the people carrier's air-conditioning the smell of shit that hung in the air was almost overpowering. Stubbs was trying to figure out what it all meant – whether he would still be getting his pay – when another, most unwelcome, thought crept into his consciousness. He was alone. Lost. In the roughest, deadliest part of the roughest, deadliest city in Latin America. And he was wearing a Sultan uniform...

From the shadows at the end of the street he thought he sensed movement...

Chapter Twenty Five

Kinsella had never seen so many worried – no frightened – faces at a race circuit paddock in his life. Half the drivers had scared themselves silly in the Saturday qualifying session, while most of the suits had something even worse to worry about, as they saw it. Even worse than flat through *Silverstone* and *Spa*, even worse than scrabbling round *Monza* at 160 mph, even worse than the image of the burning Sultan, etched into their consciousness. The suits had the nightmare vision: the biggest show of the year, the guaranteed money-spinner, billions of viewers lined up on the edge of their sofas to watch the prize fight of the century – and the star had failed to show.

Alright, the villain of the piece had done the business – so Britain would be well and truly tuned in come late Sunday afternoon. But as Kinsella had stroked the Sultan through that clean and tidy, almost effortless, pole position lap, the driver of the lead DBM was still nowhere to be seen.

The PR machine had moved into top gear: the twat from DBM was saying it was nothing, just a virus, Chico would be okay for the race tomorrow. While the Government man was saying it's not a problem, they had had assurances from the man himself that he would show – calm down people, your god will be there for you. Then there was the little big man and the suits that head the teams. All were trying their best to reassure people, all were saying it's not a problem – even Zola. And, they decided, if Chico is there to race they would let him, it was the consensus, even though it would mean him starting from the back of the grid as he had not officially qualified.

Meanwhile, some of the local papers had their own ideas, their own theories, one of which saw Chico holed up on his ranch, wracked with guilt for his part in the Solé shunt. And so the people of the Republic mourned, not for Guido Solé but for their own little martyr...

No one had asked Kinsella what he thought, but in truth he was almost past caring. Before Friday morning he might have seen it differently, Chico handing him the championship on a plate, but now it was strangely unimportant – and even more perversely that had made him quicker in qualifying. He was more relaxed at the wheel it seemed, it was natural, flowing – even the white-knuckle ride that is *Monza* was drama free – just a day at the office. But bloody quick.

He hadn't thought of Fraser since the video the day before, but now here he was in front of him, in one of the motor-homes at the heart of his enemy's camp – with Zola's blessing, with the little big man's blessing. Someone had a plan.

Fraser was not looking his dapper best and that was a fact: his eyes seemed to have been pushed back into his head and the stubble grew coarse at his chin. He slumped into a chair opposite Kinsella – who had finished swapping racesuit for civvies of khaki pants and a cream v-neck sweater. His sunglasses sat unfolded on the table, where they had sat since before Friday practice, so Fraser was able to look into his eyes. He was here to beg something, that was clear, there was something of the spaniel in those cold grey-blue peepers, it seemed to Kinsella.

"They have asked me to speak to you," he said.

"They?"

"They think they are going to lose their race."

"And..."

"Well, if there is no race you have no chance – Chico has more wins remember, and you are equal on points, he will take the championship."

"And if there is a race I win – if I score a point." He said it with no feeling, it was a matter of fact, nothing more.

"Yes." Fraser bowed his head, pulled the seat back behind him and stood up to leave, in a hurry, it seemed, to rush out to someone and say 'I told you it was useless.'

"What can I do," Kinsella said, for no other reason than if he was going to throw the championship he might as well do it in style – and maybe, just maybe, for her.

There was a helicopter waiting. On the way to the pad Fraser explained the situation. Members of other teams, one or two bosses, shouted over to him:

"Good luck Egg..."

"Nice one Kinsella..."

News travels fast in an F1 paddock, and this was certainly news:

195

the villain of the piece on his way to save the day.

"Wind him up." Fraser had said, "it's the only thing that will work on him." How right he was there, and how Kinsella had worked it on him in the past, forgetting everything, forgetting her – you fool Kinsella. But if you can make some small amends perhaps she will listen, maybe one day you can get her back.

They flew up high over Watsonville. At one point the pilot put the chopper over to the right so they could see a pall of smoke rising clear of the smog out of the Brigado quarter of the city. There had been trouble, the pilot told them, a riot. The people had heard rumours, rumours that the race had been cancelled – there was even a rumour that Chico was dead, had killed himself in a fit of remorse for his part in the Guido Solé accident. It was the sort of gallantry the people expected of the man. And, so the rumour went, the Government were covering it up – it was just the spark that the people of the Brigado needed. The Special Security Police had been called in and shots had been fired.

Once out of the city and clear of its clinging smog the helicopter descended to a lower altitude, its pilot preferring to follow the chocolate curl of a river rather than the map. Fraser explained that they would have to be quick, the weather could close in easily and ground the chopper – which was why Chico had originally elected to stay in the city over the race weekend. Staring out of the side window at the dense canopy of the forest that fringed the river on both banks, Kinsella found himself thinking about the little farm that Teresa had told him about. Her home, where he had hoped to go after the race – just as he had taken her to his place in Wales. He had imagined himself there, champion of the world. You fool Kinsella.

After half an hour of flying the forest finished, abruptly, and all there was to look at was the river and the bare red earth dotted with ugly pock marks where the trees had been uprooted by the Government logging companies. Then, in pale patches at first, there was grass, and more grass, until as the helicopter skimmed over the vein-like fan of the river's delta, the land below was once again a uniform deep green. After a few more minutes of flying the green butted against the cartoon blue of the sea, with little white bands of sand and sea to ease the shock, a symphony of colour that caused Fraser to let out an audible gasp.

"You never get used to it," he said, looking over at Kinsella.

Kinsella found himself smiling at the man, and thinking about that tape. It reminded him how out of touch F1 could be. Anywhere else it would mean nothing – political circles aside – but the sponsors want a certain sort, a certain type. Naughty was okay, he knew that, but you had to play by their rules. And Stubbs was right, a conservative conglomerate like K-Corp would drop Chico at the first hint of anything like that – as would the people of the Republic.

The pilot traced the line of the beach for a mile or two, just some hundred metres above the foaming surf. There was not a soul to be seen, just the odd black stone poking through the white sand, and – once – there was a grounded fishing boat, lying on its side, planks worn through and its superstructure rusting in paradise. Out of this wilderness of blue and green rose the ranch. First the house, two toned terracotta roof in the low sun, then the outbuildings, the paddocks – where horses panicked to the approach of the chopper – and the scrunched up grey ribbon that had to be a kart track – someone like Chico would never tire of racing machines... Or so they had always said.

The helicopter pad was close to the beach and Fraser and Kinsella had climbed out before the rotors had lost the thwacker-wacker of their momentum against the air. Tucked low, they ran from the machine and straight onto the beach so that the whistle of the chopper's turbines winding down was swiftly replaced by the rhythmic sigh of the soft surf breaking against the beach. Fraser showed no hesitation, there was no glance towards the villa, just the headlong rush to be by the sea. He continued to run, even though they had now left the noisy wash of the rotor blades far behind them. Kinsella fell in behind him, the soft sand spilling into his shoes as he jogged along the beach and filled his lungs with deep draughts of the clean sea air, a fine antidote to the poisonous smog of Watsonville just an hour or so behind him.

Chico was sitting on a big round black rock, at the apex of a dogleg of coast, where one bay met another. Other smaller rocks were gathered around the black boulder, all so perfectly round, like peas around a potato.

"He's always here." Fraser said, stopping to catch his breath some 50 metres from Chico, "I'll leave you to it, but there isn't much time, the pilot wants to get back to Watsonville before the light fails."

Kinsella walked towards the man on the rock.

"And Kinsella," Fraser shouted after him, "please go easy..."

He almost shouted back. He almost shouted back that he thought they wanted him to wind Chico up, sting him into action. But he didn't. And anyway, now he was here it all felt somehow ridiculous – he hardly knew why he had come, unless it was for Teresa, to apologise to her – for her – somehow. Nothing else made much sense.

Chico was on the top of the rock. He wore tiny blue bathing trunks and a DBM promotional T-shirt from the year before, the grey almost faded to white. His legs were curled up and clasped to his chest and Kinsella fancied that he rocked slightly to the sound of the surf breaking on the small rocks in front of him.

Chico turned to see the figure approaching, making a peak with his hand to shield his eyes from the low sun. He waved at Fraser in the background and Kinsella thought he caught the trace of a smile. Then, as he came within earshot, Chico spoke to him:

"I didn't expect to see you here."

Kinsella leant against the big rock, feeling the heat that the dark stone had sucked into itself, looking up at Chico a metre or so above him.

"No, me neither," he said.

"Are you here to persuade me to come back. If you are it's too late, it's over now."

"You have given up?" There was no venom in it, just a question.

"Yes... The accident, it was my fault."

"Bollocks," Kinsella spat back, "it's nobody's fault, it's racing – you know that. For Christ's sake, we've all known that someone was going to buy it like that sooner or later, I know I've thought about it enough..."

"But I was tired, I lifted... I'm so tired Kinsella. I've had enough."

He looked away from him, bowing his head to his knees. Kinsella watched as a little spur of surf broached the defences of a rock pool, filling it to its brim so that seaweed took on Paisley patterns, then retreating so that the weed fell black, almost hidden, against the rock. He didn't think he was about to attempt to dissuade the man, it made little sense to him – drop out tomorrow, say there's something wrong with the car, they finish on equal points, but Chico has the most wins, he is champ. Game over. The same either way. But then what he was about to do made so little sense too. For the first time in his racing life Kinsella was going to apologise. He looked up at Chico, who was staring out to sea again. The air was cool, but the low sun was still hot on Kinsella's neck, and he felt the beading of sweat around his collar.

"I'm sorry Chico," he said.

Chico laughed, and it was a real laugh, a laugh of humour.

"Sorry... sorry – what have you done?"

Kinsella shrugged.

"Unless it's the girl, is that it? Poor little Teresa. Believe me, you were doing her a favour..."

"No, I don't think so." Kinsella said.

"You were... You were. No one knows the way she's suffered..." He looked down the beach again where Fraser was at the water's edge, bending low to inspect a shell, or perhaps a little crab.

"I think I loved her you know," Kinsella said.

"You did... Why not now?" Chico looked at him again, his brown brow now furrowing in curiosity.

"It's over."

"Yes?"

"Yes. I think she still loved you – loved you and this bloody country."

Chico thought on that for a while, his face held high into the sea breeze as he seemed to let his mind play with memories. From further down the beach Kinsella could hear the pilot calling Fraser, the words whipped away by the wind, but as he turned he saw him, pointing to his watch.

"You remember Spa? When you told me. Told me she was good. Was that true?"

Kinsella nodded.

"Good. I'm glad. She never really loved me you know, it was just a thing they think is real, just the legend... Poor little girl."

Kinsella thought on that for a while, thought on what he could give the man in return, what secret he had to spill. Finally, he said:

"No, you're wrong...I think she still loves you."

Chico laughed a little laugh and shook his head slowly, and Kinsella gave more:

"You know, she asked me to throw the race, to let you win..."

For the first time there was something in those brown eyes, something he remembered from the old Chico.

"She said that?"

"Yes." Kinsella glanced at his watch, for no reason other than to break the awkwardness he felt at holding the other man's stare. "It's time I was going, are you sure you won't come, we could put on quite a show you know?"

"She asked you to let *me* win?" Chico wore a look of disbelief that was slowly dissolving into a look of disgust.

"Yes, she did, she..."

"And you would do this?" Chico interrupted.

"Maybe... I suppose I might... But I've got to go now. Goodbye Chico, and good luck." Kinsella turned and walked down the beach towards Fraser, who was now wearing an expression of pained curiosity.

"Kinsella!" Chico shouted from behind him. He turned.

"And you think *you* would be in a position to *let me* win at the Chicodrome?" He was standing on the rock now, drawn up tall, pointing at Kinsella as he emphasised the word you.

"Maybe, who knows – who will ever know?" Kinsella shouted back. Chico jumped down from the rock and trotted up to Kinsella.

"You are a fool Kinsella, do you know that? Without your games you cannot beat anyone. But I will race you all the same, if you give me your word – for what it's worth."

"Word on what?"

"You must race me, this will be my last race. I want no charade, no games – I will beat you Kinsella, and that will be that..."

"Okay, no games..." Kinsella offered Chico his hand and Chico stared down at it for some long seconds before reaching out and clasping it. They shook, each gripping the other's hand tightly, and then Fraser was with them.

"How long before the chopper goes Gordi."

"Just minutes..."

"Get my gear from the villa then."

Fraser rushed off, a massive grin on his face, the sort of grin that Kinsella would have thought the man incapable of.

"But no games Kinsella," Chico said.

"No games Chico."

Chapter Twenty Six

He had no guarantee, of course he hadn't. But he had seen the man's eyes – probably not for the first time but certainly the first time he remembered – and for some reason he believed him. Or at least he was as close as he could be to believing him. Besides, if he raced him or not Chico would still know – would still know if he drove that perfect lap. And this would be his last chance. He could hardly believe that he had almost thrown it away, dwelling on the accident. But at least time on the ranch had helped him rest. And as for Kinsella, well there was no doubt that his visit had stirred him, stirred him into action once more. It was Fraser's doing he suspected. He knew how to work Chico, knew what would make Chico angry, knew what would get him back into the car. Into the race. And now everyone was happy: sponsors, team bosses, the Government, the people... they had their show. And with half an hour to go TV sets the world over where tuning in, fastening themselves on the images from the Chicodrome. The hype machine had been super-productive and – the PR man had told him breathlessly – this was set to be the biggest single worldwide television event of the year. By far.

He thought now of the commentators across the globe, in their pre-race amble, having to explain why the lead DBM was in the last slot on the grid, alongside a Bianchi. Having to explain why Kessler sweated in the hot midday sun as he walked between the two DBMs to check on pre-race preparations – Bobby Drake second on the grid, Chico 25th. That should give them something to talk about alright. Chico was so far back that the exit of Monza was just 100 metres behind him, and over his left shoulder were the cheap seats. The seats from where the ordinary people of the Republic chanted: *Ole – ole, ole, ole – Chi-co, Chi-co...* over and over again, only pausing to break into cheers when Chico himself turned and waved to them. In front of him and to the left the great bank of grandstands that lined half the length of the straight were full to bursting point, a great carpet of colour and noise stretching down to the front of the grid and towards the first turn at *Zandvoort*. The massed T-shirts, flags and hats of the republic and of DBM was like a quilted wall of colour, shifting like vapour in the heat. The ordinary people were there, those who had worked hard to afford the ticket. There they were, chanting the name of Chico, or forging four hour friendships through their support for him, or sharing lovingly prepared food with a comrade for the afternoon – or shouting for the fire brigade to spray water on their section of the stand to cool them... Wondering how it must be for the drivers, in their layers of Nomex, in this heat.

Opposite the grandstands, above the pits in the air-conditioned hospitality boxes or on the high air-stirred balconies, sat the wealthy sponsors, and the top men from the Government and the Church. Taking in the scene, telling anyone who might listen how they had helped make it happen, showing their support for Chico with quiet applause, cooling themselves with chilled cocktails... Feeling the quickening of their pulses, wondering how it must be for the drivers.

Chico felt the heat of the tarmac through the soles of his driving boots. He had discussed it with Fraser, one stop – the tyres supplied were durable enough on this surface, even in this heat. He placed his helmet and driving gloves in the cockpit of the car, into the bowl of his seat, and then he pulled the top part of his overall down to his waist, tying its arms about him. Underneath the triple layer fire-retardant overall there was just a T-shirt, in the colours of the republic with the profile of his helmet big and bold on the front, while on the back was his signature printed big and red in an imperial flourish he had once secretly practised. There was one thing left to do before the off.

Chico started to walk up the middle of the grid, the pit wall to his right and the packed grandstands to his left, as he walked between the cars. Despite the heat all the tyres on the cars he passed were still wrapped in their electric blankets, while engineers plugged computer umbilicals into the sidepods and mechanics pumped dry ice into heating systems, or packed the sidepods with ice blocks. As he walked up the grid people from the other teams greeted him, some wished him luck, a team boss from the old days clapped his back, Thierry Michel thrust a microphone under his nose – but there was no time for that now, he apologised. And as he passed the grandstands the people there stood for him. Stood for the man who had put the Republic on the map for the right reasons – so that a multi-coloured shifting of people coming to their feet marked his progress up the length of the grid just like a slow moving Mexican wave.

It was a longer walk than he had expected, but then he had never been that far back before, not even in his first season in Formula One, not even in the junior formulae. He allowed himself a smile at the irony of it all: his last race, his worst starting position. Bobby Drake was sitting in the second DBM, the Number Eight car, a length back and diagonally opposite pole position. He tapped at the white stars on the top of the young American's crash helmet and shouted his good lucks through the open visor. Then he turned towards pole.

A swarm of photographers had gathered about him now, and the DBM PR man was busy trying to push them back. There was the first siren to clear the grid, but no one took much notice, they could not afford to miss this picture, while others on the grid – mechanics and team managers – seemed hypnotised by Chico's progress. Even the noise from the grandstand tailed off as he walked closer to the pole-sitting car – so that all eyes, all senses, were trained on Chico and Kinsella.

Kinsella had already pulled on his fire-retardant balaclava and was arranging the straps of his helmet when he looked up. There was no emotion in the Englishman's eyes, no sign that here was a man knocking at the door of the world championship. He was just a racing driver with a job to do it seemed – Chico admired that in him. Which made it easier for him to out-stretch his hand, offer it to Kinsella in full view of the packed grandstands, in full view of the teams on the grid, in full view of the world's press, in full view of the billions who watched on television. He lent over and whispered in Kinsella's ear:

"No bullshit Egg – we race."

Kinsella nodded.

"One stopping?"

Kinsella nodded.

"Okay – lap 32, it will make things easier."

Kinsella grinned, shook his head, then laughed.

"Okay Chico, you'll have your race." Then he shook Chico's hand again and turned to discuss something with his race engineer. As Chico rushed back down the grid to his car he was aware of the applause from the grandstand, like a great wave crashing against the edge of the track but never dispersing. And then he heard the engines of the other cars burst into life, first one then another, then three or four at once... By which time he was in the DBM. The stage was set.

Kinsella was strapped in and ready to go. You had to give Chico his due, he thought, he wasn't afraid to race. But this had to be a first, agreeing on the same tactics for the sake of sport – *sport*: when was the last time he'd used that word in Formula One? At any other time, in any other race, Zola would sling him out on his ear for this. But Christ, they didn't even want him to win – surely he should be allowed to lose in style? The grid was clearing, orange-shirted mechanics dragging trolley loads of equipment from in front of the Sultan, the man with his finger on the light switch about to let the cars loose on their warm up lap. Kinsella tugged at the clutch lever behind the steering wheel and selected first with the paddle, an electric-red: '1' lighting up the dash in front of him. The engine was burbling nicely behind him, and he gave it a blip or two to reacquaint himself with the feel of the throttle. He started to ease out the clutch...

"But if it's a race he wants..." He said it quietly to himself, said it as he let go of the clutch paddle and pulled his foot away from the throttle simultaneously. The car jumped forward a little, then stopped against the inertia of its own gearing. Stalled. In the mirror he caught sight of a yellow flag, waved furiously to warn the other cars of the new obstacle in front of them, while to his right the field streamed through. By the time the DBM, the last car on the grid, had passed, Kinsella's mechanics had rushed onto the grid again, inserted the remote starter and the Sultan was fired back into life. Kinsella set off in cloud of tyre smoke, and within half a lap of the Chicodrome he had joined onto the tail of the slowing field, ready to take up his new position on the grid – dead last, just behind Chico.

'It was just a mistake' he might say. It had happened to the best of them, even Schumacher some years ago, stalling on the grid – bad luck, we can't wait for you, get to the back of the class young man. As he eased up alongside the DBM on the exit to *Spa* Chico's thumb appeared over the rim of the cockpit. Yes, no bullshit now, just a race. No complications now – except for the twenty-three other cars lined up in front of them...

Chico had had this view once before and once before only. Playing on his nephew's video game, a Formula One simulation. Little Oscar had given him the Bianchi to try, on 'expert' setting, at the back of the grid: it had been near impossible. And here it was once more, but real. Multi-coloured rear wings decking ever smaller into the distance, the rows of inner tyres beading ever smaller, until they came to a point where the pole man sat: Bobby Drake in the now, in the real race. Yes, that had been classy of Kinsella. Perhaps he had misjudged the man? The Sultan had taken the slot to the right and behind him, and although Chico thrilled at the prospect of a straighter fight, the run down to *Zandvoort* would be no picnic with Kinsella laying claim to the inside line. He was already sweating, it was hot even by the Republic's standards, and he sucked at the tube that was plumbed through an aperture in the chin-guard of his helmet, connected to a drinks bottle.

Chico spotted the first of the red lights through the heat haze that hung over the grid. He tugged at the clutch paddle and selected first, the number of the gear displayed at eye level. Now was the time when seconds stretched themselves, the revs already at the right level his left foot braced against the brake pedal to prevent the car creeping forward before time. The exhaust noise of the field, straining against themselves ahead of him, was like a great wall quivering against his visor, something that he could almost feel. More red lights in the distance, four... then six... Off...

Forward motion, snapping his head back, the chassis pivoting sideways at his hips as the red band of the rev counter widens with wheelspin. A feather of the throttle – an orange flash in his peripheral vision to the right. Ahead, through banks of tyre smoke, cars are jinking left and right. Instinctively, Chico jinks left, tucking up behind the rear wing of one of the Minardis as he flicks the DBM into second. Life is a blur of impressionist brush strokes, a screaming vortex of colour, as he passes the stalled car with inches to spare – then jinks out right to see to the Minardi. Into third, and the Sultan has used its momentum from the better start to pull ahead. Fourth, and Chico has seen to four cars on the run down to the first corner. Kinsella is just ahead, on the inside, an early braking Spando between them. A car spins in the middle of the pack – a flash of pale blue broadside on, then just the tyre smoke. Chico aims for the point where the car has spun – they always spin away from where the spin begins – and he is through as others hesitate. But Kinsella is still just ahead, the tail of the orange car kicking out in a wild slide as they exit the *Zandvoort* hairpin.

Kinsella took another car on the plunge down through *Brands* and Chico followed him through – there was no doubt that some of the lesser drivers had their eyes all too firmly fixed on their mirrors with this pair starting from the back. It was a matter of showing your nose to them, let a reputation do the work, they'll back off. Either that or they'll try to make a gunslinger reputation for themselves and just make a mistake. By *Suzuka*, the flat out right-handed kink, the field had settled down a little, the challenges of the quick corners ahead forcing all but the very brave, or the very foolish, to slot into line, slot into the racing line.

Through *Silverstone* and *Spa* Chico shared in Kinsella's frustration as the car in front of them – an Arrows, he thought – took up all the road, racing in his mirrors to keep the superstars behind him for at least a lap. But then, who could blame him, his moment of glory, and the sponsors would love him for it – for there was little doubt where the attention of the TV directors would be at this moment. Anyway, they would get him out of *Monza*, on the long run down to *Zandvoort*. In the event it didn't matter. Pushing too hard into the long turn, understeer, then oversteer, then a tank slapper as the Arrows fishtailed... By the time Chico swept past the Arrows was into its spin. In front of him Kinsella was clean out of the long, long parabolic turn, but Chico matched him – ever wary of the bump where he had almost creamed the President.

Down the long straight and the first time to take stock, where the radios worked and the crew could count the other cars through. Kinsella and Chico had done well, up to 14th and 15th in the first lap sort out. But it would be more difficult from here – and that Sultan was not short on puff down the long straight either. Well, Chico couldn't complain could he – he'd said that he wanted a race...

They picked off two more that next lap, Chico staying glued to the wheel tracks of Kinsella, allowing the Englishman to forge a way through the traffic. Lap three was the same, two more – one as they went either side into *Zandvoort*, the other by default – a Ferrari spearing off and into the tyre wall at *Suzuka*. By the end of lap four the orange, silver and blue train held 7th and 8th. And, for now, the race had settled.

Chico went through it in his head: okay, nothing much to be done about Kinsella yet, his car is going well on full tanks. But that can wait, when the fuel load lightened the DBM always improved... As for the rest? Well, it's the tough cookies now, those in with a shout for points – can't expect these to roll over and play dead. And the first to see to is one of the Prosts, seven seconds down the road...

They caught the Prost three laps later, Kinsella sling-shotting past on the start-finish straight and out-braking the blue car into *Zandvoort*. Chico replicating the move a lap later. And that was the start of the gap, just a second or so, a length or two. But the invisible string between the Sultan and the DBM had been severed, and Kinsella started to pull, ever so slightly, away. He made up more time passing a Jordan, while Chico struggled for three laps to get by. By the time that Kinsella was up to fourth place it was lap 18, and Chico was down in sixth, seven seconds behind, his visor filled with an all too familiar silver and black rear wing of a McLaren.

It had become a battle within the battle. A skirmish that Chico could ill afford, and a skirmish matched by a similar fight in his head. The car was working well now, good through the turns, we can match Kinsella, no doubt about it, but the other silver car was just too damned quick down the straight... Just don't get too frustrated, don't throw it away. Fraser had come over the radio, pleading with him to pit, buy some clear space in which to drive the car to its full potential... But there was that agreement, no complications, lap 32 they had said...

The only way that Chico was going to pass the McLaren was to get a good run onto the straight, which meant braving the bump on the exit of *Monza*. Of course, he knew better than most the treachery of this particular piece of tarmac, but on lap 20 he hung back a little into the long, long turn, winding the car up through it, then gave it its head on the exit. For a moment the car was airborne, he was sure of it, and then he seemed to be heading for the furrows of the gravel trap. But the DBM held true, just throwing up a cloud of dust from the fringe of the track as its outer wheels tickled the limit of adhesion... And he was through, tucked up behind the rear wing of the McLaren, letting the other car carve its way through the air, keeping back that extra zap... Until – halfway down the straight, to shouts of encouragement from Fraser over the comms – he jinked right and pulled up alongside the McLaren. They shared the entry to the tight *Zandvoort*, but Chico had the advantage of the inside line, and he let the DBM slide wide on the exit, let it take the space the McLaren wanted.

It was a full lap before he could speak to Fraser again as radio reception was not good where the Chicodrome plunged down off the plateau. But as he came out of *Monza* the next time, there was a burst of static in his ear, then that familiar voice over the comms:

"Minus ten Chico... Minus ten to Kinsella.... Push, push..."

That new line out of *Monza* helped, and for the next few laps Chico found that he could take chunks out of Kinsella's lead. On lap 25 he was within five seconds of him, and then, coming into *Zandvoort*, he was greeted by the curious sight of two cars on top of each other. A Ferrari seemed to have clambered over the rear of another car in the braking area, both coming to rest in the gravel traps. Both of the drivers were out, and safe, arguing with each other as the marshals tried to usher them out of harm's way. Chico recognised one of the drivers, Bobby Drake, his cheeks flushed as he tossed his helmet into the gravel bed. So, third. And soon the stops...

Christ, this was a racetrack. Jesus Christ, this was a racetrack. Chico had done bloody well make no mistake. The only part of it Kinsella had a problem with was that long, long straight. Not that there was anything wrong with it, no. It made a whole heap of sense to have it there: challenging fast corner, long straight, slow corner. The recipe for overtaking, they had all said that – and he had certainly proved it in this race, up to second already. No, there was nothing wrong with that long, long straight. Except it gave him time to think. Time to glance at his instruments, time to check the ever-decreasing gap to Chico, and just too much time to think. He knew he had to throw it, throw the race somehow: for her, for the bloody sponsors... for the jet. But how could he, it wasn't in him? How could they take away a part of him, his need to win? In a way it would be better if Chico just beat him fair and square. But then that would hurt too.

It was as unnatural as if he had been asked to crash on purpose, he thought. As if he had been asked to aim the thing at a wall and drive on. It could never happen, instinct would take over, slam his foot against the brake. Christ, what did they want of him. It was too much, like putting a naked chick in front of him and ordering him not to get an erection. Balls to them... But then there was another year in a competitive car to think about, there was the jet to think about, there was Teresa to think about... And that long, long straight gave him just too much time for thinking...

He had been in the pits, up on the jacks for about five seconds when he caught sight of Chico pulling up in the DBM behind him. He watched for a moment as the silver suited mechanics swarmed over Chico's car. But then the Sultan mechanics were springing away from his own car, and he was down, off the jacks, feeding in the throttle, counter-acting the slide as the Sultan wiggled its rear under acceleration. It had been hell of a stop by the boys. Bloody quick.

A good out lap. Pretty good. Then another at full race speed as the tyres hit their optimum temperature. Out of *Monza* and onto the long straight again: look for the gap Kinsella, look for the gap...

"Ten seconds up on Chico...." He checked it against his pit board, which also displayed the gap to the lead Spando, over 25 seconds ahead and its stop done, in a different race – and who the hell would care about that one? Ten seconds then, Chico must have had a problem with the stop. A nice cushion, 30 laps to go. Thirty laps for Kinsella to make the decision. A decision he would make alone... He flicked the communications switch to the 'off' position.

Again the DBM was struggling on a full fuel load. For ten laps he had made no headway whatsoever, the gap constant at ten seconds, then stretching to twelve as he slid on the oil laid down at *Silverstone* as the engine in the lead Spando expired. He should have expected it, the blue smoke was still hanging in the air as he pitched the car into the first part of the turn. He had collected it, but it was a big moment. Chico saw the Spando driver walking through a gap in the safety fencing, his head dipped low, helmet swinging from its strap – a sure win up in smoke.

But the suits would be happy now, the sponsors would be happy now. After all, this is what the world had waited for. This was why, somewhere in India, a man had woken in the middle of the night and plugged in his little television. This was why, in the slums of the Brigado whole families would gather round the one TV set in the street. This was why in the pubs in England the football would be forgotten for an hour or two as necks craned to catch the action... Whether it would sell anymore cigarettes, any more microwaves, Chico could not say. But this was what it was all about: Chico and Kinsella down to the wire, no complications... And Kinsella was winning.

But there was still hope, and as the fuel load began to lighten the balance of the car improved, and within four laps he had shaved a second off the Englishman's advantage. And every time he passed the pits, every time he threaded the DBM through that long, long, funnel of grandstand and towering pit complex, Fraser was on the comms: *"Twenty laps – minus 11 seconds Chico..."* The task was clear, at least half a second a lap. This was it. This was the time to put it all into action. All he had learnt in years of racing karts and cars. And nothing mattered but this. All the past was gone, a life someone else lived, all the future would be away from racing cars, another life for him to live. They would judge him – he would judge himself – on this last twenty laps, and this last twenty laps alone. And Mother of God he would have it no other way.

Chico put the hammer down. For two laps he was quick, but scruffy – slightly wide out of *Silverstone*, caught out by the bump at *Monza* again – and Kinsella had responded with a quick lap of his own, but the upshot was that Chico had clawed back another second. And in the grandstands, in the spectator enclosures, in the trees where fans perched for a precarious view of their hero, they had noticed. The sea of flags that marked the crowd began to move more, the ripples from the wind, whipped up into something more splendid, something wilder, as the crowd waved the Republic flags, the Chico banners, urging him on to victory. And the next lap he knocked off another second, despite sliding fractionally wide out of *Brands*, having to lift off for a fraction of a second.

But then, for a little while, he thought there was something wrong with the car, the usual solid push of the engine on the straight supplemented by a strange pumping noise, a noise with a rhythmic cadence that seemed at one with his breathing. Fraser gave him the gap. And again on the next lap. But the lap after that was slower – one of the Bianchis baulking him out of *Zandvoort* – and the gap was unchanged. That time past the pits the noise was louder, and at last Chico recognised it: even above the noise of the engine, even through the thickness of his crash helmet, even past the cosy squash of his ear plugs – it was a country urging him on, willing him to win. Two-hundred-thousand of his countrymen chanting his name, getting louder and louder with each lap that he ate into Kinsella's lead: *Chico, Chico. Chico, Chico...*

Fraser's familiar voice came over the comms once more. But there was no gap this time, just three words: *"Do it Chico..."*

It was not as he had envisaged it, the perfect lap. He had always thought it would all be thumping in his brain, every corner like a chess move, perfectly considered, millimetre perfect in its execution, not a micron of track left unused, not a twitch of throttle gone to waste. But this was something different, something almost spiritual, as Chico seemed to float above himself, almost as if he watched himself at work. Yes, the precision was there – it was perfect after all – but the execution was effortless, time standing still for him and him alone at every braking point, every turn in point, every apex and every exit. It was more akin to enlightenment than control, seeing himself for what he really was for perhaps the first time – doing the thing that he alone did best. And as for the car, well that was just another part of him...

... Another part of him that felt out for the best grip out of *Zandvoort*, feeling the texture of the brick in the kerbing. Another part of him that prodded at the insides of the V10, stoking up the explosions, thousands of little explosions, that kept the heart-a-pumping. Another part of him that pulled the air down to him, clutching at it so that it would wrap itself around the car, keep it safe, keep it planted to the ground. He had hoped for one perfect lap, one perfect lap of the perfect track... But he had found four.

And all the time the lead was slashed, so that in no time the little dark dot on the horizon as he exited *Monza* grew bigger, grew orange, and now – with just five laps to go – he could read the branding, big and brash – smoke me! For the first time in laps Fraser was back over the comms, or at least for the first time in laps he actually heard Fraser over the comms. There were just three seconds in it, and that very lap Kinsella must have realised, over-driving, loose into *Zandvoort*, loose out of *Brands*. By the time they were halfway around *Monza*, feeding in the power through the long, long corner, climbing up the hill, Chico was within striking distance of the Sultan. And he was not about to let Kinsella get used to that fact.

Out of *Monza* he used all the road again, the car kicking and bucking as it grounded and then launched itself over the vicious bump. But the momentum gained brought the DBM right up behind the Sultan as they hit the straight again, the nose of the silver car directly under the orange rear wing. Little droplets of oil and water from the back of the other car flicked against Chico's visor while the bark of the Sultan's engine winding through the top of its range and blasting from its exhaust seemed at one with the turbulence from the dirty air spilling around Chico's head. They ran as one car at over 200 mph for half of the length of the pit straight, the noise of the crowd booming from the grandstands still audible despite the high pitched scream of the Sultan's engine just in front of him.

And then it was time. Kinsella drifted to the centre of the track, forcing Chico to go the long way round at the corner. A flick-flick of Chico's wrists and the DBM bobbed out of the Sultan's slipstream and drew alongside – making use of the slingshot effect when one car slipstreams another. Letting the car in front carve the way through the air, do the work, then hauling itself past on the power saved as it followed. They were side by side into *Zandvoort*, Chico on the left – the optimum line for a car running on its own – while Kinsella hogged the inside. They braked as one, both as late as possible, a big puff of smoke pouring off Kinsella's right front as it went light into the tight turn. Chico had the better speed, even on the dirty part of the track at the outside of the turn, and he dirt-tracked the corner, driving the DBM on the throttle, with little flicks of opposite lock. While Kinsella – in stark comparison – almost trundled through on the safer inside line. Both, though, aimed for the same exit...

Chico made it first, two wheels out on the concrete apron, but Kinsella was alongside, the front of the car sliding wide as the car pushed under acceleration. For a brief moment the two cars kissed, front wheel to front wheel, wobbled on the point of spinning, but them straightened for the dash into the left hander at *Brands*. Chico had suffered most from the brief impact, dropping back a length, but by the time they entered *Brands* and plunged down the hill for the sixtieth time he was alongside again, forcing the nose of the DBM up the inside, so that they took the turn interlocked. Chico's front right tyre directly in line with the left side wheels of the Sultan, before briefly scuffing against its left sidepod, locking still for a moment, smudging the orange black before Kinsella slid wider, the tail of the Sultan snapping out on the exit of the turn. Kinsella seemed slow to react and for an instant the Sultan veered left and was almost broadside across the bows of the DBM, before snapping back into line in front of it, now on the other side of the track.

Chico had had to slow to miss the wayward Sultan out of *Brands* but now, at least, he had the line for *Suzuka* – and yet incredibly Kinsella stayed with him, stayed alongside as both cars reached the clipping point at close to 150 mph. Stayed alongside as the suspension compressed violently in the dip at the apex of the kink, stayed alongside to the exit, two wheels on the grass, stayed alongside as the DBM drifted out towards it, slowly, inching towards the orange car that was already on the point of going off. And then, a coat of paint from the impact that would surely have tipped the Sultan into the wall, Chico feathered the throttle slightly, nothing thought through, just the natural thing to do, the human thing to do. And Kinsella was through the turn, just in front.

Chico kept close behind through *Silverstone* and *Spa*, so close in fact that once the rubber from the rear wheels of the Sultan smudged the low nose of the DBM black. And then, as they started the climb out of *Spa*, he got just too close, nudging the rear of the Sultan and breaking the endplate off his front wing as he did so, while the Sultan was pitched into a high speed tail slide as a result of the collision. For a moment or two, Chico found himself marvelling at the car control of the Englishman as he pulled the Sultan out of its broadside slide with bootfulls of power and armfuls of opposite lock.

But the damage had been done for Kinsella, the speed had been bled away, and into *Monza* Chico was alongside, ready to make the most of Kinsella's adventure. They rounded the turn as one, with Chico on the outside, the car sliding on the dirty unused line as he fed in the power up the hill, feathering the throttle to stop it from going straight off as the front end slithered because of the damaged front wing. As the two cars reached the exit of the turn they were still together, Chico with the momentum, Kinsella with the line, both aiming for the exit of the turn, both aiming for that treacherous bump at the exit of *Monza*...

Chico's world was that rough little patch of tarmac... But he knew that Kinsella's world was also that rough little patch of tarmac. As they were about to reach it as one Chico asked himself the question he had asked himself earlier – was Kinsella up for the race? Was he really racing? He knew already of course, but this was confirmed as both the cars reached the exit together, as both cars laid claim to that same patch of darker grey asphalt.

It wasn't a heavy hit, but with the bump to launch it the DBM was airborne as it hit the gravel trap. Chico could hear the tops of the ploughed gravel berms scraping against the underside of the car as the DBM skimmed over the trap. In the corner of his field of vision an orange shape was fishtailing across the road, then it straightened, then it was gone. The DBM then pitched itself sideways and the ridges of the tyres bit into the gravel so that the speed was arrested in a spine jarring lurch, great plumes of gravel cascading from the side of the car as it ploughed through the trap and out the other side. Chico tugged at the clutch and stabbed at the throttle – thankfully the engine was still running. He was just inches from the tyre wall, and through the debris fencing he caught the faces of his fans, of his countrymen, caught the pain that told him he had lost, they had lost. Tugging at the gear paddle he found first, then allowed the car to trundle around the grass strip that bordered the gravel trap. Fraser came over the comms:

"Is everything okay... If you are quick you can salvage second, but hurry..." And then some seconds later as he steered the DBM back onto the track, bucketfulls of loose gravel spilling from its sidepods:

"You did it didn't you – those laps..?"

Chico smiled, and booted the throttle just as the third place Jordan came into his view in the mirrors.

Chico had asked the question of him. Three laps to go and the world championship in sight. Are you about to chuck it all in for them, for the seat, for the jet next year? Because she had asked it of you Kinsella? No way. He had ridden the turn with him, there was no way Eoghan Egg Kinsella was backing off now. And with the cloud of dust from Chico's spin still big in his mirrors Kinsella was sure that this was the right thing to do. The one thing that was true to what he really was, a competitor, a racing driver, a player in the biggest, fastest, most ballsy game known to man. And a winner.

Nothing seemed broken from that last frantic lap, although the car was pushing into the turns a bit more so he took it a little easier. There was no hurry now anyway, Chico out of the way, way back, and no one else in sight with just two and a half laps to go.

Yes, a winner, the world champion as near as dammit, with all that would mean. No Sultan drive perhaps, no Teresa surely – but who knows, if Chico's true to his word and retires there might even be a chance at DBM again... Or there's always the Spando. Of course, all this is assuming he gets out of the Chicodrome alive, after all the fans were hardly likely to throw a party in honour of this world champion...

And then he felt it. First out of *Zandvoort*, a hesitancy in the pick up of the engine, a hiccup under acceleration. He tried to put it from his mind – that's the way it always is when you're way out in front, nothing else to think about, then the little noises grow big, you imagine you hear things, every little squeak becomes the opening bars of a fully orchestrated engine blow up.

But then there it was again, through *Silverstone*, a definite cough as he squeezed on the power. And again through *Spa* – this time the engine cutting out altogether... It burped, fired again, but only enough to get him up the hill, through the first part of *Monza*. Kinsella punched at the steering wheel as the car coasted, just enough momentum to get it to the top of the hill. And then the DBM swept by, little pieces of gravel still spilling from its undertray, the Jordan in vain pursuit a second or two later. Then silence. Just the screams of the crowd. The car rolled into the pitlane, which was slightly downhill. He remembered the pit stop and then it all made sense. Such a quick pit stop wasn't it? He flicked the radio switch to 'on'

"You bastard Zola."

"Ah, Egg, glad to see your radio is working again... I am sorry you know, but I just could not trust you to keep to our agreement..."

"So I had the boys put in a little less fuel... I'm sure you understand..."

Zola was laughing as the stricken Sultan rolled to a stop at the top end of the pit lane. And then Kinsella saw her, he was sure of it. Standing at a rail in one of the hospitality units above the pits, staring down at him, those familiar white pants, that familiar white top, the tan, sunglasses, a hat to keep the sun off her... or hide her face. She watched him for a moment as he unbuckled his harness, then turned and pushed her way through the other spectators crowded against the rail waiting for Chico to come round to begin his triumphant last lap. Zola was still talking on the radio:

"And you know Egg, next year it will be easier for you. Because you have the unfair advantage now... You know how to win..."